一生必讀的
英文小說

經典&大眾小說導讀賞析

陳超明／著

目錄

前言

"... only some work in which the most thorough knowledge of human nature, the happiest delineation of its varieties, the liveliest effusions of wit and humor are conveyed to the world in the best chosen language."

(Jane Austen's *Northanger Abbey*)

19 世紀的小說家珍・奧斯汀認為小說是以精挑細選的語言（the best chosen language），描述人性最完整的知識（the most thorough knowledge of human nature）。奧斯汀這段文字點出了小說的可貴：文字與知識的完美結合。

一般人閱讀小說總以為是研究文學作品，意境很高，內容一定要帶給我們某種啟發，所以很難去深入研究。然而閱讀小說，一方面從小說中讀到一些對於人性或社會有價值的東西，一方面還是在體會文字或學習好的語言。誠如奧斯汀所說，小說中用的是最精彩的語言、最好語言！

閱讀英文小說的好處

閱讀小說，對於文化學習有很大的助益，同時對於語言學習幫助更大，因為好的英文小說可說具備以下幾個特色：

1. 用詞精確、語言精彩

好的小說用詞優美，讓人不容易忘記，例如《飄》（*Gone with the Winds*）中的最後一句 "Tomorrow is another day." （明天又是另一天），至今仍被廣泛引用。像這些簡潔有深度又好記的句子，有涵意又影響深遠。

2. 完整的敘述邏輯

小說有好的敘述結構，長篇的小說敘述必須符合某些邏輯，要有明確合理的前因後果，才能完整地敘事。閱讀小說必須記住前後人物或情節的關係，因此好的小說會有一定的邏輯及思維，對閱讀者來說，有助於自己邏輯或思維的訓練。

3. 人類智慧與生活經驗的累積

經典或好小說，是人類永恆知識或智慧的結晶。一般人的生活經驗有限，而小說家將知識與個人經驗完整結合，提供可以思考的內容。我們可以從閱讀小說中吸收別人的智慧。

4. 批判、思考能力的培養

好的文字更可以幫助吸收，尤其透過語言的表達、文字的敘述，學習到解決問題及獨立批判思考（critical thinking）的能力。

如何訓練批判思考的能力呢？以時下青少年愛讀的小說《暮光之城》（*Twilight*）為例：

"My mother drove me to the airport with the windows rolled down. It was seventy-five degrees in Phoenix, the sky a perfect, cloudless blue. I was wearing my favorite shirts— sleeveless, white eyelet lace; I was wearing it as a farewell gesture. My carry-on item was a parka."

以這段文字的敘述，到底女主角離開她媽媽的心情是什麼？要如何用一個英文字來形容？女主角是一個中學生，她的父母離婚，媽媽有了新男友，她要離開她媽媽，是悲傷、憤怒或者有若隱若現的離愁？這些都是透過文字的閱讀，產生一些值得深思與反省的想法。

語言是有批判能力的，任何一個字可以表達自己萬千的情緒。我們可以訓練自己藉由情節去思考，去解讀它，也可以幫助個人培養解決問題的能力。

如何閱讀英文小說

閱讀好的英文小說可以幫助自己學好英文與訓練思考，但要如何開始呢？

1. 注意文字節奏與用詞

閱讀時要注意文字的節奏、遣詞用字。許多人閱讀英文小說第一個關卡是單字，實際閱讀過程中，並不需要每個單字都要查清楚。首先選擇小說時，要挑選適合自己能力的，如果這本小說有七至八成都看得懂（也就是 10 個字中只有 2、3 個生字），就可以了，如果一半以上看不懂，就不建議挑選，否則讀起來會太辛苦。

2. 培養自己的單字力

遇到生字要不要查字典？我不建議立即查字典。如果這個字不影響語意可以先跳過，如果出現到三次以上再去查字典。而且查完字典後，不要寫在小說上，這樣如再看到這個生字，覺得有印象卻又不太記得，再去查一次字典，這樣來回兩三次就會記得這個字了。如此就可以慢慢累積自己的單字量，可以提升英文小說的閱讀能力。

3. 掌握重要的用詞

重要的遣詞用字常常是小說的關鍵，小說中常用一些用法如精確的動詞、形容詞等。了解這些用詞，有助於自己以後運用英文的能力。例如 The lawn started at the beach and ran toward the front door for a quarter of a mile, jumping over sundials and brick walks. (*The Great Gatsby*)。此處使用了幾個動詞如 started、ran、jumping 等，以擬人化的動作，生動地點出了草地 （the lawn） 的生命力。

4. 結合文字與視覺的想像

閱讀小說，有如看 3D 電影，要把文字的敘述立體化，建立想像的空間。

5. 結合小說世界與自己的生活經驗

小說敘述了另一種生活，透過小說可以與自己的生活結合，才能讓文字進入腦海。

6. 選擇性的記憶優美文字

閱讀小說不需要所有的文字都要看懂或記憶下來。我們可以選擇自己最有感覺的一句話就夠了。經典的小說往往被人稱頌或傳承下來的通常都是一些精闢的字句，例如珍·奧斯汀的《傲慢與偏見》中，對「傲慢」與「偏見」所下的註解，至今仍十分適用：

Vanity and pride are different things, though the words are often used synonymously.... Pride relates more to our opinion of ourselves, vanity to what we would have others think of us.

（虛榮與驕傲是不同的，雖然這兩個字常互相混用。驕傲指的是我們對自己的看法，而虛榮則是我們希望別人對我們的看法。）

以文化層面來看，經典的英美小說表達了西方人的敘事觀點、想法，是珍貴的文化遺產，也是文明思維的結果。不論是 19 世紀或現代的英美小說更可以看到西方文化的呈現，從對家庭的疏離、個人主義興起到獨立自主的思想、批判等都有助於我們更了解西方世界的價值觀。

為何選這些書？

本書所選的 20 本小說，不全都是經典小說。我認為閱讀英文小說，不需要太過嚴肅，不是非讀經典小說不可。本書所選的小說大都是我個人的偏好。

我從大學時代開始讀英文小說，這些小說陪我度過了人生的各種不同的階段，從年輕的強說愁到中年的落寞與孤獨，這些小說都幫助自己了解更多其他人豐富的人生經歷。選讀的小說，從兒童、冒險、偵探、通俗、愛情、驚悚等，有經典的，也有通俗的。希望藉由這些小說，讓讀者也能像我一樣享受閱讀小說帶來的喜悅，更可以投入更多的想像空間。

小說與現實生活有密切的關係，很接近，但也相當程度地表達了與一般人價值觀不盡相同或者與個人生活經驗完全不同的故事。如此，我們透過閱讀小說可以補足現實生活中無法做到的遺憾，或者擁有更多的想像與期待。例如尼可拉斯‧史派克（Nickolas Sparks）的愛情小說，就可以讓許多嚮往浪漫愛情的讀者陷入故事中男女主角的愛恨情仇中。《瓶中信》是藉由男主角一封封的情深意濃的信，道出愛情故事，在現實生活中，已很少人寫信了，尤其在現代速食式的愛情，史派克滿足了現代男女追求愛情的空虛感。

如何使用本書？

您可以將本書當作該小說的導讀來閱讀，也可以當作該小說的濃縮版！

這本書包括了作者簡介、主題分析、精彩片段賞析等，可以帶著讀者細細品味小說的精髓。如果讀者想要繼續欣賞這本小說的全貌，可以去找出英文小說原著重新品讀。如果沒有時間，就可以看看本書中所寫的重要片段。而且這些都適合做為學習英文的教材。

我強烈建議，把這些小說放入人文教育課程中，讓學生去體會英美文化中的文字思維。這本書也是文學入門最好的導讀文章，讓文字的解析、意境的描述，帶著讀者走入小說想像的世界，可以啟發心靈，為自己開創更多彩豐富的英文學習境界。

政大英國語文學系教授

陳超明

《傲慢與偏見》
Pride and Prejudice
(1813)

Jane Austen

© Bettmann/CORBIS

📖 作者簡介

　　英國女性作家珍‧奧斯汀（Jane Austen, 1775 ～ 1817）在她 41 年的生命中，寫出了不少膾炙人口的小說，例如《理性與感性》（*Sense and Sensibility*）、《愛瑪姑娘》（*Emma*）、《曼斯菲爾公園》（*Mansfield Park*）等，她的文字成熟且筆觸細膩，開啟了 19 世紀英國小說的黃金時期。

　　她的小說大多以年輕女性為主角，透過自己本身的生活經驗並且靈巧運用豐富的想像力，勾畫出 19 世紀初期的年輕男女所面對的社會壓力與價值取捨。婚姻與愛情的議題，不僅是奧斯汀時期的女性所要面對的選擇，更是牽涉到整體社會價值的走向。當時的男女常常為了經濟因素而結婚，促使奧斯汀思考這種男性、女性自我成長與自我價值的重大難題，女性到底要符合社會的期許，或面對自己理性與感性的衝突，斷然地做出與社會期待背道而馳的決定呢？

　　儘管奧斯汀的小說大多以女性婚姻議題為主，但她終身未婚。奧斯汀的生活環境多所限制，父親為地方的牧師，她從小生活在只有父母親及姊妹的環境中，缺乏對於大時代變遷的第一手經驗，但是奧斯汀透過大量閱讀與敏銳的洞察力，深入觀察了英國 19 世紀糾葛的家庭關係與社會脈動，她的細膩程度，到了 21 世紀仍感動不少歐美讀者。

　　整體來說，奧斯汀的小說延續了 18 世紀小說的風格，帶點幽默風趣的措辭與對白，充滿了機智的話語常常令人拍案叫絕，對於 19 世紀的小說風格有所影響。此外，寫實的描述與細膩成熟的文字，則是她帶給 19 世紀作家最大的啟發。小說的人物在她細膩的筆觸下栩栩如生，書裡的角色就有如生活在我們周遭的人物般。對於小說，她曾有一段精彩的定義：

"...only some work in which the most thorough knowledge of human nature, the happiest delineation of its varieties, the liveliest effusions of wit and humor are conveyed to the world in the best chosen language."

(Jane Austen's *Northanger Abbey*)

（〔小說〕只是某種作品，其中對人性最完整的知識、多元的愉悅描述、智慧與幽默最生動的湧現，以最精選洗練的語言，呈現給世人！）

📖 小說介紹

"Vanity and pride are different things, though the words are often used synonymously. A person may be proud without being vain. Pride relates more to our opinion of ourselves, vanity to what we would have others think of us."

（「虛榮與驕傲是不同的兩件事，雖然這兩個字經常被等同使用。人可以驕傲卻不虛榮。驕傲指的比較傾向是我們對自己的看法，而虛榮則是我們想要別人如何看待我們。」）

此書是 19 世紀初珍‧奧斯汀的傑作，也是英國小說的經典。主要描寫兩對男女之間的戀愛與婚姻故事。對於 18 世紀末或 19 世紀初的女性，婚姻無疑是人生最重要的思考點，如何找到一個在經濟上、心靈上都能契合的伴侶，成為整部小說的關鍵（這也是當代男女關心的議題！）

📖 主題分析

小說家透過犀利的對話與細膩的人性刻畫，將兩對男女間的糾葛放在兩個關鍵的字詞 pride 及 prejudice 之上。小說的女主角 Elizabeth 第一次看到男主角 Darcy 的場景，打破傳統一見鍾情（love at first sight）的浪漫情節，一開始她就不喜歡 Darcy 的傲慢。對於家人與親戚好友以財富來評斷一個人的價值，Elizabeth 不以為然。雖然經濟的穩定對於家庭婚姻很重要，但是 Elizabeth 認為個性與情感的契合更加重要。

小說中，姊姊 Jane 是個外表美麗但個性單純的女生，一眼看上了搬來附近的闊少 Bingley，兩人這種一見鍾情的吸引，卻抵不上一些外在閒言閒語的中傷。而 Elizabeth 一見到 Darcy，對於他所表現出的男性高傲與覷睨，這位聰明的女性無法認同。對這位人人想要追求到手的男性，誤認為是個自大與傲慢的傢伙。

女主角對男性的偏見（prejudice）來自於對女性自我的驕傲（pride），她的聰明、先入為主的觀念、以及對判斷能力的自負，讓她無法好好地體諒別人。作者在此要強調每個人都有先天上的缺點，即使是聰明如 Elizabeth，也無法避免。書中的一段對話，可以呈現這方面的主題：

"There is, I believe, in every disposition a tendency to some particular evil, a natural defect, which not even the best education can overcome."

"And your defect is a propensity to hate everybody."

"And yours," he replied with a smile, "is willfully to misunderstand them."

Darcy 說：在我們每人天性中有一種罪惡的傾向（a tendency to some particular evil），一種自然的缺陷（a natural defect），這種缺點即使是最好的教育都無法克服 （not even the best education can overcome）。Elizabeth 回應說，你的缺陷就是不喜歡所有的人；而 Darcy 回笑地反擊說，而你的缺陷就是任性且故意地誤解他們（willfully to misunderstand them）。兩人針鋒相對，毫不讓步，但這也是兩人互相吸引對方的地方。

驕傲與虛榮只是一線之隔，小說人物如何透過相互的溝通與危機的處理，從誤會與偏見中，認識自己與對方，最後兩對男女取得了彼此的尊重，成就了好的姻緣。男女互諒才是堅強愛情的基礎，誠如 Darcy 最後對 Elizabeth 的告白：

"... You taught me a lesson, / hard at first, / but most advantageous. / By you, / I was properly humbled. /... / You shewed me / how insufficient were / all my pretensions / to please a woman / worthy of being pleased."

（你給我了個教訓／剛開始很難堪／但是非常有幫助。／由於你，我變得適度謙卑。／……／你讓我知道，／我的一切虛飾都不足／取悅一位值得取悅的女性。）

Elizabeth 則對 Darcy 說：

"I am a very selfish creature; / and, for the sake of giving relief to my own feelings, / care not how much I may be wounding your's."

（我是個非常自私的人；／只為了釋放自己的感情，／不在乎傷害你的感情有多深。）

小說情節的起伏，有如今天的偶像劇，但小說中的對白以及文字的使用令人激賞。

📖 精彩片段賞析

珍・奧斯汀的語言力量，一直是她的小說耐讀的主因。小說中的敘述與對話，常常充滿機智與文字的巧思。回到小說一開始，作者採用很正經的口氣，強調這個 truth 被普遍認同的程度（it is... that 的句法），並使用兩個多音節的單字（universally, acknowledge），讀起來感覺此句很正式、很盛大。以華麗的字詞與語法，誇大本故事的主題：婚姻。

"It is a truth universally acknowledged, / that a single man / in possession of a good fortune, / must be / in want of a wife.

However little known / the feelings or views of such a man may be / on his first entering a neighbourhood, / this truth is so well fixed / in the minds of the surrounding families, / that he is considered as / a rightful property of some one or other of their daughters."

✚ 閱讀提醒

閱讀這兩句，可依照以上的斷句方式，將句子拆解成小單元，然後逐段理解。第一句可以拆成較短的結構來閱讀：

這是大家所公認的事實 / 單身男子 / 擁有一大筆財富 / 一定 / 缺少個太太。

這句話看起來好像是單身男子的主觀認知：他需要一個老婆。然而下面所接的這句，以第一句的關鍵字 truth 作為第二句的主詞，形成句間非常密切的連結（transition）。其實這個「事實」並非是此單身男子的看法，而是附近鄰居（surrounding neighbourhood）的看法。第二句的反諷口氣，更凸顯第一句那種正經八百口氣的好笑。

第二句：

儘管無法探知 / 這種男子的感覺或看法 / 在他第一次踏入此社區，/ 此事實已深深印 / 在周遭家庭的心中，/ 他已被視為 / 這些家庭女兒的當然資產。

所以此單身男子欠缺一個太太，並非他自己的看法，而是這些周遭家庭父母的主觀認知：為他們的女兒找長期飯票！

第一句開場，點出婚姻與財富（fortune）的關係，第二句話則緊扣第一句，主客易位，指出真正關心資產（property）的人其實是那些父母，這也開啟了此小說的高潮：這是一場媽媽為女兒尋找夫婿的複雜遊戲。接下去的對話就是女主角的媽媽出來討論如何將自己女兒嫁給這種金龜婿：「... A single man of large fortune; four or five thousand a year. What a fine thing for our girls!」。這兩句話已成為這小說的經典名句，利用 fortune 及 property 兩個與金錢有關的字眼，點出愛情與婚姻脫離不了經濟上的考量。

閱讀此小說，並非在閱讀情節，反而是咀嚼這些文字的細節與其間段落

的連貫 （coherence），這樣，對於文字的敏感度與英語的語感就會不知不覺地強化。

此外，優美語言與人生道理的結合，也是到處可見，如下面的例子：

"... but there are very few of us who have heart enough to be really in love without encouragement. In nine cases out of ten, a woman had better show more affection than she feels. Bingley likes your sister undoubtedly; but he may never do more than like her, if she does not help him on."

（女主角 Elizabeth 和好友 Charlotte 討論男女交往。）

在此段中，Charlotte 指出：如果沒有鼓勵（without encouragement），很少人有足夠勇氣（have heart enough）真正墜入情網。十之八九，女人最好表現出比真實感覺更多的愛意（show more affection than she feels）。Bingley（小說中另一個男主角）毫無疑問地喜歡你的姊姊（Elizabeth 的姊姊 Jane）；但是，如果 Jane 沒有鼓勵他進一步的話（help him on），他可能僅僅止於喜歡她而已（never do more than like her）。可見，女性在戀愛遊戲中，其實握有主控權，好好地去表現、暗示對方，男人會很快愛上你。

此段文字利用 love、affection 、like 等不同字眼，來表達 3 個不同層次的男女感覺：love（愛）、like（喜歡）、 affection （愛意的表現）。此書點出愛情與現實的人性，在這裡只舉出數個範例，協助讀者閱讀，建議可以將優美的詞句記下、運用，如此可以豐富自己的英語辭彙與語法，並掌握段落與句間的連貫關係。

📖 結局賞析

好的小說要有好的結局，奧斯汀的小說大部分是歡樂結局（the happy ending）。敘述者以幽默的口氣跳出來，回應小說一開始 Elizabeth 媽媽 Mrs.

Bennet 急著把女兒嫁掉、最後總算完成了心願的心情：

"Happy for all her maternal feelings / was the day / on which Mrs. Bennet got rid of / her most deserving daughters. / With what delighted pride / she afterwards visited Mrs. Bingley / and talked of Mrs. Darcy / may be guessed. / I wish I could say, / for the sake of her family, / that the accomplishment of her earnest desire / in the establishment / of so many of her children, / produced so happy an effect / as to make her a sensible, / amiable, / well-informed woman / for the rest of her life...."

（快樂地感受當母親的心情，/ 這一天，/ Mrs. Bennet 趕走了 / 兩個最值得獎賞的女兒。/ 到底帶著什麼樣喜悅的驕傲，/ 日後她去拜訪 Mrs. Bingley（大女兒）/ 或談到 Mrs. Darcy（二女兒），/ 這是可以猜想到的。/ 我希望我可以說，/ 為了她家，/ 完成她最真誠的願望，/ 建立家庭，/ 為這麼多子女，/ 已引起了這麼愉悅的結果，/ 讓她成為一個有知識、/ 親切的、/ 消息靈通的女性，/ 終其一生。）

小說以 Mrs. Bennet 想要嫁女兒開始，而後已嫁女兒結束，堪稱是個完整的結局。而敘述者以 sensible、amiable、well-informed 這些形容詞來描寫帶點粗俗、聒噪、講話強勢的媽媽，諷刺與調侃意味十足，也呼應了結局的喜劇效果（the comic effect）。

適合閱讀程度：
大二以上學生及社會人士；高中生可閱讀聯經出版的珍・奧斯汀改寫版。
延伸閱讀／推薦書單、電影：
小說：
Sense and Sensibility《理性與感性》
Emma《愛瑪姑娘》
Mansfield Park《曼斯菲爾公園》

《瓶中信》

Message in a Bottle

(1998)

Nicholas Sparks

📖 作者簡介

　　尼可拉斯 • 史派克（Nicholas Sparks, 1965 ～）是個典型的聰明小孩，體育甚佳。以運動獎學金進入聖母大學（University of Notre Dame）就讀。受傷後，在母親的建議下開始小說創作。其間從事過不同工作，最後嘗試以小說寫作成為人生的重要轉折。1994 年開始創作 *The Notebook*（電影名為《手札情緣》），1995 年出版後暢銷，獲得商業上的成功。1997 年《瓶中信》（*Message in a Bottle*）大為暢銷，他從此專職寫作，辭去銷售的正職工作。其後陸續出版以書信方式的浪漫愛故事，如《最後一封情書》（*Dear John*），也獲得成功。這些暢銷的小說均被好萊塢拍成電影，結合小說與電影，推動了美國當代愛情浪漫的風潮。

　　史派克的小說大都以現代年輕人或熟男熟女的浪漫情愫開始，探討當代愛情的面面觀。作者利用傳統的書信手法，一方面引起美國當代男女的懷舊情懷，一方面重新分析愛情的元素。在現今講求速食愛情與情欲的時代裡，觸動男女間隱藏在內心的熱情，成為美國婦女間的閱讀新寵。史派克的小說被歸類為通俗小說，經常充滿濫情與新奇的大眾元素。然而他本身很重視視覺的描寫，誠如他在一次訪問中說，他是個非常偏重視覺影像的作家："I was always a fairly visual writer from the very beginning of my work."。此外，對他來說，好小說應該具備幾個特點：好的故事、好的講故事方式、原創的角色、適合故事發展的文章風格與長度。

📖 小說介紹

　　"I think that this would be meaningful to a lot of people. Nowadays, people are so busy that romance seems to be slowly dying out. This letter shows that it's still possible."

　　（我覺得這對很多人會很有意義。現在，很多人都太忙了，浪漫愛情似乎漸漸在消失，這封信顯示，還是有可能的。）

閱讀浪漫愛情小說是每個人一生都會有的經歷，隨著男女主角的悲歡離合，我們也跟著情緒起伏。濫情與感傷是這種愛情故事（或言情故事）的特色。年少歲月，總會為著這些通俗的情節，留下眼淚。我們會閱讀經典的愛情故事如莎士比亞的《羅密歐與茱麗葉》（*Romeo and Juliet*）可歌可泣，我們會也會閱讀這些通俗的愛情，放縱一下自己無知的歲月。我們暫時拋開經典，一起來閱讀，號稱最多美國婦女讀過的《瓶中信》，在繁忙的當代生活中，找尋那可能的浪漫。

史派克的愛情故事採用美國大眾愛情故事的模式，建立在異國與異地的戀情，也就是愛情永遠發生在不熟悉的人或場景上，這種浪漫（romantic）的氣氛就是激起年輕人幻想的泉源。故事從一封信開始。

📖 主題分析

✚ 愛情是命運決定的嗎？

在丈夫外遇離婚後，女主角 Theresa 渴望愛情，卻對真正的愛情感到失望。一天來到海邊，撿到了一個漂流的瓶子，裡面竟然密封著一封情書：

My Dearest Catherine,

I miss you, my darling, / as I always do, / but today is especially hard / because the ocean has been singing to me, / and the song is that of our life together. / I can almost feel you beside me / as I write this letter, / and I can smell the scent of wildflowers / that always reminds me of you. / But at this moment / these things give me no pleasure. / Your visits have been coming less often, / and I feel sometimes / as if the greatest part of who I am / is slowly slipping away.

（ 我想你，親愛的，/ 我總是如此，/ 但是今天特別強烈，/ 因為海對我歌唱，/ 唱的是我們在一起的生活。/ 我幾乎可以感受到你在我身邊，/ 當我寫這封信。/ 我可以聞到野花的香味，/ 總是聯想到你。/ 但是此刻，/ 這些事物無法給我樂趣。/ 你的拜訪越來越少，/ 有時我覺得，/ 似乎我個體最大部份漸漸流失。）

寫信的男子 Garrett 透過瓶中信來懷念其死去的妻子 Catherine，透過氣味的真實感受，寫出自己與死去妻子的不離不棄。將相思寄往大海，希望透過信件的表達，回味過去的甜蜜，但是思念越深，隨著時間的消逝，妻子的影像也越來越模糊，將妻子比喻 the greatest part of who I am 漸漸地消逝。

在這麼情欲及短暫關係的社會中，就是這樣永續的真情表達感動了 Theresa，對她而言：

"The letter obviously came from the heart. / And to think that a man wrote it! / In all her years, / she had never received a letter / even close to that. / Touching sentiments / sent her way / had always been emblazoned / with Hallmark greeting card logos."

（此信顯然出自內心，/ 想想竟然有個男人寫的！/ 在她有生之年，/ 她從來沒有接過一封信，/ 跟這相似的。/ 令人感動的情緒文字，/ 寄給她的，/ 都是印上 Hallmark 卡片的標誌。）

沒錯，當今社會，廉價的感人話語都是卡片公司現成印給我們的，在電子卡片的時代，可能簡單的滑鼠一點，就可以帶出雪萊、拜倫感人的詩句。然而這封親筆所寫情書，對 Theresa 來說，不僅是代表現代人所缺乏的真情與永恆，更是命運的主導。一封漂流數千里的真情信，竟然會落入她的手中！

之後，Theresa 將此信公布在報紙專欄裡，又獲得讀者回應，陸續接到 Garrett 這位男人的瓶中信。作者不斷地指出，愛情是命定的。Garrett 在信中不斷地強調他跟 Catherine 的相愛是與生俱來的：

"I know / that somehow, / every step I took / since the moment I would walk / was a step / toward finding you. / We were destined to be together."

（我知道，／不知怎麼了，／我每走的一步，／從我會走路那時刻開始，／都是一步步／來找到你，／我們是命定在一起。）

Theresa 也相信命運帶領她去尋找這位真情的男性，甚至在還沒有見到他時，她已經愛上了 Garrett。

將愛情與命運結合在一起，符合了現今浪漫與濫情的主軸，有如羅密歐與茱麗葉的相愛就在剎那間發生。作者不斷強調，現代人以外在條件（如身家財產、前途發展與工作職業）來定位的感情並非真感情，只有那種沒有條件，經過命運安排的愛情，才能感動人。這也就是這本小說能感動百萬美國婦女的原因。

然而，命運讓兩人在一起，命運也能主宰悲劇的發生，誠如 Garrett 在信中所言：

But now, / alone in my house, / I have come to realize / that destiny can hurt a person / as much as it can bless him, / and I find myself wondering / why—out of all the people in all the world / I could ever have loved—/ I had to fall in love with someone / who was taken away from me.

（然而現在，／孤獨地處在屋裡，／我才瞭解，／命運可以傷害一個人，／也能深深地祝福一個人。／我自己很納悶／為何在世界上所有人中／我可以愛的——／我必須愛上一個，／會被帶離開我的人。）

史派克是個擅長寫信的愛情小說家，他的幾本暢銷小說（如《最後一封情書》），將情書的古老傳統帶回到網路電子時代，這種一方面懷舊，一方面賣弄深情的通俗愛情故事，可能是都會孤寂男女的另一種文字饗宴吧！

📖 精彩片段賞析

　　愛是什麼？愛是如何產生的？愛的感覺為何？這些都是閱讀愛情故事或看愛情電影中，讀者或觀眾在內心不斷追尋的問題。而閱讀這類的愛情故事，除了感受愛情的經驗外，也不自覺地希望從中獲取一些答案。作者往往提出自己的一些看法或複製傳統的說法，然而面對這種複雜的人際關係或感情問題，大都沒有標準答案，因此追尋不斷延伸，愛情故事也不斷地創造。

　　《瓶中信》也是延續這種追尋，女主角 Theresa 追求愛情的永恆與理想的愛人：

　　As a girl, / she had come to believe in the ideal man /— the prince or knight of her childhood stories. / In the real world, however, / men like that simply didn't exist. / Real people had real agendas, / real demands, / real expectations / about how other people should behave. / True, / there were good men out there / — men who loved with all their hearts / and remained steadfast / in the face of great obstacles / — the type man she'd wanted to meet / since she and David divorced. / But how to find such a man?

　　（還是小女孩時，/ 她相信理想的男人 / ——兒童故事中的王子或騎士。/ 然而，在現實世界，/ 像那樣的男人就是不存在。/ 現實的人有現實的行程，/ 現實的需求，/ 現實的期望 / 別人如何舉止。/ 沒錯，外面有好的男人 / ——那種全心全意的去愛，/ 堅定不移，/ 面對巨大的阻礙 / 某種她想要遇到的男人，/ 自從她跟 David 離婚後。/ 但是如何去找到這樣的男人？）

　　理想中的愛人必須要能夠全心全意的付出愛（loved with all their hearts），而且在面對困難或阻礙時，能夠堅持，不會退縮（remained steadfast in the face of great obstacles）。這種理想的男人一方面有感性的能力，一方面也具對抗挫折的勇氣與毅力，情感與理性兼備的愛人正是童話故事的王子形象。然而，現實生活中，這種男人存在嗎？小說家為我們創造這種可能性，吸引了眾多的女性讀者。Theresa 閱讀了 Garrett 的幾封瓶中信後，發現這樣的男人，剎那間，為這種理想男人所惑（obsessed）：

　　Here and now, / she knew such a man existed /— a man who was alone— / and knowing that / made something inside her / tighten. / It seemed obvious / that Catherine— whoever she was— / was probably dead, / or at least missing / without explanation. / Yet / Garrett still loved her enough / to send love letters to her / for at least three years. / If nothing else, / he had proven / that he was capable of loving someone deeply / and, more important, / remaining fully committed — / even long after his loved one was gone.

　　（此地此時，/ 她知道這樣的男人存在──/ 一個孤獨的男人──/ 知道這 / 使得她心中 / 一緊。/ 很明顯地，/ Catherine ──不管她是誰──/ 大概已經死亡，/ 或至少失蹤 / 沒有解釋理由。/ 然而 / Garrett 仍愛她，/ 寄送情書給她 / 至少 3 年。/ 即使沒有其他任何事，/ 他已經證明 / 他能夠深深地愛一個人，/ 最重要的，/ 保持完整的承諾──/ 即使愛人已經消失很久了。）

　　這樣完美的男人：孤獨、深情、忠貞，實在是所有追求愛情的異性所幻想的對象。濫情的愛情小說，總是創造這種完美形象，不僅迷惑書中的女主角，也同時掌控了讀者內心對愛情的渴望，不自覺地，作者利用第一人稱的呼喊，強化了這種情緒的強度：

Where are you?
It kept ringing through her head, / like a song / she heard on early morning radio / that kept repeating itself / the entire afternoon.

　　（不斷地在她腦中迴響，/ 有如一首歌，/ 她在早上的電台聽到，/ 不斷地重播，/ 整個下午。）

Where are you?

此處的 Where are you? 不僅是女主角的呼喊，也是讀者的呼喊，作者透過這種人稱的轉換，為書中男中角，製造出場的高潮。此外，利用英文常用的比喻說法（simile，明喻），描述這樣的呼喊有如電台中強力推銷的歌曲，不斷地在腦中重播，意像簡單鮮明。

書中男主角的出場，完成了愛情的渴望與追尋，也提出了作者對於愛情的發生（love encounter），提供了浪漫的場景：

Turning toward him, / she saw that his hair had been blown back by the wind. / The coat he was wearing hung to midthigh, / unzipped. / Worn and weathered, it looked as though he'd used it for years. / It made him seem larger than he really was, / and it would be this image of him / that she could imagine remembering forever.

（面對他，/ 她看到他的頭髮被風吹起。/ 他穿的外套垂到大腿，/ 未扣上。/ 磨損、風化，/ 似乎已經用了好幾年了。/ 使得他看起來比實際大些。/ 似乎是他這種形象，/ 她可以想像永遠會記得。）

這幅充滿風霜、成熟與專情的景象，以外套的意像來代替對 Garrett 具體描寫，展現精緻的文學手法。Theresa 愛上的是自己對那個男人的想像（this image of him that she could imagine remembering forever），而非真正的 Garrett。

而男主角回應了這種深深的眼神，竟是誤認 Theresa 為其死去的太太 Catherine。

They stared at each other for just a moment, as if wondering what would come next, before Garrett finally motioned toward the boat....

"Like I said earlier, I had a wonderful time tonight," she said....

For a moment their eyes met, and for a moment he saw Catherine in the darkness.（片刻間，他們的眼神相遇。一下子，他看到 Catherine，在黑暗中）

兩人所愛上的其實都不是原始本人，而是對對方的想像，這就是戀愛的迷思嗎？作者問了一個問題：戀愛是否建立在自我的想像？Theresa 與 Garrett 的戀情注定要在想像破滅後回歸到本質，但是時間已經不等他們了！

📖 結局賞析

　　一般的大眾浪漫愛情故事都以喜劇結束，男女主角誤會冰釋，克服困難，終於找到真愛。然而，《瓶中信》這本小說卻以死亡遺憾來結束。當 Theresa 克服了自己愛情的迷思，Garrett 也企圖割捨過去的迷戀，兩人好好面對自己的真愛時，一切似乎都點出拖延的愛情只能留下遺憾。Garrett 出海向死去的老婆道別，卻死於海中，永遠無法回來擁抱 Theresa 的真情。Theresa 在最後寫給死去 Garrett 的信中，這麼說著，令所有閱讀的女性不禁滴下眼淚：

Even though I miss you greatly, /it's because of you / that I don't dread the future. / Because you were able to fall in love with me, / you have given me hope, / my darling. / You taught me / that it's possible to move forward in life, / no matter how terrible your grief./ And in you own way, / you've made me believe / that true love cannot be denied.

　　（即使我很懷念你，/ 因為你，/ 我不害怕未來。/ 因為你能夠與我相愛，/ 你已經給我希望，/ 親愛的。/ 你教導我，/ 生活是可以往前的，/ 不管你的哀傷多深。/ 你以你的方式，/ 讓我相信，/ 真愛無法拒絕。）

　　現代男女都在等待、期待真愛。史派克在這本小說以戲劇性的方式，剖析真愛的形成，才是這本濫情小說成功之處。儘管這本小說無法與珍・奧斯汀的小說並列，但是處於愛情虛幻的時代裡，去體會一下小說虛擬世界的一點真情，不也是我們人生中重要的經驗嗎？

適合閱讀程度：

大一以上學生或生活枯燥乏味的社會人士。

延伸閱讀／推薦書單、電影：

小說：

Tess of D'Ubervilles（《黛絲姑娘》）

Dear John（《最後一 封情書》）

《機械公敵》

I, Robot

(1950)

Issac Asimov

📖 作者簡介

艾薩克 ‧ 艾西莫夫（Issac Asimov, 1920 ～ 1992）是擁有猶太人血統的俄裔美國人，他是美國波士頓大學醫學院的生化學教授，對於科學教育及科學探索非常熱衷。不過他最為人稱道的，則是創造了當代美國科幻小說的傳奇，與 Robert A. Heinlein 及 Arthur C. Clarke 並列美國當代科幻小說的三巨人（The Big Three of Science Fiction）。

艾西莫夫最著名的科幻小說以基地小說（Foundation Series）、銀河帝國（Galactic Empire Series）、及機器人系列（Robot Series）為主。其小說不僅開創了某些科幻小說的類型及新的方向，更從科學出發，探索人類的未來與過去。他的科幻小說不僅融入了歷史學、人類學及文化價值的探索，更添加了懸疑小說、偵探小說等成份，讀者閱讀其科幻小說系列，可以思索不同文明與文化的價值議題，隨著情節的發展，更可以享受推理與緊張的故事鋪陳。

艾西莫夫是個多才多藝且多產的作家，他不僅在科幻小說領域中大放異彩，也寫過不少歷史研究的著作，大都以羅馬帝國為主，如 The Roman Republic, The Roman Empire 。儘管是科學出身，艾西莫夫常常自認為是人文學者（humanist），美國人文學會（American Humanist Association）就曾於 1984 年頒給他 The Humanist of the Year。他也曾經協助美國最有名的科幻影集《星際爭霸戰》系列（*Star Trek* Series）的原創者 Gene Roddenberry，擔任電影指導。其小說充滿視覺印象、具有深刻主題，也因此常成為電影的最愛，如《機械公敵》（*I, Robot*）及《變人》（*Bicentennial Man*）等。

艾西莫夫待人親切，常常四處演講，但很諷刺的是，他很怕飛行，此生僅搭乘過兩次飛機，而這種對飛行的恐懼也常出現在小說中。

他的科幻小說主題大多是人與機器人的關係及這種關係對雙方的影響，此外，對於人類生存的價值與機器文明未來發展的定位，都是作者所思考的問題。艾西莫夫為了釐清這些問題，小說中不採用太複雜的文學手法或技巧，通常以平鋪直述的方式，透過說明、動作與對白來呈現，清楚易懂。讀者一口氣讀來，會覺得非常了然暢快，無須猜測作者隱含的意象。這樣的特色，可以從他的話裡看出端倪：

"I made up my mind long ago / to follow one cardinal rule / in all my writing / —to be clear. / I have given up / all thought of / writing poetically / or symbolically / or experimentally, / or in any of the other modes / that might (if I were good enough) get me a Pulitzer prize. / I would write merely clearly / and in this way / establish a warm relationship / between myself and my readers, / and the professional critics—/ Well, they can do whatever they wish."

（我很久以前就下定決心，/ 遵守一主要原則，/ 在我所有的寫作中 / ——清楚易懂。/ 我放棄 / 任何想要 / 寫得有詩意、/ 象徵性、/ 實驗性 / 或任何其他模式 / （如果我夠好的話），可以讓我獲得普立茲獎。/ 我寧願寫得清楚，/ 這樣，/ 可以建立溫馨的關係，/ 在我跟讀者之間，/ 以及專業的批評家——/ 喔，他們可做他們想要的。）

📖 小說介紹

The Three Laws of Robotics（機器人三大定律）

1. A robot may not injure a human being, or, through inaction, allow a human being to come to harm.
   （機器人不可傷害人類，或由於不採取行動，導致人類受害。）
2. A robot must obey orders given it by human being except where such orders would conflict with the First Law.
   （機器人必須服從人類的指令，除非此指令與第一項定律衝突。）
3. A robot must protect its own existence as long as such protection does not conflict with the First or Second Law.
   （機器人必須保護自己的生存，只要不違反第一項或第二項定律。）

艾西莫夫的機器人小說，可說是科幻小說的經典，他的 *I, Robot*（電影將其改編，中文片名為《機械公敵》，儘管概念來自艾西莫夫，探討人、機器與文明的關係，但電影故事與小說差異甚大）更是奠定了機器人小說雛形與 20 世紀以來人類對機器（或電腦）的論辯基礎。整本小說其實是一系列的短篇小說組成，除了前面的介紹（introduction）外，共有 9 篇故事。故事場景在未來，整個世界大多是由機器（或電腦）運作，為人類創造一個舒適且有效率的環境。小說開始，記者以第一人稱方式，訪問美國機器人公司的首席機器人心理學家 Susan Calvin，請她回顧過去幾十年來人類與機器互動的點點滴滴。這本 *I, Robot* 是作者集結不同短篇故事而成，給予一些架構及貫穿故事的人物，並以探討機器的理性思維及人類的感性反應為主題。第一篇小說「Robbie」，寫於 1940 年，當時作者 19 歲，有感於過去小說家對於機器文明充滿懷疑與不信任，讓「科學怪人情結（Frankenstein Complex）」主導了人文學界對科學的僵化印象。對艾西莫夫來說，創造機器的目的必須是為人類服務，因此創造了機器人三大定律，來顛覆傳統「man vs. machine」的對立關係。

📖 主題分析

這 9 篇小說是以 Susan Calvin 的回憶所構成，描述她透過理性分析，解決了人類對機器的疑惑。小說以解迷（puzzles）為架構，對於人類與機器之間的感情糾葛、理性思維的盲點，環繞「機器人三大定律」的邏輯，都有深入的分析與探討。長期與機器人相處，Susan 對於理性思維充滿好奇，卻極力壓抑自己的感情想法，這位女性的機器心理學家對於機器所帶來的世界，充滿理想性的期望：

"To you, a robot is a robot. / Gears and metal; / electricity and positrons./ —Mind and iron! / Human-made! / if necessary, human-destroyed! / But you haven't worked with them, / so you don't know them. / They're a cleaner better breed / than we are."

（對你而言，機器人只是機器人。/ 齒輪與金屬；/ 電與電子——/ 理智與鐵！人類製造的！/ 如有必要，人類也可以毀滅！/ 不過，你沒有跟他們一些工作，/ 你不了解。他們更純潔、更好 / 比我們。）

作者其實探討的主要是三個機器文明以來的問題：（一）機器是否對人類有害？（二）機器的理性思維是否比人類好？（三）什麼是機器（machinery）？什麼是人（humanity）？

Susan 對於機器文明的肯定，其實並非來自長久以來的科學理性的沈迷，反而是對於人類內心孤獨的反思；她對年輕的記者說：

"Then you don't remember a world / without robots. / There was a time / when humanity faced the universe alone / and without a friend. / Now he has creatures to help him; / stronger creatures than himself, / more faithful, / more useful and absolutely devoted to him. / Mankind is no longer alone. / Have you ever thought of it that way?"

（然後你不會記得 / 沒有機器人的世界。/ 曾經有一段時間 / 人類獨自面對這宇宙，/ 沒有朋友。/ 現在人類有夥伴協助，/ 比他更強壯的朋友，/ 更忠誠，/ 更有用 / 也對他全然地奉獻。/ 人類不再孤獨，/ 你曾經那樣地想像過嗎？）

誠如，Dr. Calvin 所說的，年輕人可能都不記得沒有機器人（電腦、手機？）的世界，曾經有段時間，人類孤獨的面對宇宙，沒有朋友，現在有個夥伴來幫他，更強壯、更有用的、更忠誠的夥伴！為何我們不好好與這個夥伴（機器文明）相處呢？規範其行為（以機器人三大定律）成我們理性思維的另一半？

艾西莫夫在小說中，不斷地透過理性思維與推理，去看待人與機器互動的過程，第一篇小說中，小女孩 Gloria 與照顧她的機器人 Robbie 產生感情，引起她媽媽的恐慌，然後最後還是 Robbie 發揮其「機器性」，救了其小女主人。其中一段機器人 Robbie 要求小女孩 Gloria 講灰姑娘的故事，令人感受到人與機器之間的界限其實很低！

"Oh, I know. You want a story."

Robbie nodded rapidly.

"Which one?"

Robbie made a semi-circle in the air with one finger.

The little girl protested, "Again? I've told you Cinderella a million times. Aren't you tired of it?— It's for babies."

（「喔，我知道，你要個故事。」

Robbie 馬上點頭。

「哪個故事呢？」

Robbie 用一支手指在空中畫了個半圓，

小女孩抗議著，「還要聽？灰姑娘的故事我已經跟你說過無數次了，你沒聽膩嗎？——那是說給小孩聽的。」）

其實，艾西莫夫對於人類所創造出的機器文明也有其焦慮。在最後一篇小說 "Evitable Conflict" 中，機器人（電腦）控制整個世界，調整對第一定律的解釋，重新詮釋人類的命運。Dr. Calvin 表達對人類文明悲觀的論調：

"...our entire technical civilization / has created / more unhappiness and misery / than it has removed. Perhaps an agrarian / or pastoral civilization, / with less culture / and less people would be better...."

（我們整體的科技文明 / 製造了更多的不快樂與不幸 / 超過所移除的 / 或許農牧文明 / 較少文化 / 與較少人 / 會比較好）

"But you are telling me... / that Mankind has lost its own say in its future."

（但你告訴我……／人類喪失了對自己未來的發言權）

"It never had any, really. / It was always at the mercy of / economic and sociological forces / it did not understand— / at the whims of climate, / and the fortunes of war."

（人類從來沒有發言權，真的／人總是接受擺布／經濟與社會力量運作下／自己並不了解／，甚至在氣候的任意擺布／及戰爭的命運下。）

艾西莫夫的小說推翻 Mary Shelley 在《科學怪人》中對科學狂熱的不信任，開啟了後續科幻小說與科幻電影中更廣泛的議題：人類與機器的複雜情結、理性（機器）與感性（人類）的對立與互補。《魔鬼終結者》、《駭客任務》等電影都曾延伸討論此人類、機器及文明間的複雜關係。

本小說除了議題創新，情節起伏，小說家更透過語言的推理與邏輯的分析，幫我們解開人與機器人所面臨的難題。

科幻小說以科技的角度切入，討論人類未來的想像與理性思維的空間，常常缺乏人文的看法。然而，艾西莫夫的這本機器人小說，卻不斷地從人類感性的觀點來看邏輯思維的優缺點，也就是用人的思維去解決機器的問題。我們摘錄幾段有關機器人三大定律的理性面與矛盾面。

📖 精彩片段賞析

"If a robot can be created / capable of being a civil executive, / I think he'd make the best one possible./ By the Laws of Robotics, / he'd be incapable of harming humans, / incapable of tyranny, / of corruption, / of stupidity, / of prejudice."

在 "Evidence（證據）" 故事中，美國機器人公司的首席心裡顧問 Dr. Susan Calvin 對一位即將參選的政治人物 Stephen Byerley 這麼說：「假如機器人可以被創造／有能力成為政府首長，／我想他會成為最好的人選。／透過機器人三大定律，／他不會傷害人類，／不會專制暴政，／不會貪污，／不會愚蠢，／不會有偏見。」在故事中，Byerley 被對手懷疑已受傷死亡，複製機器人替身參選。Dr. Calvin 用盡各種不同方法仍無法證實 Byerley 到底是人或機器？這時機器人的第一定律（「機器人不得傷害人類」）證實了 Byerley 是人類，因為他在公開場合攻擊挑釁他的人類。在與 Byerley 對話時，Dr. Calvin 其實內心認為 Byerley 應是機器人替身（也是理想的政府官員）。但 Byerley 如何突破第一定律的邏輯限制呢？Dr. Calvin 從理性思維中找到其邏輯的漏洞：

Dr. Calvin rose and smoothed her dress. She was obviously ready to leave. "I mean there is one time when a robot may strike a human without breaking the First Law. Just one time."

"And when is that?"

Dr. Calvin was at the door. She said quietly, "When the human to be struck is merely another robot."

She smiled broadly, her thin face glowing. "Good-by Mr. Byerley. I hope to vote for you...."

在這段對話中，我們難得看到 Dr. Calvin 女性的溫柔，一方面起身，一方面拉平自己的衣服（smoothed her dress），其動作充滿理性，平靜地說話（said quietly），但也處處顯露其人性的一面（smiled broadly, her thin face glowing 很露骨大方地微笑，瘦小的臉興奮地亮了起來！）。她指出，原來 Mr. Byerley 可以假設挑釁他的並非人類而是機器人，這樣身為機器人的他就可以利用第二、第三定律來保護自己。這種利用假設前提的漏洞來打破規矩，是否也凸顯理性思維本身的缺陷呢？小說中不斷強調機器人思維單純的優勢，但也指出其單純的不足：

"... a robot might fail / due to / the inherent inadequacies of his brain. / The positronic brain has never equalled the complexities of the human brain."

（機器人可能會失敗，／由於／其頭腦先天的不足。／電子腦從來就比不上人腦的複雜度。

這裡說話者使用 might 表示一種推測，由於（due to）某種原因，機器人可能（might 的推測可能性低）會失敗。而第二句用現在完成式，表示過去到現在為止，電腦一直都無法跟人腦相提並論。

機器人的電腦邏輯思維單純，可以用定律來規範，但終究無法與人腦相比，在 "Runaround（繞圈子）" 的故事中，兩位機器人工程師，發現他們派出去擔任危險工作的機器人在繞圈子，甚至出現精神錯亂的現象，原來第二定律與第三定律間的矛盾讓機器人無法運作，由於第二定律，機器人必須依照人類指示去危險地帶工作，然而第三定律又要求其保護自己的存在，因此機器人依照第二定律往前，卻又依照第三定律退後，造成繞圈子。作者挑戰讀者的思維，有如偵探小說般，我們該如何解開這個矛盾的結呢？

"All right. According to Rule 1, a robot can't see a human come to harm because of his own inaction. Two and 3 can't stand against it. *They can't*, Mike."....

"What are you going to do?"

"I'm going out there now and see what Rule 1 will do. If it won't break the balance, then what the devil— it's either now or three-four days from now."

沒錯，就是使用第一定律！工程師將自己暴露在危險地帶，打破第二、第三定律的平衡性（balance），這樣就能將失控的機器人拉回正常的思維。

本故事中，描寫工程師 Donovan 冒險到外星球的烈日下面，動作驚險，重重危機，英文句中生動的動詞，夾雜人物內心的想法，讀來有身歷其境的感覺：

"He proceeded on foot, / the ground gritty and slippery to his steps, / the low gravity causing him difficulty. / The soles of his feet / tickled with warmth. /

He cast one glance over his shoulder / at the blackness of the cliff's shadow / and realized that he had come / too far to return."

（他步行前進，／每步感覺地上沙沙滑滑，／低引力讓他行進困難。／腳底／熱得發癢。／回頭一看／山崖陰影投下的漆黑，／他知道自己走得／太遠了回不去。）

此處的動詞 proceed、tickle、cast、realize 都使用得非常貼切；gritty and slippery、warmth 都是將個人感受融入行動中，也是非常傳神。閱讀時多注意這些生動動詞及一些情緒的描寫，享受閱讀的樂趣。

📖 結局賞析

小說以 Dr. Susan Calvin 的敘述為主要架構，透過其過去與機器人相處的經驗，道出了人性與機器的不同價值：理性與感性間的互動與糾葛。

"And this is all," said Dr. Calvin, rising. "I saw it from the beginning, when the poor robots couldn't speak, to the end, when they stand between mankind and destruction. I will see no more. My life is over. You will see what comes next."

I never saw Susan Calvin again. She died last month at the age of eighty-two.

（「這就是一切。」Dr. Calvin 說，起身。「我從頭看起，那時可憐的機器人還無法說話，直到最後，他們處在人類與毀滅之間。我再也看不到了。我的生命結束了，你會看到未來。」

我之後沒有再看到 Dr. Calvin。她上個月過世，享年 82 歲。）

最後一段以 see、saw 來串接，從年老的 Dr. Calvin 看到過去機器文明的發展到年輕記者的所預計的未來，作者留下一些想像的空間。

適合閱讀程度：

高三以上及社會人士

延伸閱讀／推薦書單、電影：

電影：

I, Robot（《機械公敵》，2004）

The Bicentennial Man（《變人》，1999）

《科學怪人》

Frankenstein

(1818)

Mary Shelley

Richard Rothwell © Bettmann/CORBIS

📖 作者簡介

英國女作家瑪麗‧雪萊（Mary Shelley, 1797 ～ 1851）出生於倫敦，她的父親 William Godwin 及母親 Mary Wollstonecraft 都是當時英國浪漫時期的重要作家，倡導一些自由反動的思想，影響了當代很多詩人如雪萊未來的丈夫 Percy Shelley 等人。瑪麗‧雪萊的母親生下她之後，就因大量出血死亡，這在她心中留下很大的陰影。但整體而言，她的童年仍算幸福，即使本身並未受到很多的正式教育，但由父親 William Godwin 親自教育，加上透過自己在圖書館大量閱讀，也瞭解了很多文學的發展。瑪麗‧雪萊大約是在 1813 年停留在蘇格蘭的時候認識 Percy Shelley，當時 Percy Shelley 跟妻子正處於分裂的狀況。1814 年後，兩人開始經常見面，並陷入熱戀。當時瑪麗 17 歲，Percy 21 歲。兩人在當年夏天，私奔至法國，留下 Percy 懷孕的老婆。兩人直到 1816 年 Percy 的妻子死後，才正式結婚。

瑪麗‧雪萊 1816 年與拜倫及友人一起前往日內瓦。拜倫建議他們撰寫一些超自然的故事。在一次睡夢中，她獲得靈感，開始構思這本小說。它原本是一篇短篇小說，後來在 Percy 的鼓勵下，成為現在的版本《科學怪人》，並於 1818 年出版。日後，瑪麗‧雪萊說：那年在瑞士的夏天是她從童年踏入人生的第一步：

"...the moment when I first stepped out of childhood into life."

📖 小說介紹

"A human being in perfection ought always to preserve a calm and peaceful mind, and never to allow passion or a transitory desire to disturb his tranquility. I do not think that the pursuit of knowledge is an exception to this rule. If the study to which you apply yourself has a tendency to weaken your affections, and to destroy your taste for those simple pleasures... , then that study is certainly unlawful."

（一個成熟的人，應該永遠保持寧靜、安詳的心，絕不允許激情或短暫的欲望，干擾其寧靜。我認為追求知識，不應該是例外。假如你所從事的研究會減弱你的感情，摧毀你對單純樂趣的品味……那這項研究絕對是不合法的。）

「知識的追求不應該是例外，不應該是打擊人類的情感或摧毀任何享受生活的樂趣」。這些話語，來自曾經以神自居而創造生命的 Dr. Frankenstein 的口中。《科學怪人》探討知識追求的本質。透過科學研究的過程，來分析生命的意義與人類、上帝間的關係，是一本討論「創造」（creation）議題的科幻小說。

小說以多人角度的敘述進行，情節圍繞 Dr. Frankenstein 對知識的無限追求，希望獲得生命的祕密。他利用閃電創造了生命，這是人類有史以來，無須透過男女的交配，首次從無生命中創造生命。Dr. Frankenstein 扮演上帝的角色，創造了自己的後代，但卻在恐懼中，將其遺棄。這個創造物 Monster 未受「生父」疼愛，又飽受世人鄙視，開始了殘酷的報復與殺戮。

📖 主題分析

✛ 激情與邪惡（Passion and Evil）

小說以多人敘述的觀點開始，由第一個敘述者 Walton 的海上冒險談起。在一次的海上經歷中，他救起了 Dr. Frankenstein。由他口中，聽到了科學實驗與慘酷的經歷：

No one can conceive the variety of feelings / which bore me onwards, / like a hurricane, / in the first enthusiasm of success. / Life and death appeared / to me /

ideal bounds, / which I should first break through, / and pour a torrent of light / into our dark world. / A new species would bless me / as its creator and source; / many happy and excellent natures / would owe their being to me. / No father could claim the gratitude of his child / so completely as / I should deserve their's.... / if I could bestow animation / upon lifeless matter, / I might in process of time... / renew life....

（沒有人會想像那些複雜情緒，/ 帶著我往前，有如暴風雨，/ 在最先渴望的成功中。/ 生命與死亡 / 似乎對我來說 / 是理想的界限，/ 我應該首先突破，/ 注入一股光亮的洪流，/ 進入黑暗的世界。/ 新的物種，/ 將會讚美我 / 是他的創造者與生命泉源，/ 很多快樂與卓越的本質 / 都因我而來。/ 沒有父親能得到小孩感恩，/ 這麼完整的，/ 如同我應獲得的……。/ 假如我能賜予活力 / 給無生命的物體，/ 我可以漸漸地…… / 更新生命……）

Dr. Frankenstein 對知識的追求（passions for knowledge），推展到極限，希望探索生命的奧秘，打破生與死的界限，此處將對知識的狂熱追求比喻為 hurricane，企圖為黑暗的世界注入洪流（torrent），這裡使用暴雨的意象，不僅生動的描寫出博士對知識的瘋狂，更隱含往後他可能會被這些狂風暴雨所吞噬。扮演父親（father）及造物主（creator）的角色，凸顯科學家的狂妄與虛榮。當創造物產生的剎那，Dr. Frankenstein 的恐懼與孤寂，令他遺棄了這個可怕的怪物。

小說的另一個敘述者來自這個被創造的生命（Monster）。以 Monster 命名的這個創造物，無法感受人世間的親情，充滿恨意，屠殺 Dr. Frankenstein 的親友與未婚妻。他對著創造者 Dr. Frankenstien 嗆聲說：

"All men hate the wretched; / how then must I be hated, / who am miserable beyond all living things! / Yet you, my creator, detest and spurn me, thy creature, / to whom thou art bound by ties only / dissoluble by the annihilation of one of us. / You purpose to kill me. / How dare you sport thus with life? / Do your duty towards me, / and I will do mine towards you / and the rest of mankind. / If you will comply with my conditions, / I will leave them and you at peace; / but if you refuse, / I will glut the maw of death, / until it be satiated with the blood of your remaining friends."

（所有人都厭惡可鄙的人。／我這樣被人厭惡，／我可是世上最可憐的人！／而，你，我的造物主，嫌惡並排斥我，你的孩子，／你跟我相互聯繫，／依靠連結，／僅有我們其中一人被消滅，才會解除。／你想要殺死我。／你如何敢這樣玩弄生命？／盡你對我的職責，／我也會盡我對你及其他人的職責。／如果你同意我的條件，我會放過他們跟你。／不過假如你拒絕，我將滿足死亡的胃口，／直到其喝飽了你其餘朋友的血。）

Monster 的話語充滿恨與暴力，可見其天性的邪惡；然而其哀哀地懇求親情，也令人同情，這一切是他的錯嗎？如果不是 Dr. Frankenstein 為了滿足自己的求知狂熱，創造了 Monster，這一切慘劇不會發生。然而，任何人，由於天生命運的悲慘，就能夠去殘害別人，歸罪造物主嗎？Monster 推卸責任，忽視了其本性的邪惡，是否也迷惑了讀者？讀者在閱讀兩人的各自對白，要同情誰呢？要譴責誰呢？這到底是誰的錯？作者透過多重角度的敘述觀點，創造了不同的的思維與價值觀，留給讀者不同的閱讀模式，誠如 Dr. Frankenstein 在故事結尾對第一個敘述者 Walton 所說的：

"My judgment and ideas are already disturbed / by the near approach of death. / I dare not ask you to do / what I think right, / for I may still be misled / by passion."

（我的判斷與觀念已經搞亂了，／由於死亡的接近。／我不敢要求你做／我認為對的事，／因為我可能仍然被誤導，／由於激情。）

在歌頌情感（feelings）與激情（passion）的英國浪漫主義時代裡，這部質疑 passion 價值的作品，值得讀者一讀再讀。

📖 精彩片段賞析

　　探索未知的一切是開起這本小說冒險的原動力。小說的第一個敘述者 Walton 就是在這種驅動下，將美與求知的心結合在一起：

I am already far north of London; / and as I walk in the streets of Petersburgh, / I feel a cold northern breeze / play upon my cheeks, / which braces my nerves / and fills me with delight.... / Inspired by this wind of promise, / my day dream become more fervent / and vivid. / I try in vain to be persuaded / that the pole is the seat of frost and desolation; / it ever presents itself to my imagination / as the region of beauty and delight.

　　（我已經在倫敦遙遠的北方。/ 當我漫步在彼得堡的街道上，/ 我感覺北方的冷風 / 拂在我臉頰上，/ 提振我的精神，/ 充滿喜悅…… / 受到這種微風承諾的激勵，/ 我白日夢越來越強烈、/ 越鮮明。/ 我無法被說服 (我不相信)，/ 北極是個寒冷、/ 荒蕪所在；/ 它出現在我的想像裡，/ 是個美麗與喜悅的地方。）

　　敘述者以風（wind）的意象來串場，從感受臉頰上的 breeze 到內心充滿希望的一股強烈的心情，從 wind of promise 到 fervent and vivid dream，由於心境的改變，外在的寒冷不再孤寂，而是美麗與喜悅的地方（the region of beauty and delight）。

✚ 大自然的美麗 vs. 人類的醜陋

　　大自然的美與令人驚歎的壯觀場景，也是小說中重要的線索。作者不斷強調大自然帶給人的喜悅與心靈的力量。可憐的 Dr. Frankenstein，在飽受心靈與肉體的折磨時，不斷訴諸大自然的滋潤：

In the morning / we had seen the mountains at a distance, / towards which we gradually advanced. / We perceived that the valley / through which we wound, / and which was formed by the river Arve, / whose course we followed, / closed in upon us by degrees; / and when the sun had set, / we beheld immense mountains and precipices / overhanging us / on every side, / and heard the sound of river / raging among rocks, and the dashing of waterfalls around.... / Mont Blanc, the supreme and magnificent Mont Blanc, / raised itself from the surrounding aiguilles, / its tremendous dome overlooked the valley.

（早上，/ 我們已經看到群山，從遠方。/ 面向這些山，我們慢慢前進。/ 我感覺這山谷，/ 我們蜿蜒通過，/ 被 Arve 河所圍繞，/ 我們跟著其行徑，/ 漸漸逼近。/ 當太陽落下，/ 我們看到巨大的山陵、斷崖 / 逼迫我們，從四面八方，/ 聽到河流的聲音，/ 在石頭中怒吼，瀑布的敲擊，/ 在四周⋯⋯ / 白朗峰，至高無上、壯麗的白朗峰，/ 高高聳起，/ 從四周的尖石山峰中，/ 巨大的圓頂俯視山谷。）

巨大的山峰高聳於山谷之上，更凸顯其壯麗（magnificent）與雄偉（immense）。不僅是巨大的感覺，澎湃的水聲更加強這種視覺的影響。Dr. Frankenstein 從實驗室走到大自然，從狹隘的自我追求，投入了大自然的寬闊懷抱，提升了其心靈，也鍛鍊了內心的美感經驗（the beautiful and the sublime），安慰了受傷的情感：

These sublime and magnificent scenes / afforded me / the greatest consolation / that I was capable of receiving. / They elevated me / from all littleness of feeling... / [The glacier] had then filled me / with a sublime ecstasy / that gave wings to soul, / and allowed it to soar / from the obscure world / to light and joy.

（這些令人驚愕雄偉、壯麗的場景，/ 提供我 / 最大的安慰，/ 我所能接受的。/ 將我提升，/ 從偏狹的情感中。/ 冰河因此讓我充滿 / 驚愕的狂喜，/ 給我靈魂翅膀，/ 容許它翱翔 / 出懵懂的世界，/ 來到光明與喜悅。）

這些美感的經驗（the sublime）扮演了很多角色：給我安慰（consolation）；提升我的情感（elevated me from all littleness of feeling）；讓我充滿喜悅（filled me with sublime ecstasy）；解放我的靈魂（gave wings to soul）。尤其是最後的一個動詞 soar（翱翔），點出了浪漫時代所強調的：想像力的解放。

相對於大自然的美，小說中的醜陋與怪物的描寫，也點出了人類邪惡本性：

Oh! / no mortal could support / the horror of that countenance. / A mummy again endued / with animation / could not be so hideous as that wretch. / I had gazed on him / while unfinished; / he was ugly then; / but when those muscles and joints were rendered / capable of motion, / it became a thing / such as even Dante could not have conceived.

（啊，/ 沒有凡人可以忍受 / 那容貌的恐怖。/ 一個骷髏再賦予 / 動作，/ 都沒有這個悲慘的傢伙可怕。/ 我曾盯著看他，/ 在未完成時。/ 他那時很醜，/ 但是當這些肌肉與關節 / 仍夠活動時，/ 它變成的東西，/ 即使但丁都無法想像。）

撰寫《神曲》（*The Divine Comedy*）的但丁，描寫地獄受苦的靈魂與變形的軀體，已經令人作嘔，連他都無法想像這個怪物的醜陋形體。這個醜陋的外型，反映出內心的憤怒與暴力，是否也暗示人類內心可能存在的邪惡（evil）呢？這個可怕的怪物就是科學家內心世界的縮影。怪物自己也這麼說：

At first I started back, unable to believe that it was indeed I who was reflected in the mirror; and when I became fully convinced that **I was in reality the monster that I am, / I was filled with / the bitterest sensations of despondence and mortification.**

（我確實是個不折不扣的怪物，／內心充滿／沮喪及屈辱的痛苦心情。）

大自然的美 vs. 人類的醜陋，這種強烈的對比成為本書最精彩的意象。自大的科學家，無視於自然的法則，創造了醜陋的物種，也成為近年來科幻小說與電影的主題。而這種主題是否隱含對科技文明發展的不同聲音？

📖 結局賞析

Dr. Frankenstein 最後追逐 Monster 來到了北極，終於在痛苦中死亡。小說的敘述者終於在最後的時候，親自面對 Monster。Monster 看到自己的主人也是父親因傷痛而亡，也感受到自己生命意義的消失，回顧一生，黯然道出自己的哀傷：

I was nourished / with high thoughts of honours and devotion. / But now / vice has degraded me / beneath the meanest animal. / No crime, no mischief, no malignity, no misery, / can be found comparable to mine. / When I call over the frightful catalogue of my deeds, / I cannot believe / that I am he whose thoughts were once filled / with sublime and transcendent visions of the beauty and the majesty of goodness. / But it is even so; / the fallen angel becomes a malignant devil... / I am quite alone.

（我過去受到滋養，／以榮譽及奉獻的崇高想法。／不過現在，／邪惡已經把我貶低／到最卑賤的動物之下。／沒有罪惡、惡意、邪惡、痛苦，／可以跟我的相比。／當我回想起一些可怕行為，／無法想像，／我的思想曾充滿雄偉美感與美與善的超越視野。／不過即使如此，／墮落的天使成為惡意的魔鬼⋯⋯／我相當孤寂。）

Monster 內心孤寂地吶喊，其實也代表邪惡本身的不幸：Was there no injustice in this? Am I to be thought the only criminal, when all human kind sinned against me?（難道這沒有任何的不公嗎？只有我被認為是罪犯，當所有的人類都對我犯罪？）魔鬼試圖為自己脫罪，魔鬼的犯罪難道社會沒有責任嗎？到底「邪惡」是天生的還是社會造成的，也是這本小說不斷要問讀者的問題。讀完本小說後，答案可能是更加難以確定。

適合閱讀程度：
高三以上及社會人士
延伸閱讀／推薦書單、電影：
小說：
Dr. Jekyll and Mr. Hyde（《變身怪醫》）
Invisible Man（《隱形人》）

《夜訪吸血鬼》

Interview with the Vampire
(1976)

Anne Rice

📖 作者簡介

安‧萊絲（ Anne Rice, 1941 ～）是美國當代結合恐怖與情色主題的小說家，她所創造的吸血鬼傳奇，顛覆了傳統吸血鬼故事的框架，也建立了當代恐怖傳奇的新紀元。她的作品全球銷售已經超過 1 億本，躋身美國當代最暢銷的作家行列。

萊絲大部分時間住在紐奧良（New Orleans），此地也成為她小說的大部分場景。萊絲年輕時進入舊金山州立大學念書，主修政治，後來獲得碩士學位，留在母校當講師，目睹了當時加州興起的嬉皮運動。

萊絲生長在愛爾蘭天主教的家庭，然而有段時間她屏棄了信仰，成為一個無神論者。1988 年時，她曾經因病徘徊死亡邊緣，回到了天主教的信仰。然而，萊絲並非完全接受羅馬天主教的教義，她個人支持同性戀以及依個人意願選擇墮胎的權利。

萊絲的寫作泉源來自於她對生命的質疑與神秘事物的好奇。在紐奧良及舊金山（San Francisco）兩個多元文化都市的洗禮下，她接受了多元的價值觀念，支持異質的文化論述，即使她一再強調吸血鬼並不存在，但是她的吸血鬼傳奇卻勾起了人們驚愕、好奇、渴望的心靈。

📖 小說介紹

"My vampire nature has been for me the great adventure of my life; all that went before it was confused, clouded; I went through mortal life like a blind man groping from solid object to solid object. It was only when I became a vampire that I respected for the first time all of life. I never saw a living, pulsing human until I was a vampire."

（我的吸血鬼本性一直是我生命中偉大的奇遇；之前一切非常迷惑、陰暗；我經歷凡人的生活有如盲人摸索，從一實體摸索到另一實體。成為吸血鬼，我第一次尊重所有生命。直到我成為吸血鬼，我才真正看到活生生、脈動的人類。）

　　成為吸血鬼後，所有的感官變得更加敏銳，對於周遭的環境也有不同的體驗。吸血鬼小說，如同《哈利波特》的巫師小說，充滿驚奇與冒險，成為當代最具想像力的文學世界。

　　吸血鬼傳奇從早期的《德古拉伯爵》（*Dracula*）到現在青少年浪漫愛情的《暮光之城》（*Twilight*），都充滿恐怖、懸疑、暴力的情節與氣氛。早期的吸血鬼故事大多是從受害者的觀點出發，道出吸血鬼對人性的戕害，暴力血腥的場面不斷；而近代的吸血鬼故事則從吸血鬼的自我出發，深入瞭解這種異質生命（other beings），所帶來的驚奇與想像，並談論伴隨這種異質能力所必須忍受的折磨與考驗，從吸血鬼的他者（other）觀點來看人類自我（self）生命存在或愛情的本質（如《暮光之城》等）。開啟這方面異質討論的最熱門故事，無疑是安‧萊絲的《夜訪吸血鬼》。

📖 主題分析

　　《夜訪吸血鬼》圍繞在男主角 Louis 自我追尋的過程。故事透過記者訪問，Louis 訴說自己過去幾百年的生活經歷。Louis 以第一人稱的敘述，帶領我們一步步瞭解他從人類變成吸血鬼，卻無法忘卻人性面的掙扎與痛苦。小說一開始 Louis 在兄弟死後陷入了人生的低潮，自暴自棄。這時一位名為 Lestat 的吸血鬼趁虛而入，將 Louis 轉換成吸血鬼。然而目睹 Lestat 透過殘殺人類以滿足自我的過程中，Louis 無法擁抱這種純粹以掠奪者（predator）身分的暴力本質。

　　當 Louis 的吸血鬼師父 Lestat 說：

"Vampires are killers.... / Predators. / Whose all-seeing eyes were meant / to give them detachment. / The ability to see a human life in its entirety, / not with any mawkish sorrow but with a thrilling satisfaction / in being the end of that life."

（吸血鬼是殺手……/ 掠奪者，/ 其全能的視野是用來 / 展現其超然獨立。/ 該能力能夠透視人類生命整體，/ 不是以一種傷感的憂愁，/ 而是興奮滿足 / 於該生命的結束。）

而 Louis 內心渴望「善」（good）的一面開始不斷地吶喊：

"... I was no vampire. / And in my pain, / I asked irrationally, / like a child, / Could I not return? / Could I not be human again? /... The faces of humans passed me / like candle flames / in the night dancing / on dark waves. / I was sinking into the darkness. / I was weary of longing."

（我不是吸血鬼。/ 在我的哀痛中，/ 我毫無理性地質問自己 / 像小孩般，/ 我無法回去了嗎？/ 我無法變回人類了嗎？/……人類的臉龐在我面前經過，/ 像蠟燭火光，/ 在黑夜中飛舞 / 在黑暗的波浪上，/ 我陷入黑暗，/ 我厭倦這種渴望！）

這種善與惡的、生命與死亡、渴望與厭倦的辯論不斷出現在小說之中。Louis 與另一個吸血鬼小女孩 Claudia 前往歐洲，有如美國 20 年代「失落的一代」（The Lost Generation），展開一場尋根與古典文化之旅。他們遇見了其他古文明的吸血鬼，是否找到了作為人類或吸血鬼存在的意義呢？

"And my heart beat faster / for the mountains of eastern Europe, / finally, / beat faster / for the one hope that somewhere / we might find / in that primitive countryside / the answer to / why / under God / this suffering was allowed to exist— / why / under God / it was allowed to begin, / and how / under God / it might be ended. / I had not the courage to end it, / I knew, / without that answer."

（我的心跳得更快，/ 渴望東歐的山岳，/ 最後 / 心跳加快，/ 希望某個地方，/我們可能發現/在原始的鄉間，/某些答案，/為何/在上帝之下，/這種痛苦允許存在——/，為何/在上帝之下，允許其開始，/如何/在上帝之下，/它可能結束。/我沒有勇氣結束它，/我知道，/如果沒有答案的話。）

這幾年來的小說與電影，美化了吸血鬼的一些特質，如生命的不朽、年輕貌美的外表、神奇的力量與神祕的性格，往往忽略了這些「菁英」優勢所帶來的疏離（detachment）與折磨（agony）。生命的不朽或青春美麗，或許帶來喜悅，但是看到自己愛人的衰老或是自己無法變老，無法感受人類的生老病死，生命還有什麼意義？Louis 說：

"What does it mean to die when you can live until the end of the world? And what is 'the end of the world' except a phrase, because who knows even what is the world itself?"

（死亡代表什麼意義，當你能活到世界的結束？什麼是世界的結束，除了只是一段話語外，因為誰知道世界到底是什麼？）

生命的存在意義建立在短暫與變化，沒有死亡、沒有變化的世界，如何忍受那種永生的折磨？

安・萊絲的吸血鬼其實是一群好辯的哲學家，探討善與惡、道德與藝術之間的關係，小說中也有非常浪漫的描寫。

📖 **精彩片段賞析**

到底吸血鬼的本質是否邪惡，到底吸血鬼有無道德？小說的主人翁 Louis 不斷地陷入一些道德與美學的爭辯。

他跟記者男孩之間的對話，就充滿這種價值的討論：

"I don't understand," / said the boy. / "I thought aesthetic decisions / could be completely immoral. / What about the cliche of / the artist who leaves his wife and children / so he can paint? / Or Nero playing the harp / while Rome burned?"

（「我不了解，」/ 男孩說。/「我以為美學的決定 / 可能是全然地不道德。/ 那些所謂世俗的陳腐看法，/ 藝術家拋妻離子，/ 這樣就可以專心畫畫？/ 或是尼祿皇帝彈琴，/ 焚燒羅馬？」）

"Both were moral decisions. / Both served a higher good, / in the mind of the artist. / The conflict lies / between the morals of the artist / and the morals of society, / not between aesthetics and morality."

（兩者皆是道德的決定。/ 兩者都為了一個更高的善，/ 在藝術家的心裡。/ 此衝突存在於 / 藝術家的道德 / 與社會的道德，/ 並非美學與道德的衝突。）

此回答中充滿了道德的相對觀點，也就是每個人都有其道德的看法，與社會的觀點不一定一樣，由於這種特異的（other）道德觀，也造就了藝術家獨立之人格，才能具創造力，這也說明了很多藝術家的言行與看法常常引起大眾社會的側目。此處作者用了兩個動詞，值得我們學習。served 原意指的是「為了……服務」，這裡表示前面兩件事情，達到了什麼樣的目的（serve a purpose）；另外一句 "The conflict lies between...." 也是很好使用的句法，表示「衝突存在於」，如 "The conflict lies between personal interests and social good."（衝突存在於個人利益與社會利益。閱讀小說，常常可以吸收這些好的用法與優美的詞句。

Louis 變成吸血鬼後，最大的特質在於超越了其舊有人類渾渾噩噩的認知，提升了其感官與思維的能力，語言的使用也進入了藝術的層次，使用不少優美的英文來描寫其感受：

It was well past midnight / when I finally rose out of the chair / and went out on the gallery. / The moon was large over the cypresses, / and the candlelight poured from the open doors. / The thick plastered pillars and walls of the house / had been freshly whitewashed, / the floorboards freshly swept, / and a summer rain had left the night clean / and sparkling with drops of water. / I leaned against / the end pillar of the gallery, / my head touching the soft tendrils /of a jasmine / which grew there in constant battle / with a wisteria, and I thought of / what lay before me / throughout the world and throughout time, / and resolved to go about it / delicately and reverently....

（已過了午夜 / 我終於從椅子上起身 / 走到外面的陽台 。/ 月亮大大的掛在柏樹上，/ 燭光從敞開的大門灑下。/ 厚厚的石灰柱與屋牆已洗刷白淨，/ 地板也剛清掃，/ 夏日的雨清洗了夜晚，/ 閃爍著水珠。/ 我靠在陽台的尾柱上，/ 頭輕觸茉莉花柔軟的鬚蔓 ，/ 生長於此，不斷與紫藤競爭，/ 想到展現在我面前的一切，/ 橫跨時空，/ 決定去經歷，/ 以細膩且虔誠的心⋯⋯）

這種情境與心境交雜的描寫，很多讀者都會跳過，因為與情節無關。不過，類似這種抒情方式的描寫，其實常常展現作者想要表達的訊息。人類常常忽略了周遭細膩的事物，也無法以虔誠與細膩的心去觀察大自然與外在的世界，因此透過吸血鬼視野的轉換，我們跟著體會外在環境的脈動：月光、燭光、水珠、鬚蔓、紫藤等等一切美的事物。其中一句以 "the soft tendrils of a jasmine which grew there in constant battle with a wisteria"，將 jasmine 的鬚蔓與紫藤的糾葛，用 in constant battle （不斷地爭鬥）來比喻，非常傳神。作者最後還引用了 John Milton 在《失樂園》（*Paradise Lost*）中，亞當與夏娃離開伊甸園的話語 （"The world was all before them" 整個世界在他們面前。），隱含新的生活與新的挑戰，充滿著希望也充滿著苦難（"I thought of what lay before me"）。

讀完了這一段，你是否感受到身為人類對外在事物的認知，沒有吸血鬼來的敏銳呢？吸血鬼的自我追尋才開始，也代表孤獨的自我，正掙扎於自己的內心及外在環境，各種善念與暴力、各種堅持與誘惑，正不斷地爭鬥（in constant battle）。一段情景交融的描寫，點出了此小說的主題。小說中充滿這些浪漫情境的鋪陳與文字的渲染，讀者除了進行故事冒險外，也可以多體會這些優美的片斷。不要透過逐字中文翻譯，讓我們輕輕地朗讀這一段巴黎：

"Paris was a universe whole / and entire unto herself, / hollowed and fashioned / by history; so she seemed in this age of Napoleon III / with her towering buildings, / her massive cathedrals, / her grand boulevards / and ancient winding medieval streets/ —as vast and indestructible / as nature itself. / All was embraced by her, / by her volatile and enchanted populace / thronging the galleries, / the theaters, / the cafes, / giving birth over and over to / genius and sanctity, philosophy and ware, / frivolity and the finest art."

（巴黎是屬於自己的宇宙，／完整而無缺，／被歷史雕琢成型，好似在拿破崙三世時期，／高聳的建築、／龐大的教堂、／壯麗的林蔭大道、／古老蜿蜒的中古世紀街道，／——有如大自然般巨大、永恆不滅。／擁抱一切，／不斷地創造了天才與聖潔、／哲學與器皿、／輕浮與精緻藝術。）

📖 結局賞析

小說最後的結束，以年輕記者的覺醒與悸動作為吸血鬼 Louis 的反擊！Louis 在飽受人性與異型間的道德折磨後，喪失了希望與未來。然而吸血鬼的不朽與活力，對於年輕無知的記者充滿了誘惑力，他祈求 Louis 賜給他這種神奇的力量，這不禁讓我們想起浮士德邀請魔鬼進入他的房間，定下了永遠追尋的死亡契約：

"Don't you see / how you made it sound?/ It was adventures / like I'll never know in my whole life! / You talk about passion, / you talk about longing! / You talk about things / that millions of us won't ever taste / or come to understand. / And then / you tell me it ends like that. / I tell you..." / And he stood / over the vampire now, / his hands outstretched before him. / "If you were to give me that power! / The power to see and feel and live forever!"

（「你難道看不出來，／這聽起來如何嗎？／這段冒險，／我這一生都不可能知道。／你談論到激情，／你談到熱望，／你所談的事，／幾百萬人都不可能品嚐／或瞭解。／然後／你告訴我就這樣結束，／我告訴你……」他站起來，／俯視著吸血鬼，／雙手伸展在他面前。「希望你給我這種力量，／可以看見、感覺、及永生的力量！」）

適合閱讀程度：
大二以上程度及社會人士。
延伸閱讀／推薦書單、電影：
電影：
Interview with the Vampire（《夜訪吸血鬼》，1994）
Twilight（《暮光之城》，適合高中生，2008）
The Society of S:（《驚醒之年》，適合高中生）

《暮光之城》

Twilight

(2005)

Stephenie Meyer

© Ingo Wagner/dpa/Corbis

📖 作者簡介

美國作家史蒂芬妮‧梅爾（Stephenie Meyer, 1973 ～）以《暮光之城》系列的吸血鬼小說聞名，這一系列的小說在全球已銷售超過 1 億本，被翻譯成 37 種語言。梅爾生長於亞歷桑那（Arizona）的鳳凰城，也是小說部分場景的背景。梅爾在大學時念英文系，成為作家之前，只做過一般公司的接待員工作。

據梅爾自己說，《暮光之城》的故事來自於 2003 年的一場夢。她夢到一個人類少女與一男性吸血鬼的戀愛。她將此夢境寫成故事，就成為此小說的第 13 章。在她姊妹的鼓勵下，她將此小說投稿給出版社，被多家出版社拒絕。最後由 Writers House 出版，一夕之間成為暢銷作品。2005 年出版第一本小說之後，接下去連續出版 3 本續集：《新月》（*New Moon*, 2006）、《月蝕》（*Eclipse*, 2007）、《破曉》（*Breaking Dawn*, 2008）。這 4 本書都成為美國各大排行榜的熱門作品。梅爾坦承她的吸血鬼小說受到夏綠蒂‧白朗特（Charlotte Bronte）的《簡愛》（*Jane Eyre*）所影響，其他影響她的作品包括：《傲慢與偏見》（*Pride and Prejudice*）、《羅密歐與茱麗葉》（*Romeo and Juliet*）以及《咆哮山莊》（*Wuthering Heights*）等。

一般批評家常將 J. K. 羅琳（J. K. Rowling，《哈利波特》的作者）與梅爾相提並論，兩人都是從業餘寫作出發，登上了國際書市；兩人都滿足了青少年的閱讀品味。透過神祕與驚奇的元素，創造了現代人生活中所缺乏的冒險與愛的故事。

📖 小說介紹

When life offers you a dream / so far beyond any of your expectations, / it's not reasonable to grieve / when it comes to an end.

（當生命提供你夢想，/ 遠遠超越你的期望，/ 哀傷是沒有道理的，/ 當你來到生命的盡頭。）

任何人在一生中，總是夢想生命能夠超越自己的期望，痛快地享受生命，即使要付出生命的代價。《暮光之城》一開始引用女主角 Isabella 這段話，點出面對愛情與死亡的抉擇，能夠痛快地暢飲生命，可能是我們內心的渴望。女主角在異地高中遇到了前所未有的愛情經驗，在叛逆與激情的推波下，一場神祕但非常安全的愛情之旅就這樣展開。

📖 主題分析

✚ 死亡與激情

長久以來的愛情故事都是圍繞在激情與死亡的主題上，如《羅密歐與茱麗葉》。短暫的愛情似乎得透過死亡的洗禮，才能獲得永恆。《暮光之城》也是延續這個主題，帶領年輕人去體會不同的愛情：死亡與激情都是一種極端的情緒表現，兩者有共同性，如何從死亡陰影走出來，才能體會愛情的永恆。

小說一開始，由女主角 Isabella 以第一人稱的角度，道出青少年的孤獨與無助：長久依賴的媽媽有自己的生活，而離婚的父親卻是個很難親近的人：

We exchanged a few more comments on the weather, / which was wet, / and that was pretty much it for conversation. / We stared out the windows in silence.

（我們交換了一下評論，/ 有關天氣，/ 濕濕的。/ 這大約就是我們的對話。/ 我們看著窗外，無話可說。）

來到了陌生的國度（an alien planet），Isabella 馬上被學校神祕的 Cullen 家族所吸引：

I stared / because their faces, / so different, / so similar, / were all / devastatingly, / inhumanly / beautiful. / They were faces / you never expected to see / except perhaps on the airbrushed pages of a fashion magazine. / Or painted by an old master / as the face of an angel. / It was hard to decide / who was the most beautiful /— maybe the perfect blond girl, / or the bronze-haired boy.

（我瞪著，/ 因為他們的臉孔，/ 這麼不同，/ 這麼相似，/ 都是非常 / 具毀滅性、/ 不像凡人的 / 美。/ 那些臉龐，/ 你不可能期望看到 ，/ 除非或許在時尚雜誌的霧面頁上，/ 或老師傅畫的 / 天使面孔。/ 很難決定 / 誰最漂亮 /——或許是那個完美的金髮女孩、/ 或許是那個褐色頭髮的男孩。）

美的吸引幾乎是這種類型小說必備的元素：美代表一種令人愉悅的心情，美也代表一種刺激情緒的媒介。這種一見鍾情（love at first sight），強調男女毫無物質條件（不計較出身背景、財富、家庭），而在那一剎那間，生物的本能，從外表、從感覺出發，產生了無法抵擋的致命吸引力（fatal attraction）。這本小說迷人的地方，其實就是將這種一見鍾情的致命吸引力，完整的呈現在讀者面前。讀者跟著女主角的眼神、心情變化、內心的投入，來完成這場驚險的愛情遊戲。Isabella 偷偷地望著迷人的男主角，不知不覺被他異質的行為與舉動（冷酷、孤傲）所吸引。

I couldn't stop myself from / peeking occasionally / through the screen of my hair / at the strange boy / next to me. / During the whole class, / he never relaxed his stiff position / on the edge of his chair, / sitting as far from me as possible. / I could see his hand on his left leg / was clenched into a fist, / tendons standing out / under his pale skin. / This, too, he never relaxed. / He had the long sleeves of his white shirt / pushed up to his elbows, / and his forearm was / surprisingly / hard and muscular / beneath his light skin. / He wasn't nearly as slight as he'd looked / next to his burly brother.

（我忍不住，/ 有時偷窺，/ 透過頭髮的屏障，/ 看著奇異的男孩，/ 坐在我旁邊。／整堂課，／他沒有放鬆僵硬的姿勢，／坐在椅子邊緣，／坐得離我遠遠的。／我可以看到他放在左腿上的手，／握緊拳頭，／肌肉突出，／從蒼白的皮膚下。／這，他也沒有放鬆。／他將白襯衫的長袖，／推到手肘上，／他的前臂，／令人驚訝地，／堅硬、強壯充滿肌肉，／在淺色的皮膚下。／他沒有看起來那麼纖細，／坐在他粗壯的哥哥旁邊。）

　　美與力的展現，既蒼白又健壯，凸顯 Edward 與一般高中生的不同，這樣的特異人士很快地吸引高傲且聰明美麗的 Isabella。

　　完美的愛情永遠是大眾小說讀者的最愛。然而在這些愛情中加入一點危險的因子，更提升了愛情的強度，也展現死亡與激情對比的主題。小說進入高潮時，Isabella 知道了 Edward 是異種人類，是永遠年輕、永遠俊美、嗜渴人類鮮血的吸血鬼：

I was in danger of being distracted by his livid, glorious face. It was like trying to stare down a destroying angel.

　　（我處於危險，被迷惑，他青灰色、閃亮的臉孔。好像試圖盯著一個具毀滅性的天使）

　　"Don't you see, Bella? It's one thing for me to make myself miserable, but a wholly other thing for you to be so involved."

　　（你不知道嗎？ Bella，讓我自己陷入不幸是一回事，但是將你扯進來完全是另一回事。）

He turned his anguished eyes to the road, his words flowing almost too fast for me to understand. "I don't want to hear that you feel that way." His voice was low but urgent. His words cut me. "It's wrong. It's not safe. I'm dangerous, Bella—please, grasp that."

　　（他痛苦的眼神轉向馬路，話講得太快，我幾乎無法瞭解。「我不想聽到你這麼感覺。」他的聲音又低又急。他的話打斷了我。「這是錯的，這不安全。我很危險，Bella，請妳瞭解。」）

"No." I tried very hard not to look like a sulky child.

（「不」，我努力試著，不像是個鬧彆扭的小孩。）

"I'm serious," he growled.

（「我是當真的」，他吼叫。）

"So am I. I told you, it doesn't matter what you are. It's too late."

（「我也是，我告訴過你，你是什麼不重要。太晚了。」）

　　沒錯，一切都太晚了。Isabella 已經愛上了具有致命性的吸血鬼 Edward，這場刺激、血腥的愛情故事已經轟轟烈烈展開。

　　沒有刺激的愛情不是愛情，沒有終點的激情無法昇華。Isabella 與 Edward 的愛情既危險（兩人的絕大差異及外來的阻擾）又安全（沒有性愛、又得到吸血鬼家族的保護），讀者跟隨著驚險的情節，但最終安全地看到兩人的相聚：

I touched his face. "Look," I said. "I love you more than everything else in the world combined. Isn't that enough?"

（我碰觸他的臉，「喂」，我說：「我愛你超過世上所有其他一切。這不夠嗎？」）

"Yes, it is enough," he answered, smiling. "Enough for forever."

（「永遠都夠！」）

And he leaned down to press his cold lips once more to my throat.

（他靠過來，將冰冷的嘴唇再一次印上我的喉嚨。）

📖 精彩片段賞析

　　整體小說的精彩處，其實是透過女主角的眼光與內心忐忑不安的心情，形成一個危險、刺激但又令人興奮的愛情發掘過程。

當她內心知道自己已經陷入情網，可是所愛上的人又是不該愛的。小說家並未赤裸裸的進入 Isabella 的內心，反而透過感官的描寫，點出 Isabella 的無助與迷惘：

I walked up the stairs / slowly, / a heavy stupor / clouding my mind. / I went through the motions of / getting ready for bed / without paying any attention to what I was doing. / It wasn't until I was in the shower— /the water too hot, / burning my skin— / that I realized I was freezing. / I shuddered violently for several minutes / before the steaming spray could finally relax my rigid muscles. / Then I stood in the shower, / too tired to move, / until the hot water began to run out.

（我走上樓梯，/ 慢慢地，/ 某種沉重的茫然 / 襲上心頭。/ 我進行一連串的動作，/ 準備上床，/ 沒注意到自己做了什麼。/ 直到進入沖澡——/ 水很燙，燙了我的皮膚—— / 我才感覺到自己很冷。/ 我激烈地顫抖了好幾分鐘，/ 直到水蒸氣最後放鬆了我僵硬的肌肉。/ 然後，我站在水流中，/ 太累動不了，/ 直到熱水流光了。）

熱水的流動 vs. 身體的寒冷，我們似乎也感受到這些寒冷的變化，陷入一種茫然與恍惚的境界。這種有點濫情式的寫法，正是浪漫愛情故事令人投入的主因。愛情就是令人恍惚、令人冷熱交雜出現。好好經營這類的感覺與場景，將讀者不自覺地拉入女主角的內心，就是成功的表現手法。

除了這種恍惚的心情外，挑情的場景也是這本小說的重要鋪陳：

"Tell me why you ran from me before."
（「告訴我之前為何逃開我。」）
His smile faded. "You know why."
（他的微笑消失。「你知道原因。」）
"No, I mean, exactly what did I do wrong? I'll have to be on my guard, you see, so I better start learning what I shouldn't do. This, for example" — I stroked the

back of his hand— "seems to be all right."

（「不，我的意思是，到底我做錯什麼？我也必須留心，這樣最好開始學習，哪些不應該做。這樣，比如說，」我撫摸他的手背，「似乎沒問題。」）

"Well...." He contemplated for a moment. "It was just how close you were. Most humans instinctively shy away from us, are repelled by our alienness.... I wasn't expecting you to come so close. And the smell of your throat."

（「喔⋯⋯」他想了一下，「就是你太貼近了。大部分的人類，本能上，就會避開我們，排斥我們的不同。我沒有期望你會這麼貼進。你喉嚨的味道。」）

He raised his free hand / and placed it gently on the side of my neck. / I sat very still, / the chill of his touch a natural warning / — a warning telling me to be terrified. / But there was no feeling of fear in me. / There were, however, other feelings....

（他提起他閒著的手，/ 輕輕地放在我的頸邊。/ 我坐著沒動，/ 他碰觸所產生的冷意是種自然的警告 / ——警告我要害怕。/ 但是我卻沒有恐懼的感覺，/ 在我內心。/ 卻是有其他的感覺⋯⋯）

這種帶點情欲卻又沒有性愛場景的描寫，也是這本小說成功之處。緊張、興奮、適當的愛撫與親密行為，在在都敲動青少年或浪漫讀者的心。恐怖小說家史蒂芬・金談論梅爾的小說時曾說：「很明顯地，她寫給年輕的女性，安全地結合性與愛，又刺激、又恐怖，但不具威脅性，因為沒有明顯的性愛。」

📖 結局賞析

Isabella 與 Edward 的愛情，必須接受考驗。受盡其他吸血鬼的威脅與攻擊，他們兩人總算印證了兩人的相互感覺。可是這次的追殺，看出了 Isabella 的脆弱與生命的短暫，這似乎成為兩人最後永恆愛情的障礙？ Edward 會不會將 Isabella 變成跟他一樣的 vampire 呢？這是我們讀者一直想問的問題。小說結束的時候，Edward 的回答令人疑惑。

His eyebrows rose. "Is that what you dream about? Being a monster?"

"Not exactly," I said, frowning at his word choice. Monster indeed. "Mostly I dream about being with you forever."

His expression changed, softened and saddened by the subtle ache in my voice.

"Bella." His fingers lightly traced the shape of my lips. "I will stay with you—isn't that enough?"

I smiled under his fingertips. "Enough for now."

Edward 不希望 Isabella 變成跟他一樣的「monster」（怪物）。然而，Isabella 希望跟 Edward 永遠在一起（dream about being with you forever）。唯有變成 vampire，兩人才能在一起。這是一個兩難的問題：Edward 愛上 Isabella，就是因為她人類的特質，充滿他想要的那種特殊的人類氣味。如果 Isabella 變成跟他一樣的 vampire，她是否還能吸引他呢？但是這種不平凡的愛情與吸引，卻是無法永遠延續，只能掌握現在（enough for now）。兩人的愛情難題如何解決，只能期待續集的驚喜了！

適合閱讀程度：
高一學生以上
延伸閱讀／推薦書單、電影：
小說：
New Moon（《新月》）
The Society of S（《驚醒之年》）
Harry Porter Series（《哈利波特》系列小說）

《查理的巧克力工廠》

Charlie and the Chocolate Factory
(1964)

Roald Dahl

📖 作者簡介

　　英國作家羅德‧達爾（Roald Dahl, 1916 ～ 1980）年輕時，曾參與二次大戰，是傑出的飛行軍官。達爾於 1942 年開始寫作，以他的空軍服役經驗為主。他的第一本兒童故事《小頑皮》（*The Gremlins*），也是以英國空軍的傳說迷信為主。之後，開始創作一連串深受 20 世紀小孩所喜愛的故事，包括查理的系列小說。除了兒童故事外，達爾也寫成人的恐怖小說，充滿懸疑與黑暗的一面。

　　在 40 年代，達爾因其兒童與成人故事，成為 20 世紀的暢銷作家，曾被認為是 20 世紀最偉大的兒童故事作家，2008 年，英國《泰晤士報》（*The Times*）將他列為二次大戰以來 50 位最偉大英國小說家中的第 16 名。他的小說常有令人意想不到的情節與想像力，尤其是兒童故事，以誇大的場景及帶有教化的色彩，贏得大人與小孩的青睞。

📖 小說介紹

　　They all knew it was ridiculous to expect this one poor little candy bar to have a magic ticket inside it, and they were trying as gently and as kindly as they could to prepare Charlie for the disappointment. But there was one other thing that the grownups also knew, and it was this: that however small the chance might of striking lucky, the chance was there.

　　（他們都知道，期望這麼小小的一條糖果，藏有神奇的門票在內，真是很荒謬。他們僅可能緩緩地、溫和地讓 Charlie 接受失望。不過仍然有件事，這些大人也知道，那就是：不管那驚人的幸運機會有多小，機會總是有的！）

　　機會總是有的（...the chance was there.）。抱著這種樂觀與期待的心情，Charlie 自己本人與家人能夠從貧窮的家庭中發現自己生活的樂趣，也就是這種期待，開啟了巧克力工廠的冒險。

達爾這本 1964 年描寫家境清寒的小男生 Charlie，在一次巧妙的機緣下，與另外 4 個富裕、貪婪的小孩，一起進入當地一家神奇的巧克力工廠，接受主人 Willy Wonka 的道德考驗，最後貧窮但高貴的 Charlie 通過考驗，獲得神奇的回報。整本奇幻小說（fantasy），充滿這種類型小說（如《哈利波特》、《納尼亞傳奇》、《愛麗絲鏡中遊記》）特有的因素：善與惡的對立、善報與懲罰的道德啟發、幻想與現實的矛盾。主人翁透過神奇的媒介（如月台、衣櫃、鏡子）進入奇幻的世界，展開冒險。但是閱讀這類小說的樂趣，不僅是最後的道德啟發（善念打敗惡魔），最重要的是想像力的運作。到底作者如何創造令人驚奇的場景與曲折的情節，讓青少年或成年人陶醉在這些幻想的國度裡？

📖 主題分析

✚ 驚奇的幻想，永遠是這類小說的精髓。

《查理的巧克力工廠》一開始就創造這種驚奇。可憐的 Charlie，家庭貧窮，但卻渴望巧克力，作者利用誇張的口氣，形容巧克力對他的誘惑：

... on those marvelous birthday mornings, / he would place it carefully / in a small wooden box / that he owned, / and treasure it / as though it were a bar of solid gold; / and for the next few days, / he would allow himself / only to look at it, / but never to touch it. / Then at last, when he could stand it no longer, / he would peel back a tiny bit of the paper wrapping / at one corner / to expose a tiny bit of chocolate, / and then he would take a tiny nibble—/ just enough to allow the lovely sweet taste / to spread out slowly / over his tongue.

（在那些神奇的生日早上，/ 他會小心地放在 / 一個小木盒中，/ 他擁有的。/ 珍惜它好像是一條金塊。/ 接下去幾天，/ 他只會允許自己 / 看著它，/ 但是不碰它。/ 最後，當他受不了時，/ 他會剝下一小片包裝紙，/ 在一角，/ 露出一小小片巧克力，/

然後吃一小小口，/ 足夠讓甜美的滋味，/ 慢慢散開 / 在他的舌頭上。）

　　整段使用了 3 個 tiny 來描寫 Charlie 捨不得與珍惜的心態，非常傳神。或許成人讀者會認為，一個三餐都吃不飽的小孩怎麼會渴望這種有錢人的食物！而且日後，Charlie 還運氣很好獲得進入巧克力工廠的入門票（golden ticket），此外，這個巧克力工廠沒有工人如何運作，這種種情節都不合理。

　　不合理或荒謬（absurd）的情節，其實就是驚奇的一部分，當大人質疑這一切的可能性，唯有天真純潔的小孩才會相信一切的可能，有如相信聖誕老人的存在。相信是一種希望，而相信希望（belief in hope）也是生命所賦予的意義。就是這種純潔，開啟奇幻的世界。讀者閱讀這些 absurd language and ideas（荒謬的語言與想法），必須放棄理性的思維與現實的考量，才能完全進入想像的空間。英國 19 世紀的浪漫詩人柯立芝（Coleridge）曾提到，我們要「暫時凍結那種不相信的心態（willing suspension of disbelief for the moment）」，來提升我們的心靈，接受超自然的境界：

　　... to excite a feeling / analogous to the supernatural [or romantic], / by awaking the mind's attention / from the lethargy of custom / and directing it / to the loveliness and the wonders of the world / before us.（quoted from *Biographia Literaria*）
　　（激起一種感覺，/ 類似超自然（浪漫），/ 透過引起心靈的覺醒，/ 從習慣常軌的麻木昏睡中，/ 引導心靈 / 見識這世界的魅力與驚奇，/ 在我們眼前。）（引自 Coleridge 的《文學傳記》）

　　與《哈利波特》或《納尼亞傳奇》的作者一樣，達爾試圖帶領讀者（尤其是青少年讀者），摒棄大人理性、悲觀、貪婪與勢利的心態，進入巧克力的浪漫與超自然世界，跟 Willy Wonka 一起來體驗荒謬與驚奇。Mr. Wonka 痛恨大人世界的背叛與虛偽，他需要的是小孩的純真與幻想，來經營他的工廠：

Mind you, / there are thousands of clever men / who would give anything for the chance to come in / and take over from me, / but I don't want that sort of person. / I don't want a grown-up person at all. / A grown-up won't listen to me; / he won't learn. / He will try to do things / his own way and not mine. / So I have to have a child.

（你要知道，/ 有上千的聰明人 / 願意用一切來換取進來的機會，/ 從我手上接受，/ 不過我不想要那種人，/ 我一點不想要大人。/ 大人都不會聽我的，/ 不會學習，/ 他會試圖做事，/ 以他的方法，不是用我的方法。/ 所以我要一個小孩。）

✚ 巧克力工廠的意象

巧克力工廠是個幻想的國度，是個想像力（power of imagination）的展現。有如頑童般的 Mr. Wonka 帶領 5 個小孩及其家人進入了神奇的巧克力房間（The Chocolate Room）：

They were looking down upon a lovely valley. There were green meadows on either side of the valley, and along the bottom of it there flowed a great brown river. What is more, there was a tremendous waterfall halfway along the river—

無法想像，一間巧克力房間化成一個巨大的巧克力王國，一望無際的山谷，綠草如茵，中間出現了一條巧克力河流，河中間還有一巨大的巧克力瀑布。這樣的景象，創造了驚愕的美感經驗，也正是這本奇幻小說令人著迷之處！

📖 精彩片段賞析

精彩的奇幻小說，除了想像力的展現外，文字的力量也是成功的關鍵。這本小說運用生動的文字，勾畫出視覺的影像，人物有如卡通的誇張，動作場景也栩栩如生，形成類似 3D 動畫的影像。此部小說被拍成電影，誇張的動作與生動的場景，其實在小說中已經透過文字的強化，幫導演與演員打造好了。

巧克力工廠的主人 Willy Wonka 一出現就吸引了大家的目光，其有如孩童的動作與舉止，充分流露出天真與幻想的一面：

Mr. Wonka was standing all alone just inside the open gates of the factory.
（Wonka 一個人站在工廠的敞開大門內。）
And what an extraordinary little man he was!（他多麼矮小啊！）
He had a black top hat on his head.（頭上帶個黑色高帽）
... The whole face, in fact, was alight with fun and laughter....
（整個臉，實際上，燃燒著喜悅與笑意。）
He was like a squirrel / in the quickness of his movements, / like a quick clever old squirrel / from the park.

（他像隻松鼠，/ 快速地移動，/ 像隻快速聰明的老松鼠，/ 來自公園。）
Suddenly, / he did a funny little skipping dance in the snow, / and he spread his arms wide, / and he smiled at the five children / who were clustered near the gates / and he called out, / "Welcome, my little friends! / Welcome to the factory!"

（突然，/ 他滑稽地在雪中跳舞，/ 張開雙臂，/ 對著 5 個小孩微笑，/ 他們聚在大門口，/ 他大叫：/「歡迎，小朋友，/ 歡迎來到工廠！」）

身材矮小，有如孩童，卻帶著一頂高帽，凸顯滑稽的形象。而臉上卻充滿喜感，尤其是不斷跳躍的動作。作者使用比喻性的說法，描寫他有如小松鼠，動作迅速。這種比喻的用法在兒童故事中常常使用，可以很快地將具體的視覺形象打入讀者的心中。

Mr. Wonda 雖然身材矮小，可是活力充沛，對他而言，活力與純潔就是美麗的象徵，希望為世界帶來美麗的感覺：當他帶領小朋友進入重要的巧克力房間，他說：

"This is the nerve center of the whole factory, / the heart of the whole business! / And so beautiful! / I insist upon my rooms / being beautiful! / I can't abide ugliness / in factories!"

（這裡是整個工廠的神經中樞，/ 整個產業的心臟！/ 這麼美！/ 我堅持我的房間 / 要很美。/ 我受不了醜陋，/ 在工廠裡。）

被慣壞的小孩、貪心的小孩、不滿足的小孩都是醜陋的，都沒有資格留在這個美麗的工廠裡。故事進行中，4 個「醜陋的」小孩都被踢出工廠、都被改造，只有謙虛、內心充滿感恩與喜悅的 Charlie 被留下。首先，肥胖貪吃的 Augustus Gloop 探頭狂吃巧克力河的東西，瞬間被河沖走：

"But Augustus was deaf to everything / except the call of his enormous stomach. / He was now lying full length on the ground / with his head far out over the river, / lapping up the chocolate like a dog.... / For suddenly there was a shriek, / and then a splash, / and into the river went Augustus Gloop, / and in one second / he had disappeared / under the brown surface."

（不過，Augustus 聽不到任何聲音，/ 只有他巨大胃腸的呼喊。/ 他正全身趴在地上，/ 頭向前伸到河裡，/ 舔起巧克力，有如狗…… / 突然，一聲尖叫，/ 一聲水濺，/ Augustus Gloop 掉入河中，/ 一瞬間，/ 已經消失 / 在棕色的表面下。）

此處，作者使用聲音的效果，如 the call of his enormous stomach, lapping up the chocolate like a dog, a shriek, a splash 來創造身歷其境的效果，文字與聲音的完美結合，令人感受那一剎那間的動作。此外，這裡最長的一句話 He was now lying full length on the ground with his head out over the river, lapping up the chocolate like a dog. 前面的主要句子拖得很長，透過句子的長度，來生動描寫出胖小子 Augustus 趴在地上，頭往前傾，身子拉長的影像；句子後面使用 V-ing（lapping up the chocolate），接續前面的動作（頭往前），lapping（狗舔食物）的聲音與動作更是一氣呵成。文字、聲音、視覺巧妙結合，讀起來生動有趣！

除了視覺與聲音的文字效果外，有如動畫卡通的描寫也是此本小說成功的地方。好嚼口香糖的小女孩 Violet，不顧警告，吃了神奇的口香糖大餐，瞬間變成了藍莓氣球：

But there was no saving her now. / Her body was swelling up / and changing shape / at such a rate / that within a minute / it had turned into nothing less than an enormous round blue ball—/ a gigantic blueberry, in fact—/ and all that remained of Violet Beauregarde herself / was a tiny pair of legs / and a tiny pair of arms / sticking out of the great round fruit / and a little head on top.

（但是，現在救不了她了。/ 她的身體已經脹大，/ 改變形狀，/ 速度很快，/ 剎那間，/ 已經變成一圓形的藍色大球──/ 一顆巨大的藍莓，事實上──/ Violet Beauregarde 本人所留下的，/ 只剩下細小的雙腳、/ 細小的一雙手臂，/ 突出巨大的圓形水果，/ 以及頂上的一個小頭。）

巨大（enormous, gigantic, great）與細小（tiny, little）的對比，不斷地出現在小說之中，產生一種滑稽與誇張的畫面，也構成這本小說卡通的成份。

閱讀這種類型的奇幻小說，可能不要拘泥於小說所給的道德涵義或價值觀，而是要投入神奇的幻想國度裡，不斷期待驚奇的畫面與場景的出現，開發自己的想像力。此外，更要去品嘗文字所創造出來的視覺、聲音與誇大歪曲的場景，挑戰文字與認知的極限。閱讀不僅是要讀出小說帶來的意義，更要感受這種驚奇的美感：

It was an eerie and frightening feeling / to be standing on clear glass / high up in the sky. It made you feel / that you weren't standing on anything at all.

（這是一種詭異、驚嚇的感覺，/ 站在透明玻璃上，/ 高高在天空上，/ 讓你感覺 / 好像沒站在任何東西上面。）

📖 結局賞析

小說最後，當然是珍惜一切的 Charlie 獲得了 Mr. Wonka 的信任，擁有了生平的所有幻想──巧克力工廠：

Charlie climbed onto the bed / and tried to calm the three old people / who were petrified with fear. / "Please don't be frightened," he said. / "It's quite safe. / And we're going to the most wonderful place in the world!"

（查理爬到床上，/ 試圖安撫 3 位老人，/ 他們驚嚇不已。/「別害怕，」/ 他說，/「很安全，/ 我們來到了全世界最棒的地方！」）

恐怖的冒險結束，充滿了驚喜與波折，但是最終以小孩的喜悅心情結束，那種否極泰來的痛快感，很容易引起閱讀者的迴響，闔起書，我們都會發出滿意的笑聲。

適合閱讀程度：
國中三年級以上學生及回味童真的社會人士
延伸閱讀／推薦書單、電影：
小說：
Matilda（《小魔女 Matilda》）
The Chronicles of Narnia（《納尼亞傳奇》）

《福爾摩斯的冒險》

The Adventures of Sherlock Holmes
(1891 ～ 1892)

Arthur Conan Doyle

📖 作者簡介

柯南‧道爾（Arthur Conan Doyle, 1859 ～ 1930）是位蘇格蘭的醫生，不過卻以 Sherlock Holmes 的偵探故事聞名。除了偵探小說外，他也創作科幻小說、歷史小說等。

道爾於 1882 年開始在英國普利矛斯（Plymouth）行醫，然而並不是很成功。在等待病人的時候，他開始寫小說，他的第一本小說《血字的研究》（A Study in Scarlet）於 1887 年出版，創造了 Sherlock Holmes（福爾摩斯）這個偵探角色。這個偵探基本上是以他之前的大學老師 Joseph Bell 為藍本所建構的虛擬人物。

道爾對於歷史故事非常著迷，曾經撰寫有關波爾戰爭（Boer War）的歷史書籍，然而其主要興趣仍在所謂正義的伸張。以業餘偵探的手法，去解決社會案件，滿足了道爾對維多利亞時期犯罪事件的好奇。小說的成功來自於人物的塑造：偵探 Holmes 與其夥伴 Dr. Watson（華生醫師），兩人的對比成為小說引人入勝的關鍵。而 Holmes 的科學觀察與演繹思維，恰好反應了當時社會對於理性思考與科學研究的熱潮，將科學方法運用於生活之中，解決犯罪，印證科學的功能性與即時性，滿足了讀者的好奇心。小說家以驚奇的情節吸引讀者，卻又以合乎邏輯的方式來詮釋情節發展，這種結合懸疑、驚奇與合理性的分析，建立了古典偵探小說的發展模式。

📖 小說介紹

"Life is infinitely stranger than anything which the mind of man could invent.... If we could fly out of that window hand in hand, hover over this great city, gently remove the roofs, and peep in at the queer things which are going on, the strange coincidences, the plannings, the cross-purposes, the wonderful chains of events, working through generations, and leading to the most outre results, it would make all fiction with its conventions most stale and unprofitable."

（生活絕對比人類心靈能想像的要奇怪多了。假如我們能夠攜手飛出窗戶，翱翔在這個大都市上空，輕輕地掀開那些屋頂，窺視裡邊發生的不尋常事物：奇怪的巧合、一些策劃、矛盾的行動計劃、巧妙的連鎖事件，一代一代的發生，導致怪異的結果。這會使得那些老套的小說變得索然無味、毫無利潤。）

史上最偉大的偵探 Sherlock Holmes 對老搭檔 Dr. Watson 說道：生活看起來平淡，但是如果仔細抽絲剝繭，就會發現其間的各種奇怪事物，存在於任何家庭之內，就看我們是否能細細地去觀察、推敲！周遭發生的日常事物絕對比任何小說描述精彩萬分！以不尋常的角度去看尋常的事物，到處可以發現驚奇。沿襲這種浪漫主義的傳統，Holmes 帶領我們進入犯罪的想像空間。

就是這種觀察與推敲的心思，造就了偵探小說的傳奇人物 Sherlock Holmes。 英國 19 世紀偵探小說家科南・道爾所創造的 Holmes 偵探推理小說，從最早的《血字的研究》，塑造了古典偵探小說的典範：案件發生、偵探介入、線索追蹤、嫌犯現身、解釋案情、回歸次序。所有的偵探小說大都以揭發（revelation）與解釋（explanation）的方式進行，作者先創造一個懸疑（suspense） 或謀殺案件（murder），接下去就由偵探帶領讀者去尋找線索、證據（evidence）。之後作者在讀者的認知上，製造多種可能性，然而唯有具科學及邏輯心思的偵探，才能以天才似的推理、歸納分析思考，打敗讀者，獲得真相。從 1891 年開始連載的《福爾摩斯的冒險》（*The Adventures of Sherlock Holmes*）中的 12 篇短篇小說，不以驚聳謀殺案開場，而是深入一般百姓生活，揭發一些奇怪的事物與矛盾行動，開啟了這位神奇偵探的冒險故事。

📖 主題分析

✚ 細節觀察與理性思維

《福爾摩斯的冒險》情節雖然充滿懸疑，然而其主軸並非曲折的情節，反而是偵探如何透過其驚人的觀察能力來破解謎團。誠如 Holmes 所說的：

"Indeed, / I have found / that it is usually in unimportant matters / that there is a field / for the observation, / and for the quick analysis / of cause and effect / which give the charm / to an investigation."

（的確，/ 我發現，/ 經常在一些不重要的事物上，/ 倒有些空間，/ 可以觀察，/ 可以敏銳分析 / 因果關係，/ 這賦予魅力 / 對調查工作而言。）

這裡，作者使用 It is... that 的強調句型，將 in unimportant matters 拉出來放在強調的位置上，表示「在一些不重要的事物上」，偵探經常可以找到仔細觀察與發揮分析因果的能力。

在〈身分案件〉（"A Case of Identity"）的故事中，Holmes 利用這種細微的觀察力與簡單的演繹方式（deduction），「在不重要的事物上」（unimportant things）找到證據，甚至不用出門就解決了一件離奇的失蹤案。當一位婦人來尋找失蹤的未婚夫，Holmes 要求 Dr. Watson 從外表來判斷此婦人的一些狀況。Dr. Watson 接受挑戰：

"Well, she had a slate-coloured, broad-brimmed straw hat, / with a feather of brickish red. / Her jacket was black, / with black beads sewn upon it, / and a fringe of little black jet ornaments. / Her dress was brown, / rather darker than coffee colour, / with a little purple plush / at the neck and sleeves. / Her gloves were greyish / and were worn through / at the right forefinger..."

（喔，她頭戴一頂藍灰色的寬邊草帽，/ 帽上插著一根磚紅色的羽毛。/

短外套是黑色的，/上面縫著黑色珠子，/邊緣鑲嵌小小的黑玉飾物。/上衣是黑褐色的，/比咖啡顏色還深些，/帶著一點紫色絲絨，在領部及袖子上。/手套灰色，/磨破了，/在右手食指上。）

Sherlock Holmes clapped his hands softly together and chuckled.

（福爾摩斯輕輕鼓掌，咯咯地笑著）

"...You have really done very well indeed. / It is true / that you have missed everything of importance, / but you have hit upon the method, / and you have a quick eye for colour. / Never trust to general impressions,/ my boy, / but concentrate yourself upon details. / My first glance is always / at a woman's sleeve./ In a man / it is perhaps better first / to take the knee of the trouser. / As you observe, / this woman had plush upon her sleeves, / which is a most useful material for showing traces."

（你做得真的很好。/真的，/你忽略了所有重要的地方，/不過已經掌握了方法，/對顏色觀察敏銳。/絕不可相信一般的印象，/老兄，/一定要注意細節。/我第一眼總是/看女人的袖子，/男人，/最好先看褲子的膝蓋。/誠如你觀察的，/這女人在袖子上有絲絨，/那是透露痕跡的最有用材質。）

「注意細節」，要注意有用的細節。Dr. Watson 的觀察非常細微，注意顏色，然而他的觀察沒有目標、沒有重點，只是一般的印象，用處不大。細微的觀察要與邏輯的思維結合在一起，才有其用處。從 Holmes 的觀點，女人的袖子與男人的褲子膝蓋，正是觀察一個人工作習慣與生活形態的最好證據。從證據中去推理，從推理中去找真相，就是偵探推理小說的主要樂趣。

偉大的偵探小說，挑戰讀者的想像力與推理能力，而偉大的偵探卻常常在字裡行間中嘲諷讀者的無知：聽聽 Holmes 的自誇，充滿對讀者的嘲諷：

"My name is Sherlock Holmes. It is my business to know what other people don't know."

（我叫夏洛克・福爾摩斯，我就是要知道別人不知道的事。）

"It is my business to know things. Perhaps I have trained myself to see what others overlook. If not, why should you come to consult me?"

（我的工作就是瞭解一切事物。或許我訓練自己，看出別人忽略的事。要不然，你們為何來找我？）

閱讀是一種探索（exploration），而閱讀偵探小說更是將探索的本質發揮到極致，讀者不僅要仔細咀嚼文字，更要深究任何文字所留下來的蛛絲馬跡。沒有比閱讀偵探小說更需要讀者全心投入這種文字與推理的遊戲之中。閱讀偵探小說可說是最能訓練精讀的一種閱讀方式。

📖 精彩片段賞析

一般小說的情節進行，主要以時間順序為主（in chronological order），情節依照時間的次序進行，而偵探小說的敘述結構大抵以兩線進行：一是時間的敘述結構，一是事件的敘述結構 （in topical order）。時間的敘述，大抵與傳統小說同，但是隱藏在時間敘述下面的，其實才是讀者必須去發掘的，也就是整個事件的關聯性與話題性。Holmes 的偵探冒險故事，就是以這兩線來進行：Dr. Watson 所敘述的是時間為軸線，而 Holmes 與我們讀者所關心的才是偵探事件的主題，我們就以本書的第一篇故事 〈波希米亞的醜聞〉（"A Scandal In Bohemia"）為例，來欣賞這種敘述結構的精彩片段，小說仍由 Dr. Watson 來開場，提到一位女性，讓 Holmes 感到佩服：

To Sherlock Holmes / she is always the woman. / I have seldom heard him mention her / under any other name. / In his eyes / she eclipses and predominates / the whole of her sex. / It was not that / he felt any emotion / akin to love / for Irene Adler.

（對福爾摩斯來說， / 她總是那個女性， / 我很少聽到他提到她 ，/ 用別的名字。／在他眼中，／她凌駕、超越／所有女性，／並不是／他對她有任何感情，／類似愛情的，／對 Irene Adler。）

這個神秘女性就是整篇小說的主題點（topic），整篇小說圍繞在 Holmes 與這位 Irene Adler 之間的智慧鬥法。在當時 19 世紀的英國社會中，男性代表理性思維，而女性則是感性的象徵。代表推理科學的 Holmes，當然對於感情不屑一顧，展現男性思維的自大：

All emotions, / and that one particularly, / were abhorrent to / his cold, precise / but admirably balanced mind. / He was, / I take it, / the most perfect reasoning / and observing machine / that the world has seen, / but as a lover / he would have placed himself / in a false position. / He never spoke of the softer passions, / save with a gibe and a sneer.... / But for the trained reasoner / to admit such intrusions / into his own delicate and finely adjusted temperament / was to / introduce a distracting factor / which might throw a doubt / upon all his mental results.

（一切情感，／尤其是那個特別的（愛情），／都是不容的，／對他冷酷、精準／但令人讚歎的冷靜心智。／他是，／我認為，／最完美推理、／觀察的機器，／這世界所僅見的。／不過，作為一個情人，／他一定會把自己／擺錯位置。／從來不提感情，／除了帶些嘲諷與不屑，／……但對於一個訓練有素的推理者來說，／承認這種感情侵入／他細緻且嚴謹的性格，／就是／引進了混亂的因素，／可能會質疑，／他所有心智的成果。）

理性思維與豐富情感的對立、男性與女性的鬥智、婚姻與醜聞的對比，就是本篇小說的主要敘述軸線。而 Dr. Watson 口中，Holmes 如何聽取波希米亞國王的情史、化裝假扮去探聽 Irene Adler 的作息、到最後火災事件，都是以時間的軸線來進行故事。

在時間動作的敘述結構中，我們也可以見識作者在描述事件進行，所使用明快與流暢的語言：

Holmes had sat up upon the couch, / and I saw him motion / like a man / who is in need of air. / A maid rushed across / and threw open the window. / At the same instant / I saw him / raise his hand / and at the signal / I tossed my rocket / into the room / with a cry of "Fire!" / The word was no sooner out of my mouth / than the whole crowd of spectators, / well dressed and ill / — gentlemen, ostlers, and servant-maids / — joined in a general shriek of "Fire!" / Thick clouds of smoke / curled through the room / and out at the open window. / I caught a glimpse / of rushing figures, / and a moment later / the voice of Holmes / from within / assuring them / that it was a false alarm.

（福爾摩斯已靠在沙發上，/我看到他動作/好像一個人/急需空氣。/女僕匆忙走過，/推開窗戶。/同時，/我看到/他舉起手來，/看到那暗號，/我投入煙火筒，/掉入房裡，/大叫「著火了！」/這句話一出我的口，/全部看熱鬧的人，/穿的體面的以及隨便穿的，/紳士、馬夫或僕人，/也齊聲尖叫：「著火了！」/濃煙/捲繞全室，/冒出窗外。/我看了一眼/衝出來的人群，/一會兒，/福爾摩斯的聲音/從裡面傳出，/要大家放心，/這是假警報。）

福爾摩斯接受波希米亞國王的委託，企圖從國王的情婦 Irene Adler 手中奪回兩人親密照片，故意與 Dr. Watson 設計這場火災戲。假設女人在危急時刻一定無法冷靜面對，一定會匆忙去截取這張重要照片。這一連串的動作，從 Dr. Watson 大叫著火了，圍觀者果真驚慌，作者使用幾個名詞 well-dressed and ill —— gentlemen, ostlers, and servant-maids，所謂販夫走卒、路人甲乙，將慌亂的情形點出。本段的幾個動作用得精準，更添此段動作場景的臨場感：rushed, threw, tossed, joined, curled, caught a glimpse。此外使用 no sooner... than 的句型，表示著火的話一出口，即刻引起騷動，動作連續，沒有間斷。

📖 結局賞析

　　一段男性與女性的鬥智，最後帶有女性智慧與感性的 Irene Adler 拆穿了福爾摩斯的詭計，與未婚夫帶著重要的照片遠走自由開放的美國，留下了勝利的身影。英國男性自大的理智，輸給了細膩、溫柔卻帶有智慧與解放心態的新女性。小說的結尾，呼應了小說的開頭，形成了完整的敘述結構：

And that was... how the best plans of Mr. Sherlock Holmes were beaten by a woman's wit. He used to make merry over the cleverness of women, but I have not heard him do it of late.

　　（福爾摩斯過去常常取笑女性的才智，這個事件後，他就不再如此了。）

　　作者科南·道爾在 19 世紀父權的英國社會中，透過號稱「倫敦最聰明的男人」Holmes 口中，讚美女性的思維與智慧，深具意義。

📖 福爾摩斯名言：

It is a capital mistake to theorize before one has data.　Insensibly one begins to twist facts to suit theories, instead of theories to suit facts.

　　（在沒有掌握資料前就提出理論，是個嚴重的錯誤。不知不覺地，我們就歪曲事實來遷就理論，而不是發展理論來符合事實。）

適合閱讀程度：

大一以上學生及社會人士。

延伸閱讀／推薦書單、電影：

小說：

The Hound of the Baskervilles（《巴斯克威爾的獵犬》）

Murder on the Orient Express（《東方特快車謀殺案》）

《達文西密碼》
The Da Vinci Code
(2003)

Dan Brown

© Rune Hellestad/Corbis

📖 作者簡介

　　美國作家丹‧布朗（Dan Brown, 1964～），2003 年出版的《達文西密碼》暢銷書讓他成名。布朗成長於美國新罕部夏州的 Exeter，父親是數學老師，結合數學、音樂及語言，便成為家庭的重要活動，因此布朗對謎語及神祕的興趣應該是來自於家庭的影響。父母更常常在生日或假日設計尋寶活動，讓小孩尋找他們自己的禮物，由此可見，《達文西密碼》很明顯地受到他小時候尋寶活動的啟發。

　　布朗從安姆斯特學院（Amherst College）畢業後，以音樂作為生涯規劃基礎，開始從事歌曲創作。1991 年他搬到好萊塢，希望成為詞曲作者及歌手。1993 年出版自己的第一張 CD。1993 年，布朗閱讀席德尼‧薛爾頓（Sidney Sheldon）的小說《世界末日的陰謀》（*The Doomsday Conspiracy*）後，開始創作驚悚小說。他的第一本小說 *Digital Fortress* 並未受到重視，直到第 4 本小說《達文西密碼》才進入《紐約時報》（*New York Times*）的暢銷排行榜。這本以 Robert Langdon 為男主角的小說據說為作者賺進了 2 億 5000 萬美元以上的收入。他曾說他將創作 12 本有關 Langdon 的小說。

　　這本小說的前言宣稱，本小說有關藝術作品、建築、歷史文件及祕密儀式的描述都是真實的。結合數學、藝術、歷史、宗教及符號象徵的不同知識，小說將幻想世界建構在過去與當代的歷史旋渦中。誠如布朗在一次訪問中說：

"I do something very intentional and specific in these books. And that is to blend fact and fiction in a very modern and efficient style, to tell a story. There are some people who understand what I do, and they sort of get on the train and go for a ride and have a great time, and here are other people who should probably just read somebody else."

📖 小說介紹

We fear what we do not understand.
（我們害怕我們不瞭解的事物。）

人類對於未知的事物，總是充滿恐懼。聰明的人利用各種不同的詮釋手法去解釋這些事物，於是我們有了科學、哲學、宗教、甚至於文學等不同理解生命與宇宙的種種神祕事物。這本號稱以宗教與藝術歷史為出發點的小說，就是建立在這樣的假設上。《達文西密碼》是本神祕偵探的驚悚小說（mystery-detective thriller），結合歷史小說、偵探小說與懸疑小說等各種要素，劇情懸疑且具爭議。從羅浮宮的凶殺案開始，小說的兩位男女主角，大學符號研究學者 Robert Langdon 與年輕美麗的密碼專家 Sophie Neveu 開始一連串的精彩冒險，追尋基督教最大的祕密：聖杯的傳說（Holy Grail）。

📖 主題分析

✚ 恐懼與真相（fear vs. truth）

聖杯的追尋一直是很多浪漫傳奇或冒險故事的重要母題（motif）。傳統的聖杯指的是具「神性智慧」的事物，因為這是耶穌基督最後使用的器皿。布朗利用這個追求聖杯的概念，引導讀者去追尋真相：基督信仰的真相。小說圍繞在文藝復興時期的藝術家達文西的啟蒙思維：

"Many have made a trade of delusions and false miracles, deceiving the stupid multitude."

"Blinding ignorance does not mislead us. O! Wretched mortals, open our eyes."

（很多人以欺騙及假神蹟為手段，欺騙愚昧的大眾。）

（盲目的無知指引著我們。喔！可憐的凡人們，睜開雙眼吧！）

我們必須去追尋真相，因為太多的騙局與假象蒙蔽了我們，小說引用達文西的話，要求我們睜開眼睛，看看歷史的真相。

小說家以哈佛大學的符號學家 Langdon 作為追求真相的騎士，學術的訓練要求他從複雜、糾葛的歷史與事件中，找到關聯與證據，點出了整本小說進行的脈絡與進行的軌跡：

As someone / who had spent his life / exploring the hidden interconnectivity / of disparate emblems and ideologies, / Langdon viewed the world as a web of / profoundly intertwined histories and events. / The connections may be invisible, / he often preached to his symbology classes / at Harvard, / but they are always there, / buried just beneath the surface.

　　（作為一個學者，/ 花了一輩子，/ 探索隱藏的連結性，/ 在一些分散不同的標記與意識形態中，/ Langdon 看待世界有如網路，/ 深深糾葛在一起的歷史與事件。/ 這些連結或許隱藏起來，/ 他經常這樣告訴他的象徵學班上學生 / 在哈佛，/ 但是它們總是在那的，/ 埋藏在表面之下。）

　　然而，隱藏在真相後面的，可能是令人無法承受的事實，這種恐懼的心理也跟著而來。小說中的解碼專家 Sophie 在祖父羅浮宮館長 Sauniere 被殺後，被牽扯進整個聖杯追尋的陰謀裡，隱約中，她感覺到這整體的陰謀似乎跟她的身世有關。Sauniere 生前一直想告訴她家人的背景，暗示其中有個很大的祕密。關於家人的真相與追尋聖杯的真相糾葛在一起，構成本小說的複雜結構：

"Princess...." / Her grandfather's voice cracked / with an emotion / Sophie could not place. / "I know I've kept things from you, / and I know it has cost me your love. / But it was for your own safety. / Now you must know the truth. / Please, I must tell you the truth / about your family."

　　（公主，/ 她祖父的聲音嘶啞，/ 帶著某種感情，/ Sophie 無法認出。/ 我知道我有些事沒有告訴妳，/ 我知道這讓我失去了妳的愛。/ 不過這是為了妳的安全，/ 現在，妳必須知道真相，/ 拜託，我必須告訴妳真相，/ 有關妳的家人。）

Sophie suddenly could hear her own heart. / My family? ... / His words had sent an unexpected surge of longing / through her bones. / My family! / In that fleeting instant, / Sophie saw images from the dream / that had awoken her countless times / when she was a little girl: / My family is alive! / They are coming home! / But, as in her dream, / the pictures evaporated / into oblivion.

（Sophie 突然能夠聽到自己的心跳，/ 我的家人？/ ……他的話語引起一陣意想不到的渴望，/ 一直透過她的身軀。/ 我的家人！/ 在那剎那間，/ Sophie 看到夢中的景象，/ 經常讓她數度驚醒，/ 當她仍是小女孩時：/ 我的家人還活著！/ 他們要回來了！/ 不過，就跟在她夢中一般，/ 這影像蒸發消失，/ 無影無蹤。）

老人嘶啞的聲音在她的心中，激起追求真相的渴望（longing），然而這是夢境（dreams）還是事實？此時，真相與夢境仍然模糊不清，但是對她而言，充滿了恐懼，常常令她驚醒（had awoken her countless times）。最後這些影像（真相）仍然消失，無法掌握。此處使用動詞 evaporated into oblivion 非常傳神，蒸發消失（evaporated），進入遺忘的境地，一方面敘述夢境，一方面隱含這些歷史記憶是否也為人所遺忘（into oblivion）？

不僅是小說中代表正面力量的 Langdon 及 Sophie 在追求真相，小說中隱含的另一股邪惡力量，例如 Aringarosa 主教，也覬覦聖杯的祕密與真相。

Sitting up, / Aringarosa straightened his black cassock / and allowed himself a rare smile. / This was one trip / he had been happy to make. / I have been on the defensive for too long. / Tonight, / however, / the rules had changed. / Only five months ago, / Aringarosa had feared / for the future of the Faith. / Now, as if by the will of God, / the solution had presented itself. / Divine intervention. / If all went as planned / tonight in Paris, / Aringarosa would soon be in possession of something / that would make him the most powerful man / in Christendom.

（坐直起來，/ Aringarosa 拉直黑色的教士袍，/ 露出難得的微笑。/ 這旅程 / 他很高興來。/ 我已經採取守勢很久了。/ 今晚，/ 然而，/ 規則已經改變。/ 就在 5 個月前，/ Aringarosa 還害怕 / 天主信仰的未來。/ 現在，似乎是上帝的旨意，/ 解決之道自然而來。/ 天意的介入。/ 如果一切照計畫來，/ 今晚在巴黎，/ Aringarosa 將很快擁有那個東西，/ 會讓他成為最有權勢的人 / 整個基督國度。）

穿著黑色的教士袍，Aringarosa 是否代表黑暗的力量。他對於未來（或真相）也充滿恐懼，但是掌握祕密就是掌握權力，掌握真相就是掌握知識，Aringarosa 認為上帝正在給他這種權力。

教會的介入讓聖杯追尋的複雜度增加，這不是一種歷史真相的探索，更是整個信仰的挑戰。身為歷史學家，Langdon 並非教徒，對於過去教會如何掩蓋歷史，多所批評：

No one could deny the enormous good / the modern Church did / in today's troubled world, / and yet the Church had a deceitful and violent history. / Their brutal crusade / to "reeducate" the pagan and feminine-worshipping religions / spanned three centuries, / employing methods / as inspired as / they were horrific.

（沒有人可以否認大善，/ 現代教會帶給 / 當今混亂的社會。/ 但是教會也有欺騙與暴力的歷史。/ 他們粗暴的十字軍東征，/ 「再教育」異教徒及女神崇拜的宗教，/ 持續了 3 個世紀，/ 利用各種方法手段，/ 既有創意靈感，/ 也相當恐怖。）

教會掌握了權力，掌握了真相，也能夠重新改寫歷史，隱藏真相：歷史永遠是由勝利者寫的（History is always written by the winners.）。然而即使發現了隱藏在歷史後面的真相，發覺了隱藏在經典後面的事實，又能如何呢？這不是一個歷史問題，而是一個信仰問題，Langdon 有感而發地說：

"The Bible represents / a fundamental guidepost / for millions of people / on the planet, in much the same way / the Koran, Torah, and Pali Canon / offer guidance / to people of other religions. / If you and I could dig up documentation / that contradicted the holy stories of Islamic belief, Judaic belief, Buddhist belief, pagan belief, / should we do that? / Should we wave a flag / and tell the Buddhists / that the Buddha did not come from a lotus blossom? / Or that Jesus was not born of a literal virgin birth? / Those who truly understand their faiths / understand the stories are metaphorical."

（聖經代表／一基本的指標，／對數百萬人，／在地球上，有如／可蘭經、猶太 Torah 律法、佛門 Pali 經典，／提供指引，／給其他宗教的人們。／如果你我發掘出文獻，／牴觸回教信仰、猶太信仰、佛教信仰、異教徒信仰的神聖故事，／我們該如何做？／我們應該揮舞著旗子，／告訴佛教徒，／佛陀不是來自蓮花？／或是耶穌不是由處女所生？／那些真正瞭解信仰的人，／知道這些故事都是一種象徵。）

真正執著於故事的真實性或歷史的真相，可能忽略了信仰的真正本質。

📖 精彩片段賞析

對於丹・布朗在這本小說中所提到的一些論述與所謂的歷史文件，很多的宗教學者及歷史學家都大加撻伐，認為布朗扭曲宗教與歷史，缺乏實際的論證。甚至有些學者及教徒，斥之為邪書與謊言。

然而，這是一本小說，如果把它當成一種真相的探索或是歷史的記錄，那真的是忽略了小說的本質與藝術。將小說寫的像歷史，混淆了虛構與真實的界限，模糊了真相與個人主觀意見的空間，創造了這本小說的成功之處。閱讀小說，不必將其視為歷史事件，也不是一種信仰問題，它的美學成份與語言的精彩敘述，才是我們讀小說的樂趣！此小說，一方面說要追尋真相，本身卻常常在隱藏真相，虛虛實實，製造懸疑與驚悚的場景，提供了讀者很多想像的空間，跟隨著男女主角的冒險，體會偵探小說、冒險小說與驚悚小說的各項場景。

✚ 懸疑與驚悚（suspense vs. thrill）

小說中充滿懸疑與驚悚的描述與場景。宗教殺手 Silas 拜訪 Sister Sandrine 想要探詢聖杯祕密，引起了 Sister Sandrine 的緊張與懷疑。我們擔心 Silas 是否會像之前那樣謀殺館長 Sauniere，讀者的心跟著 Sister Sandrine 懸在那：

Crouching in the shadows of the choir balcony / high above the altar, / Sister Sandrine peered silently / through the balustrade / at the cloaked monk / kneeling alone. / The sudden dread in her soul / made it hard to stay still. / For a fleeting instant, / she wondered / if this mysterious visitor could be the enemy / they had warned her about, / and if tonight she would have to / carry out the orders / she had been holding all these years. / She decided to stay there in the darkness / and watch his every move.

（蹲在唱詩班包廂的陰暗處，／就在祭壇的上方處，／Sister Sandrine 靜靜地偷看，／透過欄杆，／那位穿著斗篷的修士，／孤獨地跪在那。／內心突然的恐懼，／讓她很難維持平靜。／剎那間，／她懷疑，／是否這個神祕的訪客可能是敵人，／他們警告過她的；／是否今晚，她必須／執行命令，／這幾年來所奉行的。／她決定留在黑暗中，／觀看他的一舉一動。）

整段的敘述從 Sister Sandrine 的觀點出發，從包廂中由上往下看，完全從視覺的觀點切入，製造了整個緊張氣氛。讀者似乎也有如 Sister Sandrine 那樣，也蹲在那包廂的陰影中，感受生命的威脅！

類似的緊張場景，也出現在尋找聖杯線索的過程，作者很有技巧的使用視覺觀點切入，讓我們跟著主角一起冒險與體驗這種緊張。

Upstairs, / Sophie and Langdon exhaled in relief / to see the conveyor belt move. / Standing beside the belt, / they felt like weary travelers / at baggage claim / awaiting a mysterious piece of luggage / whose contents were unknown.... / The conveyor belt entered the room / on their right / through a narrow slit / beneath a retractable door. / The metal door slide up, / and a huge plastic box appeared, / emerging from the depths / on the inclined conveyor belt.

（在樓上，/ Sophie 跟 Langdon 舒了口氣，/ 看著輸送帶移動。/ 站在輸送帶旁，/ 他們感覺自己像勞累的旅客，/ 在行李提領處，/ 等待一件神祕的行李，/ 內容不詳…… / 輸送帶進入房間，/ 從右手邊，/ 通過一個窄口，/ 在一個伸縮門下。/ 金屬門往上滑開，/ 一個巨大的塑膠盒子，/ 從深處浮現，/ 在那條傾斜的輸送帶上。）

在焦慮的等待中，輸送帶的「緩慢」進行，加深了緊張的氣氛。這種期待快一點的心理，而畫面卻是有如慢動作的對比描寫，成了冒險故事的經典場景。英文句子使用一連串的長句，以介系詞片語來串聯（如 at baggage claim, on their right, through a narrow slit, beneath a retractable door, from the depths, on the inclined conveyor belt）更是模仿整個輸送帶的移動過程，一節一節的緩慢前進。

除了這些驚險的動作描寫外，小說中利用象徵來強化歷史與文化的深度，也是值得一讀再讀。

✚ 象徵（symbols）

談論宗教與歷史議題的小說，不可避免的會介紹一些重要的象徵意象（symbols），尤其是這本以符號為主的小說，signs and symbols 成為豐富小說懸疑情節的線索。小說中有幾個重要的意象，例如聖杯和紅髮。

聖杯（Holy Grail）

聖杯是本書中最重要的意象，代表歷史的真相，也代表信仰的祕密：

"Sophie," Langdon whispered, / leaning toward her now, / "according to the Priory of Sion, / the Holy Grail is not a cup at all. / They claim the Grail legend—/ that of a chalice—/ is actually an ingeniously conceived allegory. / That is, / that the Grail story uses the Chalice / as a metaphor / for something else, / something far more powerful." / He paused. / "Something that fits perfectly with everything / your grandfather has been trying to tell us tonight, / including all his symbologic references to / the sacred feminine."

（「Sophie，」/ Langdon 輕聲說，/ 靠過去，/「依照錫安會的說法，/ 聖杯不是一個杯子而已，/ 他們宣稱聖杯傳說 / ——那個聖餐杯——/ 其實是獨創巧思的象徵。/ 也就是說，/ 聖杯的故事使用聖餐杯 / 作為一種象徵來 / 代表其他事物，/ 某種更有力量的東西。」/ 他停下來。/「某種可以完美符合所有一切，/ 你祖父今晚一直想要告訴我們的，/ 包括所有他一直透過象徵指涉的，/ 神聖女性」）

Sophie scanned the work / eagerly. / "Does this fresco tell us / what the Grail really is?"

（她掃描作品，/ 深切地。/「那這個壁畫要告訴我們，/ 聖杯是什麼？」）

"Not what it is," / Teabing whispered. / "But rather who it is. / The Holy Grail is not a thing. / It is, in fact ... a person."

（「不是它是什麼。」/ Teabing 輕聲說。/「而是它是誰。/ 聖杯不是東西，/ 它，事實上，是一個人。」）

顛覆傳統的看法，將聖杯轉化成人的意象，這成為這本小說最引人的情節。聖杯的意象在此也達到了高潮迭起的戲劇性效果。為了凸顯這時的莊嚴性與高潮性，兩位歷史學家都使用 whispered （輕聲說）這個動詞來展現面對真相或面對上帝的一種虔誠心態！

紅髮（Red Hair）

Sophie 這位充滿神祕色彩，一身智慧與美麗的出場，贏得了 Langdon 的目光，而其紅色如紅葡萄酒顏色的頭髮，也留下伏筆，點出她在聖杯的故事中，從一位追尋者變成一位當事人，原來她竟然就是耶穌基督的後人！

Langdon turned / to see a young woman approaching. / She was moving down the corridor / toward them / with long, fluid strides... / a haunting certainty to her gait. / Dressed casually / in a knee-length, cream-colored Irish sweater / over black leggings, / she was attractive / and looked to be about thirty. / Her thick burgundy hair fell / unstyled to her shoulders, / framing the warmth of her face. / Unlike the waifish, cookie-cutter blondes / that adorned Harvard dorm room walls, / this woman was healthy / with an unembellished beauty / and genuineness / that radiated a striking personal confidence.

（Langdon 轉身 / 看到一個年輕女性接近。/ 她順著走廊，/ 向著他們，/ 邁著長長、流暢的步伐，/ 步伐堅定，令人印象深刻。/ 穿著輕便、及膝的奶油色愛爾蘭毛衣，/ 蓋住黑色的內搭褲，/ 很迷人，/ 看起來大約 30 歲。/ 她茂密、酒紅色的頭髮，/ 未梳理，/ 垂到肩上，/ 襯托出臉上的溫暖。/ 不像其他瘦骨嶙峋、呆板的金髮美女，/ 掛在哈佛男生宿舍牆上，/ 這位女性看來很健康，/ 帶有未經修飾的美 / 與真實，/ 散發出令人驚訝的個人自信。）

以金髮美女當對比，Sophie 是個健康的紅髮美女。順著長廊走來，Langdon 觀察、描述的句字也跟著拖長，製造了很好的視覺效果。

📖 結局賞析

　　小說不僅是追求聖杯的真相，也要追求 Sophia 真實身世的真相。兩者的追尋都以女性為依歸。聖杯是代表基督時代的偉大女性；Sophia 是現代充滿智慧與健康的女性，兩者都是男性眼中的「女神」。我們看到男主角 Langdon 以崇敬的心，來歌頌女性的神聖，彷彿但丁神曲中的 Beatrice 再度復活：

Raising his eyes to heaven, he gazed upward through the glass to a glorious, star-filled night.

　　（抬起眼睛，望上天空，他往上注視，透過玻璃，望向華麗、滿布星星的夜晚）

She rests at last beneath the starry skies.

　　（她最後安息，在星空之下）

With a sudden upwelling of reverence, Robert Langdon fell to his knees.

　　（帶著突然湧起的崇敬之心，Robert Langdon 跪下。）

For a moment, he thought he heard a woman's voice ... the wisdom of the ages ... whispering up from the chasms of the earth.

　　（一下子，他感覺聽到了女性的聲音……世紀的智慧……，悄然低語，來自大地的深邃。）

適合閱讀程度：
高三以上程度及社會人士
延伸閱讀／推薦書單、電影：
小說：
Angels and Demons（《天使與魔鬼》）
Final Theory（《最後理論》）

《恐懼之邦》

State of Fear

(2004)

Michael Crichton

© Peter Kneffel/epa/Corbis

📖 作者簡介

美國科幻驚悚作家麥可・克萊頓（Michael Crichton, 1942～2008）從小對寫作就非常有興趣，14 歲就在紐約時報撰寫旅遊專欄。克萊頓從年輕就想當個專業作家，大學就讀英美文學系，但不受文學老師喜歡，於是轉讀生物人類學。最後進入哈佛醫學院就讀，並且開始寫作出版。他的《死亡手術室》（*A Case of Need*）在 1969 年獲得愛倫坡小說首獎。1969 年他從哈佛醫學院畢業後則繼續進行研究。

克萊頓在 1966 年第一次出版小說 *Odds On*，敘述一家旅館的搶案，此旅館搶案以電腦科技規劃，但最後未照計畫進行。第二本小說《天外病菌》（*The Andromeda Strain*）記錄科學家追蹤外太空的微生物，造成的恐怖驚悚事件，這本小說奠立了克萊頓暢銷作家的地位。從 1970 年來，克萊頓從事各種不同驚悚小說的創作，包括歷史小說《火車大劫案》（*The Great Train Robbery*）及有關 10 世紀回教徒故事的《乘著夜幕的惡魔》（*Eaters of the Dead*）。1990 年他寫了《侏羅紀公園》（*Jurassic Park*）引起全世界的恐龍熱與基因複製議題。日後也出版其續集《失落的世界》（*The Lost World*），都陸續拍成電影，深具商業價值。

克萊頓的小說創作題材非常豐富，涵蓋各種社會與文化議題，同時充滿了驚悚與懸疑色彩。其最令人激賞的主題仍然是以科技為主。克萊頓具有深厚的科學與醫學訓練背景，他將科學知識融入小說中，創造寫實與幻想世界的模糊地帶。在小說創作中，他大量使用科學數據與科學研究。應用文學技巧，創造所謂的錯誤註解，形成真實事件的假象，常常引起科學界的質疑與批評，如《侏羅紀公園》與《恐懼之邦》（*State of Fear*）所提到的一些科學爭議，都凸顯作者對於當今科學所產生的社會、政治與人性問題，深具啟發性。

📖 小說介紹

"It's the record from the weather station at Punta Arenas, near there. It's the closest city to Antarctica in the world." He tapped the chart and laughed. "There's your global warming."

（「這是附近的 Punta Arenas 氣象站的記錄，是世界上最接近南極的城市。」他敲敲圖表，笑說：「這就是你要的全球暖化。」）

地球暖化（global warming）的議題一直是近幾年來科學家不斷辯論的議題，這本《恐懼之邦》就以地球暖化議題為主，結合恐怖主義、政治與媒體操作等主題，寫成這部生態恐怖（eco-terrorist）小說。小說的進行延續克萊頓一貫的手法，將科學數據與小說虛構情節，甚至於作家個人的評論納入，建構出真實與虛幻交雜的小說世界。讀者可以從小說中來回顧現實，也可以從現實世界的事件中，去體會小說中的懸疑氣氛與驚悚場景。這種超越寫實與現代小說的局限，提供讀者有如虛擬實境的閱讀經驗，堪稱後現代文學創作中的重要形式。小說家在序言中，直言：

This is a work of fiction. / Characters, corporations, institutions, and organizations / in this novel / are the product of the author's imagination, / or, if real, / are used fictitiously / without any intent / to describe their actual conduct. / However, / references to real people, institutions, and organizations / that are documented in footnotes / are accurate. / Footnotes are real.

（這是一部小說創作。／人物，公司、機構、團體／在這部小說中，／都是作者想像力的產品，／如果有真的，／也是虛構形式來使用，／沒有任何意圖，／來描述他們真正的行為。／然而，／任何指向真人、機構或團體，／在註解中所記載的，／都是正確的。／註解都是真的。）

作者在此強調這是一本小說（a work of fiction），整體的故事進行與人物的行為都是虛構的，但是卻又強調註解中的一切都是真實的，有憑有據，都是正確的科學論述。這是透過虛構與真實的互相重疊，來彰顯作者對這個地球暖化議題的主觀認知。

小說中，作者對於地球暖化的議題充滿懷疑。在整個小說的敘述中，作者的論述清晰可見：

一、地球暖化所植基的科學基礎並不穩固，沒有直接證據提出如何解決這個問題，如果這個問題確實存在。

二、科學家利用其科學知識，製造社會某些恐懼心態，可能利用其研究發現來配合經費申請，將科學政治化。

不管作者的論述是否屬實，但在小說骨幹中加入這類的議題爭辯或意識形態之爭，增加了本小說的質感與衝突點，提升了閱讀的樂趣。很多科學家引經據典，反駁克萊頓，說他引述錯誤，誤導民眾。但是這種科學與文學之爭，只是凸顯科學家忽略了文學家所要探討的思維。這不是誰對誰錯的問題，而是小說是否能創造一個思辨與投入的空間。這麼多人跳下來討論《恐懼之邦》，就表示這部小說是成功了。

📖 主題分析

✚ 科學的政治化（politicization of science）

小說一開始，採取克萊頓一貫的手法，進入懸疑與動作的場景，幾個恐怖分子利用一些年輕科學家的疏忽，入侵一些政府研究機構盜取重要資訊與危險武器。故事展開後，恐怖行動與政府祕密行動分別進入高潮。這些行動都圍繞著一些最熱門的生態議題：地球暖化。以地球暖化為主的恐怖行動，成為故事的主幹。男主角 Peter Evans 是一個被蒙在鼓裡的律師，參與一場國際生態求償案件。隨著劇情發展，陷入不同意識形態的團體之中，在不知不覺中，與讀者一起解開這個生態謎題。

一開始，Peter Evans 跟我們讀者一樣，一直認為科學與法律是講究證據，透過論辯或數據的說明，一切都是很清楚的。但是他忽略了人的主觀認知，一旦人認定某事應該如此發展，則經常會將所有的證據用來支撐自己的主觀認定：為了瞭解整個生態變化，Evan 接受簡報：

　　"These graphs show that carbon dioxide rose continuously, but temperature did not. It rose, then fell, then rose again. Even so, I take it you remain convinced that carbon dioxide has caused the most recent temperature rise?"

　　（這些圖表顯示，二氧化碳持續上升，但是氣溫沒有。氣溫上升，然後下降，然後又上升。即使如此，我想你還是確認二氧化碳造成最近的氣溫上升？）

　　"Yes. Everybody knows that's the cause."

　　（是的，每個人知道這是原因。）

　　"Does this graph bother you at all?"

　　（這圖表完全沒有令你困惑嗎？）

　　"No," Evans said. "I admit it raises some questions, but then not everything is known about the climate. So, no. The graph doesn't trouble."

　　（「沒有」，Evans 說。「我承認這引起一些疑問。但是有關氣候的事，不是全部都搞清楚。所以，沒有，這圖表沒有令我困惑。」）

　　（最後 Evans 下了個結論：）

　　"Because the overwhelming consensus of scientists around the world is that global warming is happening and it is a major worldwide threat."

　　（因為一致的共識，全世界的科學家，地球暖化正在發生，這是全球的主要威脅。）

　　看到真實的圖表資料顯示，二氧化碳的產生與氣溫上升的關係不大。然而，Evans 受到大眾媒體與科學研究的整體印象影響，一廂情願的相信既有的地球暖化報導。

假扮麻省理工學院（MIT）研究員身分的國際調查員 Kenner 提出了科學研究常常被歪曲或政治化的一些看法，試圖教育 Evans。他首先指出，環保團體付了他薪水，環保團體是個很有影響力的組織，接著透過邏輯論述，指出科學研究的政治化：

"Good," Kenner said. / "Now you know / how legitimate scientists feel / when their integrity is impugned / by slimy characterizations / such as the one you just made. / Sanjong and I / gave you a careful, peer-reviewed interpretation of data. / Made by several groups of scientists / from several different countries. / And your response was / first to ignore it, / and then to make an ad hominem attack. / You didn't answer the data. / You didn't provide counter evidence. / You just smeared / with innuendo."

（「很好。」Kenner 說，/「現在，你瞭解 / 正統的科學家如何感受了，/ 當他們的正直被攻擊，/ 污穢的人格歸類，/ 如你剛剛所為。/ Sanjong 跟我，/ 給你一份仔細、同儕審核過的資料解讀，/ 來自很多科學家 / 在不同國家。/ 而你的反應，/ 第一是忽略，/ 然後做人身攻擊。/ 你沒有回應資料。/ 你沒有提供反駁證據。/ 你只是抹黑，/ 使用暗諷。」）

Kenner 訴諸 Evans 的個人經驗，提出科學數據被歪曲攻擊的說明。最後連續用 3 個以 You 開始的句子，攻擊性十足，挑釁味道濃厚，挑動 Evans 薄弱的意志。

✚ 恐懼的統治（the rule of fear）

科學的政治化，依照克萊頓的邏輯，其實是科學被利用，來製造「恐懼」，對地球毀滅的恐懼。而恐懼是種手段，目的在控制。這是這本小說書名的由來：

一位研究生態政治的霍夫曼教授闖入了，在 Santa Monica 國際生態學術

研討會，進一步點醒 Evans:

"I am leading to the notion of social control, / Peter. / To the requirement of every sovereign state / to exert control over the behavior of its citizens, / to keep them orderly / and reasonably docile. / To keep them driving on the right side of the road— / or the left, / as the case may be. / Too keep them paying taxes. / And of course / we know / that social control is best managed / through fear."

（「我正要談論社會控制的觀念，/ Peter。/ 針對每個主權國家的需求，/ 去控制其人民的行為，/ 讓他們安分守己、/ 合理溫馴。/ 要他們靠右開車——/ 或靠左，/ 看情形而定；/ 要他們繳稅。/ 當然，/ 我們知道，/ 處理最好的社會控制是，/ 透過恐懼。」）

Hoffman 又繼續延伸這個主題：

"Fear," Evans said.
（「恐懼」，Evans 說）
"Exactly. / For fifty years, / Western nations had maintained their citizens / in a state of perpetual fear. / Fear of the other side. / Fear of nuclear war. / The Communist menace. / The Iron Curtan. / The Evil Empire. / And within the Communist countries, / the same in reverse. / Fear of us. / Then, suddenly, in the fall of 1989, / it was all finished. / Gone, vanished. Over. / The fall of the Berlin Wall created a vacuum of fear. / Nature abhors a vacuum. / Something had to fill it."

（「沒錯，/ 過去 50 年來，/ 西方國家維持人民 / 在永遠戰爭的狀態下。/ 恐懼另一方；/ 恐懼核子戰爭；/ 共產黨威脅；/ 鐵幕；/ 邪惡帝國。/ 在共產黨國家中，/ 剛好相反，/ 恐懼我們。/ 然後，突然，在 1989 年秋天，/ 一切結束。/ 沒了。消失。遊戲結束了。/ 柏林圍牆的倒塌，產生了恐懼的真空狀態。/ 自然界不喜歡真空，/ 必須有東西來填補。」）

Evans frowned. "You're saying that environment crises took the place of the

Cold War?"

（Evans 皺著眉頭，「你說環境危機填補了冷戰的位置？」）

這種聯合社會控制的機制建立在所謂的 politico-legal-media complex 上面（政治－法律－媒體的共生複合體）：

Politicians need fears to control the population; lawyers need dangers to litigate, and make money; the media need scare stories to capture an audience.

（政客需要恐懼來控制百姓；律師需要危險來訴訟、來賺錢；媒體需要嚇人的故事來吸引讀者。）

所以，作者問了一個很大的問題：地球暖化是真的嗎？還是這種恐怖機制的另一種操作？由學界（為了獲取研究經費）、環保團體（為了取得社會發言權）、媒體（為了恐嚇讀者）、政客（為了獲取選票）所建構出來的「科學神話」？

整本小說，除了恐怖行動的進行外，大都在解開這種恐懼機制的運作，從政府、媒體、學術機構的複雜操作。引導 Evans（也就是我們這些意志薄弱、自以為理性的讀者）瞭解這個機制的運作，成為本小說的主要情節。

但是，如果淨讀這些生態論述與政治操作，我想這本小說也是無聊透頂，成為一本非小說的小說。搭配這些生態論述，作者穿插了揭開生態恐怖行動的陰謀：生態恐怖主義者（National Environmental Resource Fund（NERF）的主任 Nicolas Drake），偷取大量毀滅性炸藥，來製造自然生態意外，引起大眾重視地球暖化的議題。Evans 與美女助理 Sarah 的冒險動作情節，就成了一個吸引人的通俗故事。

📖 精彩片段賞析

小說中，除了推理與偵探過程，尋找恐怖活動的幕後指使者外，大都停留在驚險的動作場景上。有一次，律師 Evans 跟助理 Sarah 回到老闆家尋找線索，突然：

Two powerful flashlights shone directly in their faces. Evans squinted in the harsh light; Sarah raised her hand to cover her eyes.

（兩隻強光手電筒直接照在他們臉上。Evans 在強光下，瞇著眼；Sarah 舉起手蓋住眼睛。）

"May I have the envelope, please," the voice said.

（「我可以拿那個信封嗎？」，一個聲音說）

Sarah said, "No."

（Sarah 說：「不。」）

There was a mechanical click, like the cocking of a gun.

（有個金屬卡的聲音，好像槍上膛。）

"We'll take the envelope," the voice said. "One way or another."

（「我們無論如何都要拿到信封。那個聲音說。」）

"No you won't," Sarah said.

（「不，你拿不到，」Sarah 說。）

Standing beside her, Evans whispered, "Sar-ah…"

（站在旁邊，Evans 小聲說：「Sar-ah」）

"Shut up, Peter. They can't have it."

（「閉嘴，Peter。他們不可以拿去。」）

"We'll shoot if we have to," the voice said.

（「有必要，我們會開槍。」那個聲音說）

"Sarah, give them the fucking envelope," Evans said.

（「Sarah，給他們他媽的信封」，Evans 說）

"Let them take it," Sarah said defiantly.

（「讓他們來拿吧」，Sarah 挑釁地說。）

"Sar-ah…" （「Sar-ah…」）

"Bitch!" the voice scream, and a gunshot sounded. Evans was embroiled in chaos and blackness. There was another scream. One of the flashlights bounced on the floor and rolled, pointing in a corner. In the shadows Evans saw a large dark figure attack Sarah, who screamed and kicked.

（「賤貨」，那聲音尖叫。槍聲響起。Evans 陷入混亂與黑暗中。另外一聲尖叫。一隻手電筒跳到地上，滾動，對著角落。在陰影中，Evans 看到一個巨大的黑影攻擊 Sarah，她又叫又踢。）

這段打鬥的場景，簡潔有力，將男女主角的反應及個性表露無疑：Evans 怕事、Sarah 堅定勇敢。從強光手電筒照下時，Evans 的反應是 squint，屈服在暴力下；Sarah 則是 raised her hand，有對抗的味道。之後，果然，Sarah 口氣堅定（said defiantly），而 Evans 則是 whispered。作者使用不同的動詞，生動地點出兩人不同的性格與舉止。此種男弱女強，顛覆了傳統動作小說或 007 小說電影中的刻板印象。整部小說也是等待 Evans 的堅強改變，期望他成為英雄的角色。等到他勇敢地對抗恐怖份子 Bolden，才能獲得美麗女助理 Sarah 的芳心。

最後，他們阻止了恐怖分子的活動，殺死了 Bolden，Evans 展現了英勇的一面：

Evans struggled, with the sudden strength of desperation. Abruptly, he kicked up.

（Evans 用力掙扎，突然，不顧一切的力量，瞬間，往上一踢。）

Bolden's face mashed against hot metal. He howled. His check was smoking and black.

（Bolden 的臉撞上滾燙的金屬，他哀嚎，臉頰冒煙變黑）

Evans kicked again, and get out from beneath him. Go to his feet. Standing over Bolden, he kicked him hard in the ribs, as hard as he could. He tried to kill him.

（Evans 再踢。從他下面起來，站起來，望著 Bolden。他狠狠地踢他肋骨，狠狠地。他想要殺他。）

上次是 Sarah 用力踢（kicked）歹徒，這次換 Evans 狠狠地踢（kicked him hard）。作者用 kicked 這個動詞，前後呼應了男女主角一致的動作，似乎 kicked 是英雄的招牌動作！

📖 結局賞析

小說最後，阻止了恐怖份子以海嘯攻擊加州的計畫，Evans, Sarah 與試圖挽回生態計畫的金主 Morton 回到了加州。在飛機上，看著污染的 Los Angeles，他們還有很多工作要做！

Half an hour before / they reached the California coast, / they saw the spreading brown haze / hanging over the ocean. / It grew thicker and darker / as they approached land. / Soon they saw the lights of the city, / stretching away for miles. / It was blurred by the atmosphere above.

（還有半個小時，/ 抵達加州海岸，/ 他們看到擴散的棕色煙霧 / 浮蓋在海上。/ 越來越厚、越來越黑，/ 當他們接近陸地。/ 很快，他們看到城市的光線，/ 延伸好幾里。/ 被上面的大氣遮得污穢不清。）

"It looks a bit like hell, doesn't it," Sarah said. "Hard to think we're going to land in that."

（「有如地獄吧？」Sarah 說，「很難想像我們要降落在那。」）

"We have a lot of work to do," Morton said.

（還有很多工作要做。）

The plane descended smoothly toward Los Angeles.

（飛機安穩地朝 Los Angeles 下降。）

或許地球暖化的議題被高度炒作，其實空氣污染的問題（the spreading brown haze hanging over the ocean）或是地震（earthquake）可能更值得我們恐懼吧！

適合閱讀程度：

高三以上及社會人士

延伸閱讀／推薦書單、電影：

小說：

Swarm（《群》）

電影：

The Day after Tomorrow（《明天過後》）

《格列佛遊記》

Gulliver's Travels

(1726)

Jonathan Swift

Alfred Warren © Michael Nicholson/CORBIS

📖 作者簡介

　　愛爾蘭作家斯威夫特（Jonathan Swift, 1667～1745）。其父親為律師，從三一學院（Trinity College）畢業後，即進入英國政治圈。之後進入教會服務，熟知英國政治、宗教及社會制度與運作情形，累積了日後批評英國政治與社會的素材。

　　斯威夫特一生介入英國政治旋渦，周旋於當時的兩大政治勢力（Whig and Tory）間。其間，由於不得勢，他開始著手一些短篇的諷刺作品。回到愛爾蘭後，開始帶領愛爾蘭反對英國對其家鄉的掠奪與忽視。《一個小小的建議》（A Modest Proposal）最為有名，諷刺地指出，要解決愛爾蘭的饑荒與人口過剩的問題，唯有將愛爾蘭的窮人嬰兒製成食物，餵食富人，才是上策。這種強烈控訴富人對窮人的欺壓，成為寫作的特殊風格。《格列佛遊記》（Gulliver's Travels）也帶有這種強烈嘲諷的色彩，其在 1726 年出版時，曾引起爭議，直到 10 年後，完整版本才上市。內容對於當時的英國及歐洲政治，充滿批判，可說是一本非常具有攻擊性的政治諷刺文學（political satire）。

📖 小說介紹

　　The diversion is only practiced by those persons who are candidates for great employments, and high favour, at court. They are trained in this art from their youth, and are not always of noble birth, or liberal education. When a great office is vacant either by death or disgrace（which often happens）five or six of those candidates petition the Emperor to entertain his Majesty and the court with a dance on the rope, and whoever jumps the highest without falling, succeeds in the office.

　　（這項遊戲只有那些有資格成為高位者的人才會練習。他們從小就訓練這種藝術，不一定是有高貴出身或受人文教育。當一高官位置出缺，可能是由於死亡或不名譽的事（這經常發生），5、6 個有資格的人稟求皇上，在皇上及宮廷面前，在繩索上跳舞，跳最高且沒有掉下來的人，就繼承這個位置。）

　　政府高官的位置不是因為能力而被提升，而是由於在繩索上跳舞而獲得位置（dance on the rope），這種嘲諷政治酬庸與政治小丑的荒謬情節，出現在我們一般以為是兒童青少年奇幻小說的《格列佛遊記》之中。嚴格來說，《格列佛遊記》並非小說（novel），而是盛行於 18 世紀一種敘述文類：諷刺文學（satire）。它缺乏小說中的人物、事件的因果發展與成長的要素，但由於它充滿故事敘述（narrative）的有趣與離奇情節，因此很多人都把它當作奇幻小說（fantasy）來閱讀。

　　此故事分成 4 大部分：小人國的歷險、大人國的歷險、飛島與科學院的奇遇及馬國的遭遇。故事以主人翁 Gulliver 的第一人稱來進行，敘述進入這些奇怪國度的經歷與感想。然而，一般小說中的主人翁（如之前介紹《遠大前程》中的 Pip 或《華氏 451 度》的 Montag）在故事的進行中，介入或改變的成份很大；而此故事的 Gulliver 幾乎作為旁觀者（observer），並非小說中的真實人物，其名字 Gulliver 其實也是英文字 gullible（容易受騙的）的諧音。透過這個輕易相信別人的敘述者，以看似客觀、理性的口吻，來凸顯人性或政治上的一些荒謬情事；也就是藉著外在誇大的事物，而敘述者卻不帶一絲價值判斷，來諷刺當時的英國社會。作者斯威夫特透過這些離奇的故事，檢視人類社會爭議的政治與社會價值。

📖 主題分析

✚ 人性與政治的可笑 （absurdity in humans and politics）

　　Gulliver 進入了不同的國家（如小人國 Lilliput 與大人國 Brobdingnag），

由於其身材的差異，更凸顯了人與人相處間的矛盾與社會衝突。他在小人國時，得知這個國家的戰爭是由於打蛋事件，讓兩大強權成為世仇：

... two mighty powers / have ... been engaged in a most obstinate war... / It began upon the following occasion. ... / the primitive way of breaking eggs, / before we eat them, / was upon the larger end; / but his present majesty's grandfather, / while he was a boy, going to eat an egg, / and breaking it / according to the ancient practice, / happened to cut one of his fingers. / Whereupon the emperor his father published an edict, / commanding all his subjects, / upon great penalties, / to break the smaller end of their eggs.... / It is computed / that eleven thousand persons have at several times suffered death, / rather than submit to break their eggs at the smaller end.

（兩大強權，/ 已經進行這場頑強的戰爭⋯⋯ / 事情是這麼開始的⋯⋯ / 最原始打蛋的方式，/ 在我們吃之前，/ 是打在較大（較鈍的）的那邊；/ 然而現在皇上的祖父，/ 小時候，要吃蛋的時候，/ 打蛋 / 依照舊傳統，/ 不巧割傷了手指。/ 因此，其父親發佈命令，/ 要求所有子民，/ 依照嚴格規定，/ 要打在較小（較尖的）的那一頭⋯⋯ / 據統計，/ 約有 11,000 多人因此在不同時期慘遭死亡，/ 而不願意在較小的那頭打蛋。）

此種不同的打蛋方式到後來成為兩國的宗教信仰與意識形態，而兩個國家由於堅持這種意識形態之爭，打了長久戰爭。從外人觀念來看，這是一件莫名其妙、荒唐至極的理由。但是看看人類歷史上所發生的戰爭，不正是這種「我認為我比較聰明，你應該聽從我的指示」這樣的驕傲心態與意識形態所產生的嗎？歐洲的宗教戰爭、二次大戰等都是明顯的例子。

政治的可笑與人性的墮落隨處可見。作者透過大人國的驕傲國王口中，嚴厲地批判了文明國家（此處指英國）的虛偽：

He was perfectly astonished with / the historical account I gave him of our affairs / during the last century, / protesting / "it was only a heap of / conspiracies, rebellions, murders, massacres, revolutions, banishments; the very worst effects / that avarice, faction, hypocrisy, perfidiousness, cruelty, rage, madness, hatred, envy, lust, malice, and ambition, could produce...." / "My little friend Grildrig, ... / you have clearly proved, / that ignorance, idleness, and vice, are the proper ingredients for qualifying a legislator; .... / I cannot but conclude / the bulk of your natives / to be the most pernicious race of little odious vermin / that nature ever suffered / to crawl upon the surface of the earth. "

（他非常震驚，／對於我給他有關我們的歷史描述，／過去整個世紀，／斷言指出：／「這只是累積／陰謀、叛亂、謀殺、屠殺、革命、放逐／以及最惡劣的一切行為後果，／由貪婪、黨派內鬥、虛偽、背信、殘忍、憤怒、瘋狂、仇恨、忌妒、慾望、惡意、及野心所產生。／我的小人朋友……／你很清楚的證明，／無知、怠惰、邪惡是培養國會議員的最適當元素……／我不得不下個結論，／你們這群住民，可說是最惡毒、令人嫌棄的壞蟲，／大自然容忍／其在地球表面上爬行。」）

　　Brobdingnag 的國王列出了人類歷史與社會中所出現過的一切惡行（conspiracies, rebellions, murders, massacres, revolutions, banishments）　與所有人性中的醜陋（avarice, faction, hypocrisy, perfidiousness, cruelty, rage, madness, hatred, envy, lust, malice, and ambition），這些名詞強有力地挑戰 Gulliver 的良知，也讓 21 世紀的我們看到了自己的醜陋。我們到底從歷史中學到了什麼？大人國國王所言，是否還是不斷地在人類歷史上一再演出？

　　作者對於人類社會的嘲諷，不僅在於人性與政治環境，也涉及到學術界與知識份子，Gulliver 來到了飛島 Laputa 及 Lagado 的科學研究院，看到了一些科學家，脫離現實，為研究而研究的可笑與荒謬行為。

　　格列佛的旅程，在 18 世紀理性主導的時代，充滿了突破理性思維的想像空間，從敘述者格列佛進入小人國、大人國後，由於身材的落差，產生了視覺與觀點的不同，讓我們可以從新審視很多不一樣的價值觀。

📖 精彩片段賞析

在大人國中，有次 Gulliver 觀察到一位奶媽哺育小兒，他發現：

I must confess / no object ever disgusted me so much as / the sight of her monstrous breast, / which I cannot tell what to compare with, / so as to give the curious reader / an idea of its bulk, shape and colour... / This made me reflect upon / the fair skins of our English ladies, / who appear so beautiful / to us, / only because they are of our own size, / and their defects not to be seen / but through a magnifying glass, / where we find by experiment / that the smoothest and whitest skins look / rough and coarse, and ill coloured.

（我得承認，/ 沒有什麼東西令我更加噁心，/ 看到這麼巨大的乳房。/ 我不知跟什麼相比，/ 才能讓好奇的讀者，/ 知道它的體積、形狀及顏色⋯⋯ / 這使得我回想起 / 我們英國女性的美好肌膚，/ 看起來很美麗，/ 對我們來說，/ 只是因為他們體型與我們一樣，/ 缺點沒有看見。/ 但如果透過放大鏡，/ 我們從實驗得知，/ 最平滑、白皙的皮膚看起來 / 粗造、不平、顏色醜陋。）

美醜之間的判斷，其實是距離與觀點的不同。放大美麗的事物產生了歪曲的視覺，不同的角度對於美麗的價值觀絕對有不同的判斷標準。人類站在不同的角度，對於熟悉的事物會產生全新的看法。

格列佛的奇遇不僅在於大小人國，進入空中島國（Laputa, flying island）後，他又面臨不同價值觀的挑戰。這次，他要問我們：什麼是理性的知識？

Their houses are very ill built, / the walls bevel, / without one right angle in any apartment; / and this defect ariseth from the contempt / they bear for practical geometry, / which they despise / as vulgar and mechanic, / those instructions they give / being too refined / for the intellectuals of their workmen, / which occasions perpetual mistakes. / And although they are dexterous enough / upon a piece of paper / in the management of the rule, / the pencil, and the divider, / yet in the common actions and behaviour of life / I have not seen a more clumsy, awkward, / and unhandy people... / Imagination, fancy, and invention, / they are wholly strangers to, / nor have any words / in their language / by which those ideas can be expressed ....

（他們的房子蓋得很差，/ 牆壁傾斜，/ 任何公寓中沒有一個筆直的角落，/ 這些缺陷來自於輕蔑，/ 他們對實用幾何，/ 他們鄙視為粗俗及太工匠，/ 他們所給的指示太精密，/ 對工人的腦力，/ 造成不斷的錯誤。/ 雖然他們熟於，/ 在紙上，/ 處理尺、/ 筆、及圓規，/ 然而在一般生活事物上，/ 我沒有看過更笨拙，/ 更不靈巧的人。/ 想像力、幻想及創新，/ 他們完全陌生，/ 也沒有任何字眼，/ 在她們的語言，/ 可以表達這些觀念……）

飛島的居民大都為天文學家（astrologists）與音樂家（musicians），對於數學運算與音樂原理非常熟悉，但是他們瞧不起實用的學問（practical geometry），對於實際的蓋房子與日常生活（ common actions and behaviour of life）也無法掌控。以抽象的理論來處理實際的事物，落實到生活上，則是一場災難。此外，他們不事生產，但利用飛島的空中優勢，控制地上的居民提供其日常生活用品與食物。這種菁英份子的理論暴政（theory tyranny），其實也常出現在當代知識份子治國的迷思之中。以觀念、理論治國，不瞭解庶民的需求與感受，國家出現了類似 Laputa 的不切實際，只能在空中飛翔（the island is floating in the air）。

不僅是飛島的居民脫離現實，Lagado 的研究學院也充滿了令人噴飯的幾項研究：

He had been eight years upon a project / for extracting sunbeams out of cucumbers, / which were to be put into vials / hermetically sealed, / and let out to warm the air / in raw inclement summers.

（他已經 8 年進行計畫，/ 萃取陽光從小黃瓜，/ 將放在試管中，/ 密封好。/ 以後釋放出來溫暖空氣，/ 在天氣惡劣的夏天。）

His employment from his first coming into the Academy / was an operation / to reduce human excrement / to its original food....

（他第一次進入研究院的工作就是，/ 進行 / 濃縮人類排泄物 / 至原始的食物……）

There was a most ingenious architect / who had contrived a new method / for building houses, / by beginning at the roof / and working downwards to the foundation, / which he justified to me / by the like practice of those two prudent insects, / the bee and the spider.

（有個非常具創意的建築師，/ 發明一種新方法，/ 來蓋房子，/ 先從屋頂開始，/ 然後往下蓋到地基，/ 這種方法，/ 他證明給我看，/ 類似兩種精明昆蟲的運作：/ 蜜蜂及蜘蛛。）

這些研究看似合乎邏輯，但深入思考，卻覺得不切實際。作者 Swift 透過 Gulliver 的眼光，觀察到這些不可思議的研究，其實在探討一個嚴肅的問題：什麼是知識？從理性思維的觀點來看，唯有實用可行的方法或有用的創意，才是真正的知識與智慧。Swift 所要檢驗的正是希臘時期柏拉圖（Plato）所倡言的：未經實務檢驗的知識並非知識（Knowledge unexamined is no knowledge.）。

在最後的旅程，Gulliver 來到了馬國（Houyhnhnms），在此國度裡，馬（horse）是理性思維、溫和的代表，而人類則是粗鄙的物種（yahoo）。透過人馬的互換位置，作者提出了幾個問題：理性的基礎為何？人的本質為何？當我們社會上充滿「理盲」的批判，這最後的旅程值得我們一讀再讀：

As these noble Houyhnhnms are endowed by nature with a general disposition to all virtues, and have no conceptions or ideas of what is evil in a rational creature, so their grand maxim is to cultivate reason, and to be wholly governed by it.

（他們最崇高的座右銘是培養理性，完全由理性主宰。）

📖 結局賞析

　　小說的結局，Gulliver 與先前的旅程不同，他不再是個客觀的觀察者。他已經受到馬國文化的影響，開始厭惡人類的生存與價值，他無法忍受人類（yahoos）的粗鄙與庸俗，這種對人類愚蠢的最大指控，可能是這本小說最令人感到反諷的地方：

　　"... when I behold a lump of deformity and diseases / both in body and mind, / smitten with pride, / it immediately breaks all the measures of my patience; / neither shall I be ever able to comprehend / how such an animal / and such a vice / could tally together."

　　（……當我看到一大堆畸形與疾病，/ 同時存在身體與心靈中，/ 為驕傲所苦，/ 馬上我就無法忍受；/ 我也無法理解，如此的動物，/ 如此的邪惡，/ 如何能搭配在一起。）

　　身為人類的 Gulliver 無法忍受人類的愚蠢與邪惡，矛盾的存在點出了其理性的盲點與人類的困境。

適合閱讀程度：
大一以上及社會人士；高中以下可以閱讀簡易版或電影版。
延伸閱讀／推薦書單、電影：
小說：
The Chronicles of Narnia（《納尼亞傳奇》）
The Lord of the Rings（《魔戒》）
電影：
Gulliver's Travels（《格列佛遊記》，2010）

《人鼠之間》

Of Mice and Men

(1937)

John Steinbeck

© Hulton-Deutsch Collection/CORBIS

📖 作者簡介

美國作家約翰‧史坦貝克（John Steinbeck, 1902 ～ 1968）。1962 年獲得諾貝爾文學獎，他的重要著作包括《憤怒的葡萄》（*The Grapes of Wrath*）、《伊甸園之東》（*East of Eden*）、《人鼠之間》（*Of Mice and Men*）等。史坦貝克生長在加州的中產階級家庭，離開史丹佛大學（Stanford University）到紐約，想要成為作家卻遭受挫折。他回到加州，受父親支助，專心寫作。直到 1935 年 *Tortilla Flat* 發表後，經濟才開始穩定。

史坦貝克的小說是以加州為背景，描寫中西部地區下階層勞工的生活，尤其是美國遭遇經濟大蕭條（Great Depression）期間，移動勞工的艱困生活。小說同情工人生活的無助，對於資本主義與社會多所批判。對於生活辛苦的勞工如何保持其尊嚴與無奈的命運掙扎，有深入的描寫。1962 年諾貝爾文學獎頒獎時，他曾說：

"... the writer is delegated / to declare and to celebrate man's proven capacity / for greatness of heart and spirit— / for gallantry in defeat, for courage, compassion and love. / In the endless war against weakness and despair, / these are the bright rally flags of hope and of emulation. / I hold / that a writer who does not believe in the perfectibility of man / has no dedication nor any membership in literature."

（作家被賦予 / 陳述並歌頌人類既有的能力，/ 追求心靈與精神的偉大—— / 追求在失敗中的英勇行為、勇氣、同情與愛。/ 在無止盡的對抗懦弱與失望的戰爭中，/ 這些都是明亮鼓舞士氣、希望與競爭的旗幟。/ 我堅信，/ 任何作家，如果不相信人類完美性，/ 就無法奉獻或參與文學。）

📖 小說介紹

"Guys like us, / that work on ranches, / are the loneliest guys in the world. / They got no family. / They don't belong no place. / They come to a ranch / an' work up a stake / and then they go inta town / and blow their stake, / and the first thing you know / they're pounding their tail on some other ranch. / They ain't got nothing / to look ahead to."

（像我們這樣的人，/在農場工作，/是世上最孤獨的人。/沒有家人，/不屬於任何地方。/來到一家農場，/工作賺了點獎金，/然後來到另一個城鎮，/花掉那些錢。/首先你知道的是，/他們又到另一個農場做事，/他們沒有什麼，/可以往前看的。）

流浪的農工（migrant farm workers）沒有任何未來可以期望（... got nothing to look ahead.）。在這本描寫美國 30 年經濟大蕭條窮人悲慘命運的小說中，1962 年美國諾貝爾文學獎得主史坦貝克，透過小說中的主角 George 道出窮人的最大悲哀：沒有未來。《人鼠之間》以兩個在加州農場打工的難兄難弟 George 及 Lennie 的生活為主，即使兩人並無血緣關係，但親密的友誼與互相的依存，成為本故事最感人的重心。

📖 主題分析

✚ 人與人之間的友誼 vs. 環境的漠然

小說一開始，就以類似溫馨田園的景色來引出自然環境的美：

A few miles south of Soledad, / the Salinas River drops in / close to the hillside bank / and runs deep and green. / The water is warm too, / for it has slipped / twinkling over the yellow sands / in the sunlight / before reaching the narrow pool. / On one side of the river / the golden foothill slopes / curve up to / the strong and rocky Gabilan mountains, / but on the valley side / the water is lined with trees—/ willows fresh and green / with every spring.

（在 Soledad 南方幾哩的地方，/ Salinas 河落下，/ 靠近山坡岸邊，/ 流得又深又綠。/ 水也很溫軟，/ 因為從上滑下，/ 閃爍在黃沙上，/ 在陽光底下，/ 直到抵達淺淺的水塘。/ 在河的一邊，/ 黃金色的山丘斜坡，/ 往上蜿蜒到 / 堅硬的 Gabilan 山陵，/ 而在河谷這邊，/ 河水沿線一排樹木，/ 柳樹活力十足、充滿綠意，/ 隨著每次跳躍。）

這段文字簡單輕快，作者使用幾個生動、活力的動詞如 drops、runs、slipped、twinkling、reaching、curve up 等點出了河流與大自然的生命。此外，一些顏色如 green、golden 都令人感覺整個大自然環境的生命力與希望。然而接下去出場的兩個主角卻是缺乏大自然的這種綠色與金黃色的活力：

Both wore black, shapeless hats / and both carried tight blanket rolls / slung over their shoulders. / The first man was small / and quick, / dark of face, / with restless eyes / and sharp, strong features.... / Behind him walked / his opposite, / a huge man, shapeless of face, / with large, pale eyes, / with wide, sloping shoulders; / and he walked heavily, / dragging his feet a little, / the way a bear drags his paws.

（兩人戴著不成型的帽子，/ 扛著緊捆的毛毯，/ 背在肩上。/ 第一個人很瘦小，/ 動作敏捷，/ 臉黑，/ 眼神不安，/ 容貌突出、堅毅……/ 在他後面走的，/ 跟他完全相反，/ 巨大，面貌不明顯，/ 眼睛很大、蒼白，/ 肩膀寬大、下垂。/ 走路步伐沉重，/ 拖著腳，/ 有如一隻熊拖著大爪。）

這裡呈現的兩個人物，顏色灰暗，拖著腳步，無之前大自然的生動活潑。兩種場境點出了本小說的主題：人 vs. 環境；灰暗 vs. 活力，儼然有些自然主義小說的成份：大自然對於人的存在是冷漠的，而人的命運受到環境的主宰，無法擁有自我的意志。一般讀者在閱讀小說時，常常跳過這些景色（scene）

或人物（character）的描寫，僅著重情節（plot）的鋪陳。其實，小說在一開始透過這些場景的介紹與人物的出場，已經隱含故事發展的主軸。

　　小說中的小個子 George 與大個子 Lennie 兩人相依為命，到處流浪，在農場打零工，面對外在環境與社會的冷漠，僅有兩人的堅強的友誼及對未來的憧憬（買一塊屬於自己的地），支撐他們繼續活下去：

George went on, / "With us it ain't like that. / We got a future. / We got somebody to talk to.... / We don't have to sit in no bar room / blowin' our jack / jus' because we got no place else to go...."

　　（George 繼續說，/「我們不像那樣。/ 我們有未來。/ 我們有人可以講話，……/ 我們不必坐在酒吧裡，花光我們的錢，/ 只是因為我們沒有地方可以去。」

Lennie broke in, / "But not us! / An' why?/ Because... Because I got you to look after me, / and you got me to look after you, / and that's why." / He laughed delighted. / "Go on now, George!"

　　（Lennie 插嘴，/「我們不是！/ 為何？/ 因為……因為我有你可以照顧我，/ 你有我可以照顧你。/ 這就是為什麼！」/ 他笑得很開心，/「繼續講，George！」

"O.K. / Someday— / we're gonna get the jack together / and we're gonna have a little house / and a couple of acres / an' a cow / and some pigs and—"

　　（「是的，/ 有一天 /——我們會有錢，/ 我們將可以擁有一間小屋，/ 一兩畝地、/ 一隻母牛、/ 幾隻豬——」）

　　即使在困苦與悲觀的環境之中，他們擁有彼此，幻想未來能夠擁有自己的土地。兩人的對話，即使充滿天真的話語與不成熟的想法，但卻展現那種純真的友誼。然而這種希望與堅強的友誼，在碰到外在充滿敵意的環境，漸漸破滅。

　　小說中的 Lennie 是個智能不足的憨直大個子，喜歡撫摸柔軟的事物如老鼠。但是柔軟的老鼠常在其不經意的強壯手掌中捏死。老鼠與人之間（of mice and men）的脆弱關係、溫柔與強壯（soft and strong）的對比，希望與死亡（hope and death）的交錯，構成了這本小說溫馨卻又感傷的情節。

　　在窮苦的時代裡，在大自然冷漠的空間裡，窮人悲慘、感人的故事，永遠是這時代裡最撼動人心的題材。描寫社會邊緣人的小說中，《人鼠之間》強調美國夢（American dream）的破碎，而存在於人與人之間，最值得珍惜的就是：希望與友誼。

📖 精彩片段賞析

　　「希望」是這些社會邊緣人賴以生存的精神糧食。天真的 Lennie 經常要求 George 描述未來的生活——他們可以擁有自己的土地與小動物：

Lennie said, "Tell about that place, George."

（「告訴我那個地方，George。」）

"I jus' tol' you, jus' las' night."

（「我告訴過你了，昨天晚上。」）

"Go on—tell again, George."

（「繼續講，再說一遍，George。」）

"Well, it's ten acres," said George. / "Got a little win' mill. / Got a little shack on it, / an' a chicken run. / Got a kitchen, / orchard, / cherries, / apples, / peaches,... / They's a place for alfalfa / and plenty water / to flood it. / They's a pig pen—"

（「喔，那地方大概有 10 畝。/ 有個小風車，/ 有間小屋，/ 還有養雞場，/ 小雞跑來跑去，/ 有個廚房、/ 果園、/ 櫻桃、/ 蘋果、/ 桃子⋯⋯。/ 有個地方種苜蓿，/ 水很多 / 可以灌溉，/ 還有個豬圈——」）

"An' rabbits, George." ...

（「還有兔子，George。」）

George's hands stopped / working with the cards. / His voice was growing warmer. / "An' we could have a few pigs. / I could build a smoke house / like the one gran'pa had, / an' when we kill a pig / we can smoke the bacon and the hams, / and make sausage an' all like that."

（George 的手停止 / 玩牌。/ 聲音越來越溫馨。/「我們可以養幾隻豬，/ 我可以蓋個燻製房，/ 就像爺爺以前的那個。/ 我們殺了豬後，/ 可以煙燻豬肉火腿，/ 做個香腸什麼的。」）

"... We'd just' live there. / We'd belong there..."

（「……我們就住在那，/ 我們屬於那個地方……」）

每當兩個難兄難弟做完白天的苦工，George 不斷編織兩人的美國夢，好好奮鬥存錢，可以擁有自己的土地、找到自己歸屬的地方。這種類似宗教儀式（rituals）的不斷自我肯定與憧憬理想天堂的做法，正是這些社會邊緣人的「美國夢」。就連年老的農場幫工 Candy 也被感染，要求加入，即使知道這些都是遙不可及：

"S'pose I went it with you guys. / Tha's three hundred an' fifty bucks / I'd put in. I ain't much good, / but I could cook / and tend the chickens / and hoe the garden some. / How'd that be?"

（「假如我跟你們一起，/ 那就是 350 塊，/ 我可以投入。/ 我不是很行，/ 不過我可以煮飯，/ 照顧雞群，/ 花園鋤草，/ 這樣如何？」）

老人誠懇的話語令人動容。George 燃起了希望，3 人剎那間為自己的希望、想像感動：

They all sat / still, / all bemused / by the beauty of the thing, /each mind was popped / into the future / when this lovely thing should come about.

（他們坐在那，/ 一動也不動，呆住了，/ 這一切的美。/ 每個心思突然 /

進入未來，／這些美妙的事情可能發生！）

　　此處的 lovely thing 指的是他們的夢想與希望。看著未來，這一切都是美的展現（the beauty of the thing）。

　　然而這種美感被外來的誘惑所破壞了！農場年輕主人 Curley 的太太寂寞孤獨，常常找這些窮苦的勞工搭訕。在一次意外中，強壯但智力不足的 Lennie 扭斷了女主人的頸部。這個死亡意外，真是上蒼的作弄，毀了這些邊緣人的希望！接近故事尾聲時，George 帶著 Lennie 逃離農莊，但是如何 Curley 一幫人的追殺，George 與 Lennie 必須付出慘痛的代價。小說最後一章利用水蛇的死亡象徵 Lennie 最後的命運：

A water snake glided smoothly up the pool, / twisting its periscope head / from side to side; / and it swam the length of the pool / and came to the legs of a motionless heron / that stood in the shallows. / A silent head and beak / lanced down / and plucked it out by the head, / and the beak swallowed the little snake / while its tail waved frantically.

　　（一條水蛇平穩地滑出水池，／轉動其潛望鏡的頭，／左右擺動。／然後游過水池，／來到了一動也不動的蒼鷹腳下，／站在淺水中。／寧靜的頭與嘴／筆直射下，／截取它的頭，／嘴吞下小蛇，／其尾巴瘋狂地搖晃。）

　　作者利用強有力的動詞描寫水蛇在剎那間死於蒼鷹嘴中，其中 lanced down、plucked it out、swallowed 一氣呵成，凸顯死亡的快速與生命的脆弱。

　　George 與 Lennie 間的友誼，是一件令人動容的場景。儘管幼稚且強壯的 Lennie 常常讓他們兩人失掉工作，George 雖抱怨卻仍堅守著 Lennie：

George still stared morosely at the fire. / "When I think of the swell time / I could have without you, / I got nuts. / I never get no peace."

　　（George 哀傷地瞪著柴火。／「當我想到美好時光，／沒有你，／我就會發瘋，/得不到任何安寧。」）

　　Lennie still knelt. He looked off into the darkness across the river. "George, you want I should go away and leave you alone?"

　　"Where the hell could you go?"

　　一句「你能去哪？」（Where the hell could you go?）道出了兩者間的依存關係。George 願意守著一個智能不足的大漢，來自於內心對 Lennie 真誠付出的感動：他自白說：

　　"... One day / a bunch of guys was standin' around up on the Sacramento River. / I was feelin' pretty smart. / I turns to Lennie and says, / "Jump in." / An' he jumps. / Couldn't swim a stroke. / He damn near drowned / before we could get him. / An' he was so damn nice to me / for pullin' him out. / Clean forgot / I told him to jump in. / Well, I ain't done nothing like that no more."

　　（……有一天，/一堆人站在沙加緬度河的河邊。/我覺得自己了不起，/我轉向 Lennie，說/：「跳下去。」/他就跳了。/一點都不會游泳。/他幾乎快淹死了，/我們救他起來。/他對我超好的，/將他拉出來。/完全忘記/是我叫他跳下去的。/喔，從此我就不會做這種事了。）

　　Lennie 這種毫無心機的忠誠與友誼打動了 George，也加深 George 永遠照顧這位容易受傷的兄弟。兩人的堅強友誼成為這個冷酷世界中為唯一溫暖，也是這本小說令人動容之處。

📖 結局賞析

　　然而面對這兩位情感真誠的兄弟，卻不是美好的未來，而是殘酷的現實。當 Lennie 在意外中殺死了女主人後，兩人逃離農莊。這次 George 知道他們無法逃避，為了避免 Lennie 落入農場主人的追殺，也為了維持 Lennie 對未來美好的想像，他毅然決然地開槍，結束了 Lennie 的一生：

And George raised the gun / and steadied it, / and he brought the muzzle of it close to the back of Lennie's head. / The hand shook violently, / but his face set / and his hand steadied. / He pulled the trigger. / The crash of the shot rolled up the hills / and rolled down again. / Lennie jarred, / and then settle slowly forward / to the sand, / and he lay / without quivering.

（George 舉起槍，/ 穩住。/ 將槍口靠近 Lennie 的頭後。/ 手劇烈顫抖，/ 然而，他板起臉來，/ 手穩了。/ 扣下扳機。/ 槍擊的巨響響徹山陵，/ 轟然回音。/ Lennie 震動，/ 然而慢慢地前傾，/ 倒在沙上。/ 躺在那，/ 沒有抖動。）

一槍斃命，減少了 Lennie 的受苦與受辱（...he lay without quivering.）。與其死在外人手中，George 忍痛結束了好友的生命。這一切的悲慘結束，不正是作者一直在強調的，面對所有的逆境，這些弱勢的勞工，如何在這些對抗中，保留一些 gallantry, courage, compassion and love。

適合閱讀程度：
高三以上學生及關心弱勢的社會人士
延伸閱讀／推薦書單、電影：
小說：
The Grapes of Wrath（《憤怒的葡萄》）
Green Miles（《綠色奇蹟》）

《遠大前程》

Great Expectations
(1860 ～ 1861)

Charles Dickens

📖 作者簡介

　　查爾斯·狄更斯（Charles Dickens, 1812 ～ 1870），可說是英國維多利亞時期最受歡迎的作家。狄更斯的小說如《孤雛淚》（*Oliver Twist*）、《塊肉餘生錄》（*David Copperfield*）、《雙城記》（*A Tale of Two Cities*）都是膾炙人口的佳作，奠立他在英國文學的不朽地位，號稱英國小說的泰斗。回應當時的社會問題，狄更斯的小說深入英國的中下階層，描寫這些人物的困難遭遇。小說的主角往往是孤兒（或孤女），在這個變動的時代裡，如何堅強奮鬥，最後建立一個美好的家庭。狄更斯的小說可說是社會小說，從小人物的觀點出發，挖掘當時英國的社會問題，小說家不僅具有敏銳的觀察力，更充滿社會關懷，從人性出發，發覺愛與親情的重要性，不僅贏得 19 世紀讀者的心，更能感動幾個世紀的讀者，從其人與人的互動中，體會人性的堅強一面，令人動容。其文字內容已成為英美世界的重要文化思維及家庭價值。

　　狄更斯的小說一方面以寫實的手法，將中下層的人物、生活忠實呈現，一方面運用滑稽、誇張的小說技巧，凸顯這些人物的特質，可說是將小說提升到藝術的層次。他在《塊肉餘生錄》的序言中，曾說：

It would concern the reader little, perhaps, to know / how sorrowfully the pen is laid down / at the close of a two-years' imaginative task; / or how an Author feels / as if he were dismissing some portion of himself / into the shadowy world, / when a crowd of the creatures of his brain are going from him for ever. / Yet, I had nothing else to tell; / unless, indeed, / I were to confess... / that no one can ever believe this Narrative, / in the reading, / more than I believed it in the writing.

　　（讀者可能不太會想知道，／這隻枝筆多麼痛苦地被放下來，／在兩年的想像力的工作後，／或是想知道，作者如何感受，／好像打發身體的一部分／進入幽暗的世界，／當一群腦中的人物永遠離他遠去。／然而，我沒有其他話可說，／除非，／我要坦白說，／沒人，在閱讀中，／會像我在寫作中，／那麼相信這個故事。）

對於狄更斯來說，他的小說都是他生命的一部分，也是他的小孩。他全心全力的創作，希望激起讀者對人性的重視。

📖 小說介紹

I was too cowardly to do what I knew to be right, as I had been too cowardly to avoid doing what I knew to be wrong. I had had no intercourse with the world at that time, and I imitated none of its many inhabitants who act in this manner. Quite an untaught genius, I made the discovery of the line of action for myself.

（我太懦弱，以至於不敢做一些我知道是對的事，就好像之前，我太懦弱，以致於不敢避免做些錯的事。那時，我跟這個世界沒有什麼接觸，我無法仿效世界上這麼做的居民。我完全是個沒人教的天才，自己發掘行為的準則。）

狄更斯的《遠大前程》主人翁 Pip 在小說中不斷地強調其懦弱的一面，缺乏對外在世界的認知與長輩的指導，道出了孤兒成長的心酸與孤獨。這本小說可說是狄更斯嘔心泣血之作，也是他對人性描述與青少年成長的深入探討。延續 19 世紀小說模式，這是一本孤兒成長小說（Bildungsroman），以第一人稱敘述，從兒童、青少年，到成年。小說主角 Pip，透過回憶與自我的省思，道盡這段成長過程的喜悅與痛苦：如何面對家裡姊姊及其他外界大人的心靈與肉體的欺壓；如何面對那段沒有結果的情感生活；如何認識自己的虛榮與勢利。在第一人稱的敘事中，Pip 交錯運用英文的現在式與過去式，呈現現在的心情與回顧的感想，時態的轉換讓讀者了解時空背景的替換。主角的回憶有如幻燈片般一幕幕地出現，情節中充滿驚奇，到底是誰給 Pip 財富，讓他能夠一夕間成為倫敦上流社會的紳士？到底女主角 Estella 情歸何處？到底 Pip 是否能夠重新面對自己？

這種種的一切，不僅反映出 19 世紀英國孩童與青少年的成長歷程，更觸動了全世界青少年與成年人的感情世界。青少年所面對的外在與內心世界的掙扎，都可以透過這本小說中，得到清晰的影像。在過去幾十年來，這本小說的張力與充滿衝突的情節，被英美導演所欣賞，不斷拍成電影，也有不同的名稱，如《孤星血淚》與《烈愛風雲》等；近年來流行於青少年的《哈利波特》小說，似乎可以在此本書中找到很多的場景與呼應。

📖 主題分析

✚ 忠誠友情 vs 財富地位

Pip 在困苦受虐的環境中成長，幸好其憨厚的姊夫 Joe 付出了友情與關心，讓他似乎認命的生活注入一點溫暖：

"But I did mind you, Pip," / he returned, / with tender simplicity, / "When I offered to your sister to keep company, / and to be asked in church, / at such times / as she was willing and ready / to come to the forge," / I said to her: / "And bring the poor little child. / God bless the poor little child," / I said to your sister, / " there's room for him / at the forge!"

（「不過，我確實掛心你，Pip」／他回說，／帶著溫柔純樸。／「當我要求與你姊姊作伴，／進入教堂，／那時，／你姊姊同意也準備／來工廠」，／我告訴她，／「把可憐的小傢伙帶來，／願上帝祝福這個小傢伙，」／我告訴你姊姊，／「有空間給他，／在工廠裡。」）

I broke out crying / and begging pardon, / and hugged Joe round the neck: / who dropped the poker to hug me, and to say, / "Ever the best of friends; ain't us, Pip? / Don't cry, old chap!"

（我突然哭出來，／要求原諒，／抱住 Joe 的頸部，／他放下火鉗來抱我，說，／「我們永遠是最好的朋友吧？／Pip，別哭，小傢伙。」）

.... Young as I was, / I believe / that I dated a new admiration of Joe / from that night. / We were equals afterwards, / as we had been before; / but afterwards at quiet times / when I sat down looking at Joe / and thinking about him, / I had a new sensation of feeling / conscious that I was looking up to Joe / in my heart.

（儘管那時還小，/ 我相信 / 我開始對 Joe 充滿新的讚佩，/ 從那晚。/ 我們之後還是平起平坐，/ 跟之前一樣。/ 不過之後，/ 在寧靜的時刻，/ 我坐下來看著 Joe，/ 想著他，/ 我有股新的悸動，/ 我知道我尊敬 Joe，/ 打從心底。）

Pip 對 Joe 的感情與悸動，在進入上流的倫敦社會後，跟著瓦解。Pip 背叛了之前 Joe 對他付出的忠誠與友情，開始追求虛幻的愛情與社會地位。一次，Joe 來拜訪 Pip，Pip 對老友的冷漠，對 Joe 笨拙的言行感到羞恥，令讀者感到鼻酸：

"Here Joe's hat / tumbled off the mantelpiece, / and he started out of his chair / and pick it up, / and fitted it to the same exact spot. / As if it were an absolute point of good breeding / that it should tumble off again soon."

（Joe 的帽子，/ 從壁爐架上跌落，/ 他從椅子跳起來，/ 撿起來，/ 塞回原來的地方，/ 好像那完全是一種好的教養，/ 隨時會再度掉下來）。

Pip 以 Joe 的不合適的帽子來比喻為一種「好教養」，使用 tumble（看來很笨拙跌落的動作），可以看出 Pip 那種瞧不起鄉下人的虛榮心態。離開前，Joe 說出了小說中最富哲理的一段話：

"Pip, dear old chap, / life is made of ever so many partings / welded together, / as I may say, / and one man's a blacksmith, / and one's a whitesmith, / and one's a goldsmith, / and one's a coppersmith. / Divisions among such must come, / and must be met / as they come."

（Pip 老兄，/ 人生是由很多分隔組成，/ 銲接在一起，/ 就像我說的。/

某人是鐵匠，／某人是錫匠，／某人是金匠，／某人是銅匠，／這之間的區分一定會來臨的，／也必須面對，／當他們來臨的時候。）

　　獲得財富的 Pip 已經成為金匠（goldsmith），而帶有土氣的 Joe 仍是那個純樸憨厚的鐵匠（blacksmith），兩人已處於不同的社會階層，必須面對區分（divisions）。狄更斯透過 Pip 與 Joe 之間的關係改變，嚴厲地批判上流社會的虛假。當我們擁有財富與地位，穿著名牌、進出豪宅與時尚餐廳，我們是否會開始瞧不起那些仍穿著土氣、不知社交應對的純樸老友呢？到底誰才是真正的紳士（gentleman），穿著體面、談話高雅的 Pip？還是穿著老土、卻充滿愛心的 Joe？

　　Pip 的救贖並非來自於對愛情的追求，而是對遠大前程（great expectations）假象的破滅。

📖 精彩片段賞析

　　這本小說另外一個精彩的主題，圍繞在愛情（love）與激情（passions）的衝突與矛盾。Pip 的墮落除了財富的誘惑外，對 Estella 的激情迷戀也是其中的主因。青少年的 Pip 第一次看到美麗的 Estella，由於自卑與自憐，對於冷酷無情的 Estella，產生了無可救藥的迷戀。對他而言，Estella 的垂青代表其人生中另一個最大的期望（great expectations）。小說中很多精彩的描寫都是放在 Pip 對這種虛無愛情的執著。

✚ 愛情與激情（love and passions）

I took the opportunity of being alone in the courtyard, / to look at my coarse hands and my common boots./ My opinion of those accessories was not favorable. / They had never troubled me before, / but they troubled me now, / as vulgar appendages.... / I wished Joe had been rather more genteelly brought up, / and then I should have been so too.

（我利用獨自在庭院的機會，/ 看看自己粗糙的雙手及粗俗的鞋子，/ 對這些配件並無好感，/ 之前從來沒有困擾我，/ 但是現在卻困擾我，/ 有如低俗的附加物，/ 真希望 Joe 應該較有教養，/ 而我也是。）

She came back, / with some bread and meat / and a little mug of beer. She put the mug down on the stones of the yard, / and gave me the bread and meat / without looking at me, / as insolently as I were a dog in disgrace. / I was so humiliated, / hurt, / spurned, / offended, / angry, / sorry ... / that my tears started to my eyes. / The moment they sprang there, / the girl looked at me / with a quick delight in / having been the cause of them.

（她回來，/ 帶著麵包、肉、/ 及一小杯啤酒，/ 將杯子放在院子的石頭上，/ 給我麵包及肉，/ 沒有看我一眼，/ 無禮地視我如卑賤的狗。/ 我如此被差辱、/ 受傷、/ 輕斥、/ 觸怒、/ 憤怒、/ 難過……/ 淚水湧上眼眶。/ 淚水流出的剎那，/ 女孩望著我，/ 帶著短暫的喜悅，/ 是她引起我的淚水。）

Pip 跟美麗的 Estella 相遇，第一次感受到出身及外表的卑微（to look at my coarse hands and my common boots）。他希望他姊夫 Joe 及自己應該更有教養些。此處使用假設法（had been rather more genteelly brought up 及 I should have been so too），表示應該如此但事實並非如此，充滿無奈與難過的心情。此外，被漂亮的 Estella 鄙視，從差辱（humiliated）到憤怒（angry）、難過（sorry），層層的心情，讀者也不禁與 Pip 一樣留下淚水，同情這位小男生的處境。

Pip 不幸地落入 Estella 的摧殘，而 Estella 也不過是當地富婆 Miss Havisham 報復男人的工具。Estella 被訓練成無法付出感情、無法體會愛情的冷酷女性。她自己使用本書中最有名的一個暗喻（metaphor）來說明個性的形成：陽光與黑暗的對比，她對養母 Miss Havisham 說：

"I begin to think," said Estella,.../ "If you had brought up your adopted daughter / wholly in the dark confinement of these rooms, / and had never let her know that there was such a thing as the daylight / by which she has never once seen your face / — if you had done that, / and then, for a purpose, / had wanted her to understand the daylight / and know all about it, / you would have been disappointed and angry?"

（如果你扶養你的養女 / 完全在這些房間的黑暗中，/ 從來不讓她知道有陽光這種東西，/ 她無法透過陽光看到你的臉，/ 假如你這麼做，而為了某種目的，/ 你現在要她瞭解陽光，/ 徹底瞭解，/ 你不會失望生氣嗎？）

一個從未見過陽光的人如何去體會陽光的熱力與光亮，一個從未體會感情與愛情的女孩，如何去付出感情？

相對地，從鄉下來的 Pip 即使一時被財富地位所迷惑，其內心所存的善念，轉化內心對 Estella 的渴望，即使知道 Estella 是個沒有心的女性（a girl without a heart），仍願意付出；真心的告白，令人動容：

".... You are part of my existence, / part of myself. You have been in every line I have ever read, / since I came here, / the rough common boy / whose poor heart you wounded even then. / You have been in every prospect / I have even seen since /—on the river, / on the sails of the ships, / on the marshes, / in the clouds, / in the light, / in the darkness, / in the wind, / in the woods, / in the sea, / in the streets. / You have been the embodiment of every graceful fancy / that my mind has ever become acquainted with.... / Estella, to the last hour of my life, / you cannot choose but remain part of my character, / part of the little good in me, / part of the evil. / But, in this separation / I associate you with the good, / and I will faithfully hold you to that always, / for you must have done me far more good / than harm, / let me feel now what sharp distress I may. / O God bless you, / God forgive you!"

（你是我生命的一部分，/ 是我的一部分，/ 你存在於我所讀的每一行字裡，/ 自從我來此，/ 那個粗俗的男孩，/ 你曾傷害其可憐心靈。/ 你存在於所有視野中，/ 我曾看到的 / ——在河上、/ 在船帆上、/ 在溼地裡、/ 在雲端、/ 在光亮中、/ 在黑暗中、/ 在風裡、/ 在樹林裡、/ 在海裡、/ 在街道上。/ 你一直以來象徵所有優雅的想像，/ 我內心所能熟悉的一切……/ Estella，直到我生命的最後時刻，/ 你仍是我的一部分，/ 我內心的一點善，/ 也是邪惡的一部分。/ 但是，在此分離的時刻，/ 我只想到你的善，/ 我永遠忠實地對你如此，/ 因為你對我做的善絕對大於 / 對我的傷害，/ 現在我感受到強烈的悲痛。/ 願上帝祝福你，/ 願上帝原諒你！）

就是這點善的聯想（the good），這點能夠體諒 Estella 悲哀一生的心情，Pip 原諒了 Estella，而 Estella 也在多年的受苦中成長，她說：

... when suffering has been stronger / than all other teaching, / and has taught me to understand / what your heart used to be. / I have been bent / and broken, / but — I hope— / into a better shape.
（苦難已經強過了 / 其他的教訓，/ 教我瞭解 / 之前你的心。/ 我已經被折服、/ 被馴服，/ 不過——我希望—— / 變成更好。）

Estella 要求 Pip 的原諒，希望他們還是好朋友：

"Be as considerate and good to me as you were, and tell me we are friends."

📖 結局賞析

小說的結尾，引起了不同的爭辯。狄更斯原始的悲劇結尾，引起了出版商及讀者的反彈，最後他修改了結尾：Pip 與 Estella 歷經了多年的風霜，回到了兒時的地方，現場一片廢墟，但卻充滿了再復甦的那點感情：

I took her hand in mine, and we went out of the ruined place; and as the morning mists had risen long ago when I first left the forge, so, the evening mists were rising now, and in all the broad expanse of tranquil light they showed to me, I saw no shadow of another parting from her.

（在晚霧延展的寧靜光線中，我看不到跟她分手的陰影。）

光線與陰影的對比（lighr vs. shadow），帶出兩人未來可能的相愛，既寫實又浪漫。

適合閱讀程度：

大一以上學生及社會人士；

高中生可以閱讀簡易版（如聯經出版的《遠大前程》）

延伸閱讀／推薦書單、電影：

小說：

David Copperfield（《塊肉餘生錄》）

Harry Potter（《哈利波特》）

電影：

Great Expectations（《烈愛風雲》，1998）

《織工馬南傳》

Silas Marner

(1861)

George Eliot

📖 作者簡介

英國女作家喬治‧艾略特（George Eliot，本名 Mary Ann Evans，1819～1880）是英國維多利亞時期的重要作家，寫過 7 本小說，其中《米德鎮》（*Middlemarch*），描寫一個小鎮中 4 對男女的故事，曾被批評家評為英國文學史上寫的最好的一本小說。艾略特從小就展現不凡的智力，勤於閱讀。她的父親不吝嗇投資小孩教育，將她送到住宿學校，她 17 歲時，母親過世，開始與姊妹經營管理父親的莊園。儘管其所受正式教育不長，但透過大量閱讀，艾略特開始投稿當時的重要雜誌 *Westminster Review* 最後成為該雜誌的助理編輯。也就是在此雜誌工作其間，認識了已婚的 George Henry Lewes，從此與其相知相守，直到 Lewes 過世，艾略特長期跟他同居，不受到家人諒解。

艾略特甚早開始寫作，從投稿 *Westminster Review* 就開始小說寫作。她的第一本長篇小說《亞當‧比德》（*Adam Bede*）在 1859 出版，馬上獲得文壇與市場肯定。之後，她便開啟 15 年的寫作生涯，出版了重要作品如《弗洛斯河上的磨坊》（*The Mill on the Floss*）、《織工馬南傳》（*Silas Marner*）等。《織工馬南傳》的寫作靈感來自於艾略特自己的生活感觸。由於她與 Lewes 的不倫關係，得不到家人、社區與教會的諒解，因此他失去了過去對宗教與價值的信念，開始了一連串的思考與追尋，企圖透過寫作，尋回失去的信心。

艾略特的小說充滿深度的思考，其語言展現成熟與複雜的思維架構。閱讀她的小說，不僅要體會其細膩的思維，更要體會語言所展現的曲折與纖細的含義，適合較成熟的讀者。她的小說，情節不算複雜，但人物內心的勾畫頗為多面。勾畫的人物都是周遭可見，但有待我們讀者慢慢去發掘。她在《亞當‧比德》這本小說中說過：

I want a great deal of those feelings / for my everyday fellow-men, / especially for the few / in the foreground of the great multitude, / whose faces I know, / whose hands I touch.... （*Adam Bede* Ch. 17）

（我想要這些感情，／賦予我每天的夥伴，／尤其是那些少數／　存在大眾間的，／那些人的臉我認識，／那些人的手我碰過。）

📖 小說介紹

A child, more than all other gifts
（孩子，勝過其他的禮物）
That earth can offer to declining man
（是這個世界能帶給凋謝的人）
Brings hope with it, and forward-looking thoughts.
（帶來希望與前瞻的看法）

— Wordsworth

　　《織工馬南傳》的一開始就引用了英國浪漫詩人華茲華斯（William Wordsworth）的詩，歌頌小孩的純真是大人世界的希望。小孩的確是世上最尊貴的禮物，帶給人類希望與信心。《織工馬南傳》是小說家本身經驗的一部分，艾略特曾經歷宗教信仰的喪失與不同文化價值的衝擊，這是一段如何心靈獲得滋潤，生命重新獲得意義的故事。

📖 主題分析

✚ 人 vs. 社區

　　小說一開始，我們看到主人翁 Silas 過著孤苦、卑微的生活，離群索居，沒有任何朋友：

His life had reduced itself / to the functions of weaving and hoarding, / without any contemplation of an end / towards which the functions tended.... / Strangely / Marner's face and figure shrank and bent themselves / into a constant mechanical relation / to the objects of his life, / so that he produced the same sort of impression / as a handle or a crooked tube, / which has no meaning / standing apart. / The prominent eyes / that used to look trusting / and dreamy, / now looked / as if they had been made / to see only one kind of thing / that was very small, / like tiny grain...; / and he was so withered and yellow, / that he was not yet forty, / the children always called him "Old Marner"

（他的生活已經簡化／到織布與囤積的功能，／沒有思考特定目標，／這些功能所指向的……／很奇怪的，／Marner 的臉跟身體萎縮、彎曲，／變成持續的機械動作，／有如他生活中的一些物體。／因此他給人的印象／有如是手把或曲管般，／沒有意義，／單獨存在。／突出的眼睛，／過去看來令人信任，／充滿夢想，／現在看來似乎變成，／只能看一種東西，／非常眇小，／有如小穀粒……；／他如此凋謝、泛黃，／不到 40 歲，／小孩總是叫他「老馬南」。）

此處，作者使用了幾個枯萎、萎縮的意象，來形容 Silas 所過的生活，例如 reduced、shrank、bent、withered、yellow、crooked tube、tiny grain 等等字眼，又以機械性的動作來表示 Silas 過著如行屍走肉的生活，如 a constant mechanical relation、a handle、a crooked tube 等。最後以小孩與老馬南來產生強烈的對比。

這些強烈的意象很清楚的勾畫出主人翁可悲的生活。然而 Silas 之前的生活並非如此，他曾在教會奉獻服務。但是，在一次教會指控他偷竊黃金後，他喪失了對社區人群的信任，從此過著獨居的生活："He seemed to weave, like the spider, from pure impulse, without reflection."（他總是織布，好像蜘蛛，出自純粹的本能，沒有思考。）

生命意義的消失，迫使 Silas 與社區的隔閡。他生命中唯一意義就是數錢：

"But now, / when all purpose was gone, / that habit of looking towards the money and grasping it / with a sense of fulfilled effort made a loam / that was deep enough / for the seeds of desire; / and as Silas walked homeward / across the fields / in the twilight, / he drew out the money / and thought it was brighter / in the gathering gloom."

（但是現在，/ 當所有目的消失，/ 向錢看、並緊緊抓住金錢的習慣，/ 帶有一絲成就，成為沃土，/ 夠深可以 / 發育欲望的種子。/ Silas 走回家路上，/ 越過田野，/ 在黃昏中，/ 他拿出金錢，/ 覺得錢更加明亮，/ 在天色漸漸暗下來時。）

✚ 從失望到希望：擁有孩子的喜悅與希望

抓住金錢是否可以代表一切呢？ Silas 的未來難道要沈淪在金錢與機械般的生活中嗎？ 15 年過去了，有天，Silas 回到家發現他辛苦累積的錢（也是他現在生活唯一的重心）被偷了。這次，失錢的打擊卻換來村民對他的同情與安慰，過去大家覺得他是孤僻的，可是現在社區開始重視他的感覺，其中一個村民 Mr. Macey 來拜訪他，安慰他：

"Come, / Maser Marner, / why, you've no call to sit amoaning. / You're a deal better off / to ha' lost your money... / You might ha' made up for it / by coming to church reg' lar..."

（「別這樣了，/ Master Marner，/ 欸，你沒必要坐在這哀傷。/ 你可能變得更好，/ 掉了那些錢⋯⋯ / 你可以補救，/ 固定來上教會。」）

邀請他上教會代表村民對他的接受，也漸漸回復了 Silas 失去的社區友誼支柱。

然而，對 Silas 最大的回報與救贖，來自一個嬰兒 Eppie。村裡有錢人家生的私生子，意外的進入了 Silas 冷清的家，從此 Eppie 成為 Silas 與村民、外在世界溝通的媒介，也成為他生命的目標：

Silas began now / to think of Raveloe life entirely / in relation to Eppie: / she must have everything that was a good in Raveloe; / and he listened docilely, / that he might come to understand better / what this life was, / from which, for fifteen years, / he had stood aloof / as from a strange thing, / wherewith he could have no communion.... / And now something had come to replace his hoard / which gave a growing purpose to the earnings, / drawing his hope and joy / continually onward / beyond the money.

（Silas 開始 / 看待 Raveloe 的生活，/ 完全跟 Eppie 有關。/ 她一定是擁有 Raveloe 美好的一切。/ 他溫柔地傾聽，/ 或許更能理解自己的生活，/ 對於他自己的生活，/ 過去 15 年來，/ 他離得遠遠的，/ 好像那是很奇怪的東西，/ 完全沒有聯繫……/ 現在，某個東西取代他的積蓄，/ 漸漸賦予金錢的目的，/ 帶領他的希望及喜悅，/ 持續往前，/ 超越金錢。）

對 Eppie 的付出，讓他感受愛與信任，出自內心的話語，他已經回復到過去對人的熱情、對生活的喜悅：

"Eh, my precious child, the blessing was mine. If you hadn't been sent to save me, I should ha' gone to the grave in my misery. The money was taken away from me in time; and you see it's been kept— kept till it was wanted for you. It's wonderful—our life is wonderful."

沒有 Eppie，Silas 的生命將在哀傷結束。第一次的偷竊事件，他喪失了信心；第二次的偷竊，卻帶給他生命的喜悅。Eliot 是個充滿生命探索的作家，透過簡單的故事，敘述生命的態度與哲理，以下我們閱讀更多這些雋永的話語。

📖 精彩片段賞析

艾略特的小說頗富生活哲理，即使背景在 19 世紀的英國，但是描寫人類喪失信心，喪失社會的關心，而將自己封鎖起來，陷入某種 obsession（迷戀、困惑）的狀態，不正是當代都會或網路社會常常出現的現象嗎？

小說主角的變化來自於跟社區之間的互動，當一個人對社會或過去的記憶漸漸消失，他對現在也是無法掌握的。作者是這樣來描寫 Silas 如何與社區脫離了：

"...the past becomes dreamy because its symbols have all vanished, and the present too is dreamy because it is linked with no memories."

（過去變成有如夢般，因為所有的象徵都消失了，現在也有如夢般，因為連接不到任何記憶。）

當過去一切有價值的象徵沒有了，我們所信仰的價值消失了，過去就不再具體；而現在也因為找不到過去的記憶，成為沒有實體的存在。這段話說明了人類歷史的延續性，也說明了人類建立價值信念的重要性。艾略特經常在這些從日常生活或是個人經驗的體會中，提出了這些令人深省的話語。

主人翁 Silas 的價值與信念的失去後，他沉入了另一種生活的形態：簡化自己的生活成為有如動物般的行動：

Then there were the calls of hunger; / and Silas, / in his solitude, / had to provide his own breakfast, dinner, and supper, / to fetch his own water / from the well, / and put his own kettle on the fire; / and all these immediate promptings helped, / along with the weaving, / to reduce his life / to the unquestioning activity of a spinning insect. / He hated the thought of the past....

（有時肚子餓，/ Silas，/ 孤獨中，/ 必須準備自己的早餐、中餐、晚餐，/ 拿自己的水，/ 從井裡，/ 將水壺放到火上，/ 這些及時的刺激活動，協助他，/ 與織布一樣，/ 降級他的生活 / 到紡織昆蟲的盲目行動。/ 他痛恨想到過去……）

　　這種生活的形態，對於現代都市人是否非常熟悉？上班、下班、吃三餐、喝水等，沒有過去，沒有未來，有如打轉忙碌的昆蟲般。

　　除了機械性或動物性的行為外，自我封鎖的社會疏離人，其實還會進入某種迷戀的狀態。有如日本的御宅族（otaku）沉迷於某種收集或執著上，Silas 除了織布外，還非常著迷於金幣的收集。然而金幣的收集，並非有如守財奴一般的固守財富，而是對某些事物的執著讓他產生一種歸屬感：

But / what were the guineas to him / who / saw no vista / beyond countless days of weaving?/ It was needless for him to ask that, / for it was pleasant to him / to feel them in his palm, / and look at their bright faces, / which were all his own; / it was another element of life, / like the weaving and the satisfaction of hunger, / subsisting / quite aloof from the life of belief and love / from which he had been cut off.

　　（但是，/ 金幣對他有何意義？/ 他是這麼個人，/ 看不到未來，/ 在無盡的織布歲月外。/ 無須問他這個問題，/ 因為對他而言是很愉悅的，/ 感覺這些金幣在他手中，/ 看著他們閃閃發亮的表面，/ 這些都是他的。/ 這是生活的另一個要素，/ 有如織布或解餓，/ 維持生存，/ 遠離信仰與愛的人生，/ 而那些是他被切斷的。）

　　作者除了描寫他的生活之外，還會很仔細地探討這種現象的意義，協助讀者思考類似的生活或人生問題，也讓讀者能夠從周遭的環境去感受，去回顧自己的生活，這是閱讀這本小說的最大樂趣。當然這種讀法，需要我們慢慢、反覆咀嚼每句話及每個字，精讀的功力就是這樣培養出來，對於英文文字的體會也是從這個地方培養。我們再讀以下這一段，當 Silas 自己收藏的金幣被偷了，他氣急敗壞的去尋找鄰居協助。作者帶領我們看到 Silas 從內心漸漸開始的細微轉變：

"This strangely novel situation / of opening his trouble to / his Raveloe neighbors, / of sitting in the warmth of a hearth / not his own, / and feeling the presence of faces and voices / which were his nearest promise of help, / had doubtless its influence on Marner, / in spite of his passionate preoccupation / with his loss. / Our consciousness rarely registers the beginning of a growth within us / any more than without us: / there have been many circulations of the sap / before we detect / the smallest sign of the bud."

（這奇怪新奇的情況，/ 開放自己的問題給 / 他 Raveloe 的鄰居，/ 坐在火爐的溫暖中，/ 並非自己的，/ 感受面孔與聲音在面前，/ 這是最能協助他的希望，/ 無疑的影響到 Marner，/ 儘管他強烈地想著自己的損失。/ 我們的意識 / 很少去記錄到內在變化的形成，/ 也不會去注意我們的外在；/ 很多樹液已經在流動，/ 在我們發覺 / 樹芽長出的小小徵兆之前。）

以樹液的流動來比喻些微的變化，不管是內在的或外在的（within us or without us），都是在不知不覺中產生。先敘述狀況，而後以一句具體比喻的話語（... there have been many circulations of the sap ....）來作結論，可見作者歸納與總結的能力甚強，也能從小地方點出人性的共同點。此處使用一個英文比較難的句法：rarely... any more than（表示前後的兩個事件都是一樣的 rarely 很少做到）。作者句子很長也有點複雜，但就是利用這種複雜的句法來表現其繁密的思維。

類似的用法與思維不斷出現在小說中，描寫 Silas 受到領養小孩 Eppie 的影響，整段話有如詩句般，句法重疊，聲音節奏優美動聽：

As the child's mind was growing into knowledge, / his mind was growing into memory:/ as her life unfolded, / his soul, / long stupefied in a cold narrow prison, / was unfolding too, / and trembling gradually / into full consciousness.

（當孩子的心靈漸漸接受知識，／他的心靈也漸漸接受記憶，／當她的生命展開，／他的靈魂，／長久呆滯在冰冷狹小的監獄中，／也漸漸展開。／漸漸顫動，進入完全的意識中。）

作者用了兩個對稱字詞 growing into、unfolding，最後使用動詞 trembling 表示心靈漸漸復甦，開始顫動，也隱含一點點的不安與緊張。使用三個 into 產生節奏，製造詩的感覺。

好的文字需要細嚼慢嚥，艾略特的小說文字充滿了那種細膩的情感，值得回味。

📖 結局賞析

從疏離到歸屬，Silas 完成了自己人生的追尋，也表現了小說家自我價值的肯定。呼應浪漫詩人華茲華斯的危機處理模式，從兒童、從記憶、從童年找回愛與信心，主人翁 Silas 告訴我們生命歸屬的重要：

Unlike the gold / which needed nothing, / and must be worshipped in close-locked solitude— / which was hidden away from the daylight, / was deaf to the song of birds, / and started to no human tones / — Eppie was a creature of endless claims / and ever-growing desires, / seeking and loving sunshine, / and living sounds, / and living movements; / making trial of everything, / with trust in new joy, / and stirring the human kindness / in all eyes that looked on her.

（不像金幣，／無所需求，／必須在閉鎖的孤獨中膜拜──／遠離陽光，／聽不到鳥兒歌聲，／對於人類的聲調／── Eppie 是個生命體，／無止盡的需求，不斷成長的渴望，／追求喜愛陽光，／活生生的聲音，／活力的行動，／嘗試所有的事物，／期待新的喜悅，／激起人類仁慈之心，／在所有看著她的眼睛裡。）

最後，作者要求我們不要執迷於冷冰冰的物體如金幣，而要去感受需要你擁抱、需要你去關懷的小孩或周遭的朋友。對於沉迷於網路遊戲或某些物品收集的御宅族來說，走出戶外，擁抱陽光、聽聽大自然的聲音、多接觸你的親人，才是尋找歸屬感最好的方法。從物品或虛擬的世界是尋找慰藉，失去的東西可能更多。

適合閱讀程度：

大三以上學生及社會人士；高中程度可以閱讀簡易版。

延伸閱讀／推薦書單、電影：

小說：

Jane Eyre（《簡愛》）

Jude the Obscure（《石匠玖德》）

《必需品專賣店》

Needful Things

(1991)

Stephen King

📖 作者簡介

　　史蒂芬・金（Stephen King, 1947～），是美國當代多產且讀者群非常廣大的恐怖小說作家（horror fiction writer）。截至 2011 年，他總共寫了 49 本小說，很多都拍成電影，如最近的《捕夢人》（*Dreamcatcher*）、《1408》、《迷霧驚魂》（*The Mist*）、《綠色奇蹟》（*Green Miles*）等。金在早期擔任中學老師時，就對神祕故事產生興趣，並且不斷以短篇小說投稿到雜誌，最後《魔女嘉莉》（*Carrie*）受到出版社青睞，這是他第一部長篇小說。從此之後，金的驚悚小說獲得市場歡迎，成為美國當代最受歡迎的恐怖小說作家之一。

　　金的恐怖小說涵蓋的主題甚廣，這本小說則以緬因州的一個虛擬小鎮為場景，敘述在這個以白人為主的小鎮中，居民受到外在或內心的邪惡攻擊，成為美國社會的集體夢魘。金認為人類恐懼的事物其實並非僅存在一些恐怖詭異的世界，而是到處可見。我們周遭的環境，仔細觀察，充滿了令人感到驚悚的事件與場景，這些都是美國社會或人類內心世界的投射。他的恐怖小說經常探討心理的層次，大量使用心理學、宗教、科學、民俗傳說、社會學等理論與實證，分析人類內心恐懼的來源。他在《恐懼國度》（*Kingdom of Fear*）一書的前言裡，曾提到最令人恐懼的十大事物，都成為其恐怖小說的主要骨幹：

"Fear of the dark; fear of squishy things; fear of deformity; fear of snakes; fear of rats; fear of closed-in places; fear of insects (especially spiders, flies, beetles); fear of death; fear of others (paranoia); fear for someone else."

📖 小說介紹

Times changed; methods changed, faces, too. But when the faces were needful they were always the same, the faces of sheep who have lost their shepherd, and it was with this sort of commerce that he felt most at home, ... He charged them with what they could afford—not a penny more or a penny less. Each according to his means was Mr. Gaunt's motto, never mind each according to his needs, because they were all needful things, and he had come here to fill their emptiness and end their aches.

（時代改變，方式改變，臉孔也改變；但是那些有所需求的臉孔，千古不變，有如失去牧羊者的羊群面孔。就是這種交易方式，他覺得很自在……。他索取他們能負擔的價格，不多一分也不少一分。每個人都依照自己的能力付出，這是高特先生的座右銘，不管每人有什麼需求，因為這些都是他們所需要的東西。他到此處來填補他們的空虛，結束他們的痛苦。）

這些都是他們所需要的東西（they were all needful things），恐怖大師史蒂芬‧金這部探討人類醜陋與脆弱本性的驚悚小說，點出了每人內心的渴望：我們都有所需求、內心有所空虛。這部 1991 年出版的《必需品專賣店》延續作者長久以來，強調恐懼來自內心的邪惡與墮落，帶領我們進入人性實驗室，進行一場善與惡之間的鬥爭。

小說的場景發生在一個寧靜的小鎮 Castle Rock。當邪惡入侵，我們親眼目睹從小孩到老年人，在貪婪的誘惑下，逐漸被污染、邪惡化的過程，這不是外星人的入侵，也不是邪靈附體，而是人性的轉換，也是人性的考驗。道德的抉擇（moral choice）永遠是這類小說的重要關鍵，面對所喜愛的東西放在眼前（例如長久以來渴望的棒球卡、貓王的照片等），如何做出選擇常常是我們現代人需要面對的問題。「必需品專賣店」滿足了我們對物質的需求，但是史第芬‧金告訴我們：天下沒有白吃的午餐。面對自己的物質欲望，這次不是要付出金錢，而是付出靈魂。這種對當代資本主義（capitalism）及物質主義（materialism）的批判，非常強烈，也點出了當代人對於物質欲望的追求其實是一種靈魂的付出。

📖 主題分析

✚ 靈魂的交換、魔鬼的交易

從《浮士德》到《歌劇魅影》，我們看到西方文學傳統中，對於魔鬼的誘惑又期待又怕受傷害的矛盾心態。然而人類在這些人性的考驗與魔鬼的挑戰中，不斷地屈服與挫敗，難道是人性的脆弱？還是邪惡力量的巨大呢？小說一開始，敘述者談到小鎮中的一些小衝突，漸漸會演變成大災難，這些都是人類私心的作祟，也是魔鬼運作的空間：

"We bump up against each other / every now and then, / but mostly things go along all right. / Or always have, / until now. / But I have to tell you a real secret, / my friend; / it's mostly why I called you over / once I saw you were back in town. / I think trouble / — real trouble— / is on its way. / I smell it, / just over the horizon, / like an out-of-season storm / full of lightning."

（我們互相碰撞，/ 經常，/ 但是大都相安無事，/ 都是如此，/ 直到現在。/ 我必須告訴你一個真正的祕密，/ 我的朋友；/ 這就是為何我叫你來，/ 一看到你回到鎮上。/ 我想麻煩 / ——真正大麻煩—— / 要來了。/ 我聞得到，/ 就出現在地平線上，/ 有如一場不該在季節中出現的暴風雨，/ 滿布閃電。）

這段敘述，作者使用幾個代名詞（We, I, you），並稱呼讀者 my friend，將敘述者以鎮民的角度，邀請讀者進入小鎮中（I called you over once I saw you were back in town），成為鎮民，接受必需品專賣店老闆 Mr. Gaunt 的誘惑。以 an out-of-season storm full of lightning 來比喻小鎮所要面對的魔鬼誘惑，非常傳神。

Mr. Gaunt 對鎮民 Hugh 說："Do you know something, Hugh? The world is full of needy people who don't understand that everything, everything, is for sale... if you're willing to pay the price." Mr. Gaunt（魔鬼的化身）開了一家必需品專

賣店，針對所有人的需求，提供貨物，滿足他們的渴望。他認為這個世界充滿內心需求的人（The world is full of needy people....），所有事物都是可以出賣的，只要你願意付出代價（pay the price）。這種誘惑任何人都很難拒絕，試問，當一個當季的 LV 包放在眼前，你只要伸手去拿，而且代價只是要你開個小玩笑或作弄別人，就可以滿足擁有名牌包的慾望，有誰可以抵擋這種誘惑呢？但是這個小小的代價，就是我們墮落的開始。魔鬼也正在進行盜取人類靈魂的工作：

"Mr. Gaunt thought of himself / as an electrician of the human soul. / In a small town like Castle Rock, / all the fuse-boxes were lined up / neatly side by side. / What you had to do was / open the boxes... / and then start cross-wiring.... / All it took was / an understanding of human nature,.... / People always thought / in terms of souls, and / of course he would take as many of those as he could / when he closed up shop."

（Mr. Gaunt 覺得自己是 / 人類靈魂的電工，/ 在 Castle Rock 這種小鎮，/ 所有的保險絲盒一個一個 / 整齊排列，/ 要做的只是打開盒子，/ 然後接線⋯⋯ / 完成這一切 / 必須瞭解人性⋯⋯ / 人們總是思考 / 以靈魂的角度，/ 當然他會帶走越多的靈魂，/ 當他歇業關門時。）

✛ 邪惡力量的入侵純樸心靈或小鎮（evil vs. innocence）

邪惡入侵純樸的心靈一直是美國文學中重要的主題，馬克吐溫（Mark Twain）的《神祕陌生人》（*The Mysterious Stranger*, 1916）以及《讓小鎮墮落的人》（*The Man That Corrupted Hadleyburg*, 1900）即是類似的故事。史第芬・金除了延續這種美國文學傳統之外，更勾畫人性的另一面。他從心理分析的層次，來描素迷戀（obsession）與強迫症（compulsion）的整體過程，常人可能無法想像鎮民如何對棒球卡或是某些陳舊事物的迷戀，但是迷戀是一種上癮的過程，從小慾望的滿足產生了成就感，這種不斷去填補空虛的心靈，不斷需要產生成就感，也是人類墮落的一項主因。而強迫症則不僅是迷戀的病態行為，更是自我慾望、外在環境與道德感的複雜糾葛。作者藉著小男孩（innocence 純真的象徵）對於棒球卡的迷戀（evil 邪惡入侵）來勾畫出，在這種善惡鬥爭中，人性其實很脆弱：

My card. My Sandy Koufax card it's gone.
（我的卡片。我的 Sandy Koufax 卡片不見了！）
It wasn't. / He knew it wasn't, / but he also knew / he would not be able / to go back to sleep / until he'd checked / to make sure / it was still there, / in the looseleaf binder / where he kept / his growing collection of Topps cards / from 1956. / He had checked it / before leaving for school yesterday, / had done so again / when he got home, / and last night, / after supper,/ he had broken off / playing pass in the back yard / with Stanley Dawson / to check on it once more. / He had told Stanley / he had to go to the bathroom. / He had peeked at it one final time / before crawling into bed / and turning out the light. / He recognized / that it had become a kind of obsession with him, （這已成為一種迷戀）/ but recognition did not / put a stop to it. （但是，發覺此事卻無法停止這種迷戀。）

　　這麼精彩簡潔的文字，不必要字字翻譯成中文。試著拆成短小易懂的片段，並忽略某些專有名詞或不懂的單字，慢慢去體會這些文句的力量。本段中，作者不斷重複用了很多 He had + Ved 的句型，配合小男孩不斷去查看棒球卡的焦慮心態，重複的句法與重複的動作互相搭配，且配合故事主題的進行，語言結構與內心世界完美結合。
　　驚悚小說起源於早期的歌德式小說（Gothic novels），描寫罪惡與內心的恐懼，充滿神祕與幽靈的場景。史蒂芬·金導入現代心理學的分析模式，結合西方傳統魔鬼的意像與罪惡心裡的分析，創造了當代的幽冥世界（twilight zone）。
　　一個好故事，不僅需要好題材，其實更需要一個會講故事的人（story-

teller）。史蒂芬‧金這個很會說故事的人一開始扮演路人甲的角色，道聽途說，東扯西扯，指出本書隱藏的風暴，這種輕描淡寫及風趣寫實的開始，卻預告了小鎮未來的瓦解：

"It's the same here as where you grew up, most likely. People getting bet up over religion, ... people carryin secrets, people carryin grudges ... and even a spooky story every now and then, ... to liven up the occasional dull day."

（這裡跟你成長的地方大致差不多。大夥兒不是對宗教興奮緊張……就是心中藏著祕密、或是心懷怨恨，有時來個恐怖故事，活潑一下無聊的日子。）這是個美麗的小鎮，跟美國任何小鎮差不多，"Trouble and aggravation's / mostly made up of ordinary things, / did you notice that? / Undramatic things." （紛爭煩惱 / 大都是來自一些平凡無奇的事，/ 你有沒有發現，/ 一些無關痛癢的事！）

故事敘述者（narrator）從這裡開始，警告我們：

Keep an eye on everything. You've been here before, but things are about to change. I know it. I feel it. There's a storm on the way.

（注意所有一切。你曾來過此處，不過情況將要改變，我知道、我感覺得出來，暴風雨就要來臨了！）

📖 精彩片段賞析

✝ 恐懼與溫馨

"Hello?" he asked uncertainly, still standing in the doorway. "Is anybody here?"

He was about to grasp the doorknob and pull the door shut again when a voice replied," I'm here."

A tall figure— what at first seem to be an impossibly tall figure— came through a doorway behind one of the display cases. The doorway was masked with a dark velvet curtain. Brian felt a momentary and quite monstrous cramp of fear. Then the glow thrown by one of the spots slanted across the man's face, and Brian's fear was allayed. The man was quite old and his face was very kind.

必需品專賣店的老闆 Gaunt 第一次出現，由小男孩 Brian 主觀的印象引出，夾雜懸疑（The doorway was masked with a dark velvet curtain. 門口掛著深色天鵝絨的帷幔）、恐懼 （a momentary and quite monstrous cramp of fear 那間怪異的恐懼抽痛）與信任（Brian's fear was allayed 布萊恩的恐懼減輕了。）

滿懷幻想的 Brian 首先踏入這家店，一映入眼臉的是個很高、一個高得不像話的人出現在展示櫃後面，令人恐懼。然而一道亮光斜照（slanted across）在那人臉上，減低了整體的恐怖感。那道亮光來自天花板的投射燈（spots），以動詞 slanted across（斜照），而非直射（shine upon），來呈現光線打在那人臉上產生一種柔和（kind）的感覺，映照出他的面容慈祥（His face was very kind.），非常精彩，這種又詭異又溫馨的情境，一直貫穿整個故事。小說中的魔鬼 Gaunt 一方面給人陰森恐怖的感覺，一方面又常以溫柔的聲音及形象來安慰、腐蝕人心。

✚ 懷疑與墮落

小說中另一個精彩的描述，在於呈現小鎮人物如何陷入互相的猜忌與懷疑之中，如何產生不信任感，開始展開瘋狂的報復。小鎮的老師 Sally 滿心期待跟未婚夫分享婚姻生活，然而一封捏造的親密信摧毀了她對愛情與婚姻的信任，對未婚夫的不信任，引進了邪惡的心思，她喪失了純真：

All of her former complacency now rose up to mock her, and a voice which she had never heard before today suddenly spoke up from some deep chamber of her heart: The trust of the innocent is the liar's most useful tool.

（她之前的那種滿足感現在全部浮現上來嘲弄她，內心深處傳來之前沒聽過的聲音：純潔之人的信任，是騙子最有力的工具。）

✚ 渴望與需要的不同

小鎮中唯一理性正直的警長 Alan，也差點因為內心強烈的復仇心理，淪為魔鬼的工具。他的老婆小孩因車禍喪生，對他而言，獲得真相是永遠無法滿足的欲望。而魔鬼 Gaunt 利用他這種喪妻喪子的傷痛所產生的罪惡感，幾乎摧毀了他的理性。最後有賴其女友 Polly 要他拿掉那種誘惑人渴望。

"I have to go, Polly," he said. His own voice seemed to be coming to him from far away.

（他的聲音似乎來自遠方）

"No you won't!" she cried. Suddenly she was furious with him— furious at all of them, all the greedy, frightened, angry, acquisitive people in this town, herself included.

（「不，你不能，」她大叫。突然，她對他很生氣，氣憤這鎮裡所有的人，所有貪婪、受驚嚇、憤怒、貪得無厭的人，包括她自己。）

"... What's the one thing in all the world, the one useless thing, that you want so badly that you get it mixed up with needing it? That's your charm, Alan— that's what he's put around our neck."

（那是什麼東西，那個無用的東西，你很想要，因此誤認為那是你需要的。那就是迷惑你的東西，Alan，那就是他（魔鬼）掛在你頸部的東西。）

我們想要的（what we want）與我們需要的（what we need），兩者並不相同，想要的並不一定是需要的，Polly 點出了人性的謬誤，我們的渴望造成了惡魔的入侵，那些渴望的事物不是真正的 needful things（必需品）。小男孩 Brian 所渴望的棒球卡，真的是必需品嗎？我們要（want）的名牌，真的是我們的必需品（needful things）嗎？

　　小說的精彩處，在於敘述者不斷地利用文字的語意來挑戰我們的思維，各種字詞的使用（如 slant, rise up, want, need）並不難懂，但從上下文語意來推敲，都可見作者的用心。小說最後，玩世不恭的敘述者又回來了，告訴我們另個小鎮也要開個新店，滿足大家內心的希望。欲望永遠不會停息，罪惡永遠虎視眈眈（The devil never dies.）

📖 結局賞析

　　小說最後，警長 Alan 從自己的憤怒中清醒，瞭解了魔鬼 Gaunt 的陰謀，與小學老師 Polly 聯手，搶回了魔鬼手中的鎮民靈魂，將惡魔逐出小鎮：

The Gaunt-thing hissed / and shook its claws at them.
（怪物 Gaunt 嘶嘶吼叫，/ 揮動爪子。）

Alan picked up the bag / and backed slowly into the street / with Polly by his side. / He raised the fountain of light-flowers / so that they cast an amazing, revolving glow / upon Mr. Gaunt and his Tucker Talisman. / He pulled air into his chest—/ more air than his body had ever contained before, / it seemed. And when he spoke, / his words roared from him / in a vast voice which was not his own. / "Go Hence, Demon! / YOU ARE CAST OUT FROM THIS PLACE!"

（Alan 提起袋子，/ 慢慢退到街上，/ Polly 在他旁邊。/ 他舉起光芒的花束，/ 投下驚人旋轉的光芒，/ 照著 Gaunt 跟他的 Tucker 符咒。/ 他吸了一口氣進胸腔，/ 超過身體能容納的，/ 似乎。/ 他一開口說話，/ 字字洪亮，/ 不是自己的聲音：「滾吧，惡魔，/ 你被逐出這個地方！」）

The Gaunt-thing screamed / as if burned by scalding water. / The green awning of Needful Things burst into flame / and the show-window blew inward, / its glass pulverized to diamonds.

（怪物 Gaunt 尖叫，/ 彷彿被沸水燙傷。/ 必需品專賣店的綠色遮陽篷陷入烈焰，/ 櫥窗向內爆破，/ 玻璃粉碎成閃閃發亮的鑽石。）

回到了自己的良心，恢復了自己的心智，Alan 與 Polly 才有神奇力量驅趕惡魔。最後場景，回到史蒂芬·金最喜歡的壯觀場景，充滿戲劇性的轉折與特效，滿足了讀者最後的期待。

適合閱讀程度：
大一以上學生或生活枯燥乏味的社會人士。
延伸閱讀／推薦書單、電影：
小說：
Thinner（《變瘦》）
The Man That Corrupted Hadleyburg（《讓小鎮墮落的人》）
The Phantom of the Opera（《歌劇魅影》）
電影：
Needful Things（《必需品專賣店》，1993）

《大亨小傳》

The Great Gatsby

(1925)

Scott Fitzgerald

📖 作者簡介

費茲傑羅（Scott Fitzgerald, 1896 ～ 1940）早年就讀於普林斯頓大學（Princeton），但成績不好，並未畢業。1917 年入伍當兵，當時正值第一次世界大戰尾聲。其間從事寫作，於 1920 年出版第一部小說《塵世樂園》（*This Side of Paradise*），一夕成名。1925 年出版的《大亨小傳》（*The Great Gatsby*）更是讓他成為文壇的名人。成名後，費茲傑羅陷入一連串的財富追逐與浮華享受中，有如《大亨小傳》中所描述的情景。最後在 1940 年死於心臟病，得年 44 歲。

費茲傑羅身處美國 20 年代，也就是所謂的美國爵士時代（the Jazz Age）。第一次世界大戰的混亂與摧毀，對當代美國社會產生很大的震撼。參與戰爭的這一代訴諸奢華享受與頹廢心態，作為空虛心靈的補償。費茲傑羅忠實地反應這股風潮，勾畫出那種無奈與空虛的時代：宴會的燈光閃爍，對應著外在世界的漸漸黑暗：

"The lights grow brighter as the earth lurches away from the sun."

📖 小說介紹

In my younger and more vulnerable years my father gave me some advice that I've been turning over in my mind ever since.

"Whenever you feel like criticizing any one," he told me, "just remember that all the people in this world haven't had the advantages that you've had."

（在我年輕、容易受傷的歲月，父親給我些忠告，迄今仍不斷在心中思索：

「任何時候，你想要批評某人，」他告訴我，「只要記住世界上所有人並未擁有你所擁有的優勢。」）

美國小說家費茲傑羅在美國 20 年代出版這本《大亨小傳》，描述美國爵士時代中，從財富的追求到道德的空虛，偉大的美國夢（the great American dream）興起、幻滅。透過敘述者（Nick）第一人稱的故事，讀者見證了小說主角 Gatsby（蓋茲比），忠實追求夢想、追求愛情，最後卻身亡的悲慘過程。

小說中講故事的 Nick 來自中西部的望族，對於暴發戶 Gatsby 大肆揮霍、炫耀財富的行為，充滿批判，可是接觸到了 Gatsby 純真的一面，他開始重新思考人的價值與物質的虛幻。Nick 對 Gatsby 本人及故事的態度，其實非常矛盾，有時批判 Gatsby 的價值觀與道德的侵犯，有時又羨慕、美化 Gatsby 的純真愛情，故事以懷舊、哀悼的心情展開，回應了他爸爸告訴他的那句話：世界上所有人並未擁有你所擁有的優勢。

📖 主題分析

✝ 財富的追求 vs. 道德的淪喪

追求財富是每個人的夢想，不管是世家或新起富豪，奢華的生活形態，都透過不同的意像來呈現，敘述者以漂浮（floating）的意像來呈現貴婦的生活，堪稱是神來之筆：當 Nick 去找他的舊時好友 Tom 跟她老婆 Daisy，踏入豪宅，進入眼簾即是這幅非常超寫實的景象：

The only completely stationary object / in the room / was an enormous couch / on which two young women were buoyed up / as though upon an anchored balloon. / They were both in white / and their dresses were rippling and fluttering / as if they had just been blown back in / after a short flight around the house. / I must have stood / for a few moments / listening to / the whip and snap of the curtains / and the groan of a picture / on the wall. / Then there was a boom / as Tom Buchanan shut the rear windows /and the caught wind died out about the room / and the curtains and the rugs and the two young women / ballooned slowly to the floor.

　　（唯一完全靜止的物體 / 在房裡，/ 是一巨大沙發，/ 在上面兩個年輕女性飄浮，/ 好像是停泊的氣球。/ 他們兩人穿著白色，/ 衣服飄動起伏、隨風飄揚，/ 好像剛被吹進來，/ 在房裡短暫的飛行之後。/ 我一定在站在那，/ 好幾分鐘，/ 傾聽窗簾拍打、劈哩叭啦的聲音，/ 牆上畫畫的呻吟聲。/ 然後突然砰一聲，/ 湯姆、巴克南關上後窗，/ 陷在房裡的風一下消失，/ 窗簾、地毯以及兩位年輕女性 / 像氣球般慢慢降到地上。）

　　這段以 balloon 來描寫貴婦，非常貼切，不僅描寫她們的虛浮（buoyed up），也誇飾她們驕傲（高高在上），整段以聲音的運作（rippling and fluttering, the whip and snap of the curtains, the groan, boom），彷彿爵士樂的節奏，襯托出時代的輕飄與富裕，最後由 Tom 的現實關門動作，讓這些貴婦回到人間，既寫實又夢幻，點出了這些有錢人的生活形態。

　　但是這種虛浮誇示的生活形態，看在 Nick 的眼中，其實非常庸俗，他看著 Gatsby 的豪宅與豪宴：There was music from my neighbor's house through the summer nights. In this blue gardens men and girls came and went like moths among the whisperings and the champagne and the stars. 這些男女有如飛蛾一般，穿梭在耳語、香檳與星星之間，追逐聲色，享受夜生活，生命卻是短暫的。

　　Nick 營造了這些有錢人的生活形態，但也沒有忘記另一個世界的荒蕪：窮人的世界，這是一個充滿灰燼的山谷：

This is a valley of ashes / — a fantastic farm / where ashes grow / like wheat into ridges and hills and grotesque gardens; / where ashes take the forms of houses and chimneys and rising smoke / and, finally, / with a transcendent effort, / of men who move dimly and already crumbling / through the powdery air. / Occasionally a line of gray cars / crawls along an invisible track, / gives out a ghastly creak, / and comes to rest, / and immediately the ash-gray men swarm up / with leaden spades / and stir up an impenetrable cloud, / which screens their obscure operations / from your sight.

（這是個充滿灰燼的山谷，／──有如奇特的農莊，／沙灰成長／猶如小麥進入山脊、山丘、怪誕的花園，／灰燼佔據了屋子、煙囪、裊裊上升的燻煙，／最後／以一種超自然的方式，／襲上人們，／這些人在灰暗中移動，／已經粉碎在粉狀的空氣裡。／有時，一長串的灰色車子／爬上一條幾乎看不見的小道，／傳來詭異的煞車聲，／停了下來，馬上，灰色的人們蜂湧／擁著沉重的鏟子，／攪動起穿不透的雲層，／隱藏了他們隱晦的操作，／離你的視線。）

以聲音來描寫有錢人，以顏色（灰色─死亡、暗淡的顏色）來勾畫窮人的世界；有錢人的世界是輕快的、飄浮的，窮人的世界是沉重的、詭異的；有錢人的世界充滿生命，窮人的世界籠罩死亡陰影。那長串的灰色車子，帶來一群灰色的人，攪動泥土，所謂 obscure operations，代表埋葬與死亡。

兩種世界的對比，在小說中不斷的出現。然而有錢人的世界一定是美好的嗎？有錢的 Tom 以金錢框住拜金的老婆 Daisy，而 Gatsby 也試圖以炫耀財富來重新獲取 Daisy 的愛情，追求年輕時的浪漫激情，悲劇就由此發生。撞死人的 Daisy 不敢負責，遂由偉大的愛人（Great Gatsby）抵命。財富的累積只是讓我們看見有錢人的懦弱與道德的淪喪：Nick 最後批評 Tom 及 Daisy 這批人的虛偽：

I couldn't forgive him [Tom] or like him but I saw that what he had done was, to him, entirely justified. It was all very careless and confused. They were careless people, Tom and Daisy—they smashed up things and creatures and then retreated back into their money or their vast carelessness or whatever it was that kept them together, and let other people clean up the mess they had made....

（他們是些爛傢伙，Tom 跟 Daisy，把東西砸爛了、把人糟蹋了，然後退縮到自己的錢堆裡。）

《大亨小傳》的故事其實環繞著書中的大人物 Gatsby 與 Daisy 的戀情，從 Gatsby 口中我們得知，年輕的時候，他們陷入一段熱戀，然而追求享受與經濟穩定的 Daisy 轉而嫁給了有錢的 Tom。這段挫折，迫使 Gatsby 認為只有財富才能喚回 Daisy 的愛情，這種財富與愛情的糾葛、夢想與現實的矛盾，才是小說中令人唏噓的地方。

📖 精彩片段賞析

對 Gatsby 而言，5 年前的相戀無疑是一輩子的承諾，當他描述那天晚上與 Daisy 的浪漫夜晚，彷彿是一場舊式愛情電影的重播：

... One autumn night, five years before, / they had been walking down the streets / when the leaves were falling, / and they came to a place / where there were no trees / and the sidewalk was white with moonlight.... / His heart beat faster and faster / as Daisy's white face came up to his own. / He knew that when he kissed this girl, / and forever wed his unutterable visions / to her perishable breath.... / Then he kissed her. / At his lips' touch / she blossomed for him like a flower / and the incarnation was complete.

（一個秋天晚上，5 年前，/ 他們走下街道，/ 樹葉飄落，/ 來到了一個地方，/ 樹木消失，/ 月光染白了人行道。 / 他心跳得越來越快，/ 當 Daisy 白皙的臉靠上他。/ 他知道，一吻了她，/ 就永遠連結他那無法道出的一切前景，/ 給她消失的氣息⋯⋯/ 然後，他吻了她，/ 在嘴唇的接觸中，/ Daisy 為他綻放，/ 有如花朵，/ 人如其名，完全地轉化。）

這段初戀的經過，由 Gatsby 透過回憶道來，聽在小說敘述者 Nick 耳中，有如不真實的電影情節。然而，對 Gatsby 來說，這種外界聽來非常廉價的濫情畫面，正是支撐他 5 年來不計一切代價、以不法手段來賺錢。希望以豪宅來贏回 Daisy 的心。此段的描述，套用了很多廉價電影情節的場景，如 autumn night, leaves were falling, the sidewalk was white with moonlight 等，其他的動作，如 His heart beat faster and faster; at his lips' touch, she blossomed for him like a flower 等都是一般愛情電影的老套，看起來非常不真實。作者希望透過這種看起來不真實的場景，告訴我們 Gatsby 就是生活在這種濫情（sentimental）、浪漫（romantic）與幼稚（naïve）的幻覺（illusions）之中。

即使情節描述老套，作者還是字字斟酌，如 his unutterable visions（他無法說出的一切想像與前景），相對於 Daisy 那種可以被摧毀的呼吸氣息（perishable breath），指出：Gatsby 未可知的視野與前景，竟然綁在 Daisy 隨時可以改變的呼吸上，以 vision 的長久對上 breath 的短暫，非常有意思。此外，最後以花朵的綻放來描寫融入愛情的 Daisy，但作者又說 for him，所以這是 Gatsby 自己的感受，並不一定是 Daisy 的體驗。最後說 incarnation is complete，作者耍了個文字的遊戲，由於 Daisy 的名字代表一朵菊花，所以當她有如花朵綻放時，她就是完成了人身肉體完全轉化花朵的過程，這是 incarnation 的過程。濫情的描寫中，帶有一點不真實的感覺，難怪聽完後的 Nick 說：I was reminded of something— an elusive rhythm, a fragment of lost words, that I had heard somewhere a long time ago.

即使，我們讀者跟 Nick 一樣，對於 Gatsby 所敘述的故事感覺不真實，然而對於 Gatsby 那種執著與過去那種揮之不去的情感，我們還是非常的感動：為了與 Daisy 再見一面，費盡苦心，等了 5 年，請 Nick 安排一場下午茶會：

"We haven't met for many years," said Daisy, her voice as matter-of-fact as it could ever be.

（「我們 5 年未見了，」Daisy 說，口氣很事務性，非常無趣。）

"Five years next November"

（「到 11 月才 5 年」）

The automatic quality of Gatsby's answer set us all back at least another minute.

（Gatsby 自動回答的口氣讓我們很尷尬：把時間拉回至少 1 分鐘，大家停在那！）

I had them both on their feet with the desperate suggestion that they help me make the tea in the kitchen....

（我讓他們回神過來，急忙建議他們幫我到廚房泡茶……）

He followed me wildly into the kitchen, closed the door, and whispered: "Oh, God! " in a miserable way.

"What' s the matter?"

"This is a terrible mistake," he said, shaking his head from side to side, "a terrible, terrible mistake."

"You' re just embarrassed, that' s all," and luckily I added: "Daisy' s embarrassed too."

"She' s embarrassed?" he repeated incredulously...

"You' re acting like a little boy," I broke out impatiently.

（「你表現得像個小男孩」，我不耐煩地叫出。）

這場相會可以看出 Gatsby 的笨拙與純真，也可以見識 Daisy 那種虛榮與失去愛情的悔恨：Gatsby 帶他們回他的豪宅，展示財富：

"They' re such beautiful shirts," she sobbed, her voice muffled in the thick folds. "It makes me sad because I' ve never seen such— such beautiful shirts before."

（「這是好漂亮的襯衫」，她低泣，聲音掩蓋在厚厚的衣疊中。「我覺得很難過，因為我從來沒有見過——這麼漂亮的衣服。」）

Daisy 的哭泣，絕不是看到漂亮的衣服，而是要掩飾與 Gatsby 再度相見的情緒，她所喪失的一切，埋藏在她心中的感情。過去由於無法堅持自己的愛情，放棄了愛情，以財富為主要考量，而現在面對昔日的愛人，以財富炫耀，心情真是百感交集。

Daisy 的婚姻建立在財富上，面對丈夫的外遇也僅能暫時忘卻，一個愛慕虛榮的女性，只有金錢才是安全的：

"Her voice is full of money," he said suddenly.
（「她的聲音充滿金錢。」）

That was it. / I'd never understood before. / It was full of money— / that was the inexhaustible charm that rose and fell in it, / the jingle of it, the cymbal's song of it.... / High in a white palace the king's daughter, / the golden girl.

（沒錯，就是這樣。/ 我之前從來不瞭解。/ 那聲音充滿金錢── / 那種無窮盡的魅力，一高一低，/ 叮叮噹噹、清脆的響聲。…… / 高高在上，有如住在白色皇宮的國王女兒，/ 黃金女孩。）

儘管瞭解 Daisy 是個拜金的女人，Gatsby 卻仍對愛情充滿幻想，對理想的美國夢充滿憧憬。但是 Gatsby 卻非恐怖情人，對 Daisy 的情感建立在幻想與浪漫上。他充滿樂觀，認為他的財富，可以重建 5 年前與 Daisy 的愛情，迎向未來，以為自己可以開創不一樣的人生。

📖 結局賞析

小說最後，敘述者 Nick 回顧 Gatsby 的一生，幡然醒悟：Gatsby 代表這個時代的矛盾，沉迷於過去，卻又要抓住現在。逝去的、過去的一切仍然永遠壓著我們，我們不斷的往前，卻被不斷地拉回過去：

Gatsby believed in the green light, / the orgastic future that / year by year / recedes before us. / It eluded us then, but that's no matter — / tomorrow we will run faster, / stretch out our arms farther.... / And then one fine morning— / So we beat on, / boats against the current, / borne back ceaselessly into the past.

（Gatsby 相信綠色的燈光，/ 充滿歡樂的未來，/ 年復一年，/ 在我們面前退縮。（美好的未來）逃避我們，╱ 但是沒關係──╱ 明天，我們會跑得更快，╱ 手臂伸得更遠……╱ 然後，一個美好的早上──╱ 所以，我們繼續逆風而行，╱ 船頂著浪，╱ 卻不斷地被拉回到過去。）

適合閱讀程度：
高三以上學生及社會人士
延伸閱讀／推薦書單、電影：
小說：
Vanity Fair（《浮華世界》，William Makepeace Thackeray）

《麥田捕手》

The Catcher in the Rye

(1951)

J.D. Salinger

📖 作者簡介

　　沙林傑（J. D. Salinger, 1919 ～ 2010）在美國文壇的名聲主要建立在《麥田捕手》這本小說。生長在紐約的曼哈頓，從高中開始就寫小說，其求學過程並不順利，曾多次退學，日後參與哥倫比亞大學夜間寫作班，才找到寫作的興趣。他曾參與二次世界大戰，戰爭的經驗對他日後小說創作產生很大的影響。

　　沙林傑對寫作與電影充滿興趣，但早期的作品並未獲得太大的重視，直到 1951 年出版《麥田捕手》，奠定了他在文壇的地位。小說出版之後，評論不一，有些書評認為這是了不起的作品，有些書評則認為這是本不道德的書。但是爭議的話題，讓這本書在出版後，高居美國紐約時代暢銷書排行榜30周，一再重印。至今這本麥田捕手仍受到美國青少年讀者的喜愛，每年銷售達數10 萬本。

　　沙林傑擅長描寫青少年的疏離感與迷失，這大概跟他自己成長的經驗有關。他在求學的過程中歷經波折，更能體會青少年的孤寂感。晚期的沙林傑非常低調，避免公開曝光，然而其爭議的小說永遠是美國讀者討論的話題。
📖

小說介紹

　　"... I'm standing on the edge of some crazy cliff. What I have to do, I have to catch everybody if they start to go over the cliff— I mean if they're running and they don't look where they're going I have to come out from somewhere and catch them. That's all I'd do all day. I'd just be the catcher in the rye and all."

　　（……我站在某個瘋狂懸崖邊緣，我必須做的，我得抓住每個人，如果他們開始走過懸崖——我是說，如果他們奔跑，沒看到往哪裡，我得出來抓住他們。這就是我整天做的，我就是麥田捕手。）

沙林傑的《麥田捕手》從出版後評價不一，由於小說中使用不雅語言並且主題是疏離、頹廢，因此有些美國中小學圖書館將它列為禁書；但也因為小說深入探討美國青少年內心的孤獨與自我救贖的努力，很多美國批評家將其視為與《頑童歷險記》（*The Adventures of Huckleberry Finn*）、《大亨小傳》（*The Great Gatsby*）等並列為美國文學中最完美的 3 本小說（The Three Perfect Books）。此本小說的爭議性其實來自於所呈現的真實性，小說具體展現美國 5、60 年代青少年的次文化，從不雅語言、叛逆到失落，點出了美國文學中很重要的主題：喪失天真（loss of innocence）。

📖 主題分析

這是一本第一人稱的小說，敘述者就是故事的主人翁，高中生 Holden。小說打破傳統 19 世紀小說的敘述模式，不從小時候或家庭背景交代，而是從人生中的重要轉淚點開始：他被當了 4 科，被學校退學——

"I forgot to tell you about that. / They kicked me out. / I wasn't supposed to come back / after Christmas vacation, / on account of I was flunking four subjects / and not applying myself and all. / They gave me frequent warning / to start applying myself / — especially around mid-terms, / when my parents came up for a conference / with old Thurmer— / but I didn't do it. So I got the ax."

（我忘了告訴你，/ 他們把我踢出。/ 我不用回來，/ 在聖誕節假期過後，/ 因為我被當掉 4 科，/ 不用功。/ 他們常常警告我，/ 要好好用功，/ 尤其是在期中，/ 那時我父母來學校會談 / 跟校長 old Thurmer—— / 不過我沒做，/ 所以我被開除了。）

這是男主角講話的口氣，很隨性地道出自己想法，非常口語，不重視文法，但是青少年無所謂的口氣（They kicked me out; So I got the ax.），可以看出反叛的性格。

　　Holden 是所謂後段班學生，成績不好，但卻仍充滿對人的期待與付出：當他離開學校回到紐約，走出車站，他回憶：

　　"The first thing I did when I got off at Penn Station, I went into this phone booth（電話亭）. I felt like giving somebody a buzz.（想要打電話給某人）I left my bags right outside the booth so that I could watch them, but as soon as I was inside, I couldn't think of anybody to call up.（一進入電話亭，卻想不起要打給誰。）"

　　那種無法跟人聯繫，那種無法與人溝通的感覺，令人難過。」

　　小說的主題圍繞在主角內心的衝突，一方面他想透過性與愛情進入成年人世界，而一方面又覺得大人世界太過虛偽：他對妹妹說：

　　"Oh, God, Phoebe, don't ask me. / I'm sick of everybody asking me that," / I said. / "A million reasons why. / It was one of the worst schools I ever went to. / It was full of phonies. / And mean guys."
　　（「喔，菲比，別問我，/ 我討厭別人問我這些，」/ 我說，/「有很多原因，/ 那是我讀過最爛的學校，/ 一堆虛假的人，/ 齷齪的人。」）

　　Holden 的問題在於無法以肯定的態度面對人生，他一直害怕面對自己喜歡的事物：他跟妹妹 Phoebe 的對話，可以看出這種害怕面對改變與成長的恐懼：

　　"You don't like anything that's happening."
　　（「你不喜歡周遭發生的一切」）
　　It made me even more depressed when she said that.
　　（我覺得更加沮喪，當她這麼說。）

"Yes I do. Yes I do. Sure I do. Don't say that. Why the hell do you say that?"

（「我喜歡。我喜歡。我當然喜歡。別這麼說。你為何這麼說？」）

"Because you don't. You don't like any schools. You don't like a million things. You don't."

（「因為你不喜歡，你不喜歡學校，你不喜歡很多東西。你不。」）

"I do! That's where you're wrong— that's exactly where you're wrong! Why the hell do you have to say that?" I said, Boy, was she depressing me.

（「我喜歡，這件事你錯了。你真的錯了，你為何這麼說？」我說。天啊，她令我心情沮喪！

"Because you don't," she said. "Name one thing."

（「因為你不喜歡。」她說。「指出一件事。」）

"One thing? One thing I like?" I said. "Okay."

（「一件事，我喜歡的一件事，」我說。「好啊。」）

"The trouble was, I couldn't concentrate too hot. Sometimes it's hard to concentrate."

（「問題是，我無法專注，有時，真的很難專注下來！」）

　　這段敘述夾雜著兩人的對話與 Holden 內心的描寫，口頭上的回答與內心的想法互相矛盾，成為強烈對比：一方面不承認自己的負面思維 （Yes I do. Yes I do. Sure I do.），可是內心世界又是無法否認妹妹講的話（It made me even more depressed when she said that.）。這樣的故事敘述，大概也只有這種第一人稱的手法才能表現出來。無法知道自己喜歡什麼，對於一切改變的事物充滿又無助與憤怒，正是青少年叛逆與頹廢的主因。

　　儘管 Holden 帶些悲觀的人生態度，但是其內心仍保有純真（innocence）。與女朋友 Jane 一段快樂回憶，充滿純潔的愛情 ，相對於日後對性的探求，可看到對 innocence 的渴望：

"I held hands with her all the time, for instance. / That doesn't sound much, /

I realize, / but she was terrific / to hold hands with. / Most girls / if you hold hands with them, （大部分的女孩，如果你牽她們的手）/ their goddam hand dies on you, （牽她們的手，你變得沒有感覺了）/ or else / they think / they have to keep moving their hands / all the time.... / Jane was different. / We'd get into a goddam move / or something, / and right away / we'd start holding hands, / and we wouldn't quit / till the movie was over. / And without changing the position / or making a big deal out of it. （無需改變姿勢或大作文章）/ You never even worried, / with Jane, whether your hand was sweaty or not. / All you knew was, / you were happy. / You really were."

就是這種純真，讓他想當扮演「麥田捕手」，拯救那些即將喪失純真、即將墮落懸崖的少年：

"I have to catch everybody if they start to go over the cliff.... I'd just be the catcher in the rye and all."

青少年的成長矛盾來自於：跟成人世界的脫節，卻又不得不面對成人世界的複雜。小說中的男主角 Holden 正是處於那種希望保持純真，卻又不得不面對虛偽的成人世界。閱讀此本小說，最好的方法是順著敘述者的口氣，對著自己大聲朗讀，而不是把它當成教材或是高中讀本來研讀文法句型。

📖 精彩片段賞析

✚ 主人翁的第一人稱敘述方式

"If you really want to hear about it, the first thing you'll probably want to know is where I was born and what my lousy childhood was like, and how my parents were occupied and all before they had me, and all that David Copperfield kind of crap, but I don't feel like going into it, if you want to know the truth."

小說一開始，主人翁 Holden 建立起獨特的說話口氣，充滿叛逆（I don't feel like going into it, 我不想談論那些東西），卻很直接的想要說出內心的話（if you want to know the truth）。這段的語言文字玩弄傳統的小說敘述模式：一開始讀者以為說故事的人要講述他的出身與家庭背景：

"where I was born / and what my lousy childhood was like, / and how my parents were occupied / and all before they had me, / and all that David Copperfield kind of crap."

（我在哪裡出生，/ 我差勁的童年如何，/ 我父母在做些什麼，/ 他們生我之前，/ 那些 David Copperfield（狄更斯小說中的孤兒人物）的那些廢話。）

在這段充滿調侃的話語後，敘述者使用一個 but 的語氣轉換，推翻了前面所提的這些傳統小說的開場白。這是個非常別出心裁的前言，讓我們感受敘述者對周遭環境的嘲諷態度。接下去的故事就尋著這種角度，開始解剖成人世界的虛偽及 Holden 的疏離與孤獨。

✚ 拒絕成長

鄙視大人世界的虛偽，Holden 遇到困難便退縮到自己幻想的國度。他期望那種永遠不變的感覺，永遠純真的感覺。所以，自然歷史博物館裡面的一切，對他而言就是那種不變的象徵：

"The best thing, though, in that museum was that everything always stayed right where it was. Nobody'd move.... Nobody'd be different. The only thing that would be different would be you."

（在那博物館裡最棒的是，一切都是維持原來的樣子。沒有人會動，沒人會不同。唯一不同的是你。）

　　這裡敘述者使用 you 而不使用 me，代名詞的轉換，指的是別人（you），不是自己（me），期望改變的不是我，而是別人。

　　學校老師 old Spencer 在 Holden 要離開學校時，很誠懇地告訴他一些社會的規矩，但是這些規矩，對於叛逆且成績不好的退學生，是否能適用呢？Holden 內心充滿質疑。

"Life is a game, boy. Life is a game that one plays according to the rules."
（人生是種遊戲，人生是種遊戲，依照某些規則來玩。）

"Yes, sir. I know it is. I know it."
（是的，先生，我知道，我知道。）

"Game, my ass. Some game. / If you get on the side where all the hot-shots are, / then it's a game, / all right—I'll admit that./ But if you get on the other side, / where there aren't any hot-shots, / then what's a game about it? / Nothing. No game."
（真是遊戲喔。/ 如果你站在高手這邊，/ 那就是種遊戲，/ 沒錯，我承認。/ 不過要是你站的那一邊，/ 沒有任何高手，/ 那算什麼遊戲，/ 一切都沒，沒戲了。）

✝ 尋找自己的真誠

　　很多讀者或批評家一直認為此小說的主人翁過於消極，對於生命充滿悲觀，其實整本小說，我們要從青少年的角度去解讀，去體會邊緣少年失敗與無法溝通的困境。Holden 的內心，仍充滿令人感動的真性情，幾段真誠的告白令人動容：

"What really knocks me out / is a book, / when you're all done reading it, / you wished the author that wrote it / was a terrific friend of yours / and you could call him up on the phone / whenever you felt like it."

（真正能打到我的 / 是書本。/ 每次讀完一本書，/ 真的希望寫作的作家 / 是好朋友，/ 可以打電話跟他聊聊，/ 當想要的時候。）

此外，Holden 對他死去弟弟 Allie 的情感也表現在下面這一段如詩般的描寫中：不忍看到弟弟孤單地躺在墓地裡，遭受雨水侵蝕，而所有訪視者躲在車裡。那種虛偽的探視，令他難過：

"When the weather's nice, / my parents go out quite frequently / and stick a bunch of flowers / on old Allie's grave. / I went with them a couple of times, / but I cut it out. / In the first place, / I don't enjoy seeing / him in that crazy cemetery... / we were there / when it started to rain. / It was awful. / It rained on his lousy tombstone, / and it rained on the grass on his stomach. / It rained all over the place. / All the visitors that were visiting the cemetery / started running like hell / over to their cars. / That's what nearly drove me crazy.... / I just wished he wasn't there."

（天氣很好時，/ 我父母經常會去，/ 插一束花 / 在 Allie 的墓上，/ 我跟他們去了幾次。/ 不過我不再去了。/ 首先，我不喜歡看他 / 在那個莫名其妙的墓園，……/ 有次，我們在那，/ 開始下雨。/ 很糟，/ 雨下在他那差勁的墓，/ 下在他肚子上的草地，/ 下得到處都是，/ 所有拜訪墓園的訪客，/ 開始像瘋子似的 / 奔回自己的車子，/ 那真是令我發瘋……/ 我真希望他不在那。）

Holden 對弟弟的珍惜，來自於對純真童年的懷念，唯有從那裡走過，才能真正瞭解童年的真誠與少年的憧憬。看著其妹妹 Phoebe 對事物的追尋，他有如下的感受：沒錯，所有的小孩都在追尋美好的事物（此處以 gold ring 金戒指為象徵），我們都擔心他們會摔倒，但是我們都沒說話。Holden 認為小孩子要追尋他們要的東西，最好隨他們去做，不插手，如果他們跌倒了，那就跌倒吧。但是，如果你說什麼，那就非常糟糕！讀者，你認為呢？放手讓小孩去嘗試，還是處處擔心小孩的跌倒呢？這裡可以看出東西方對於管教小孩的不同！

"All the kids kept trying to grab for the gold ring, and so was old Phoebe, and I was sort of afraid she'd fall off the goddam horse, but I didn't say anything or do anything. The thing with kids is, if they want to grab for the gold ring, you have to let them do it, and not say anything. If they fall off, they fall off, but it's bad if you say anything to them."

（所有的孩子都不停地嘗試抓住金戒指，老妹菲比也是，我有點怕她會從那該死的馬上跌下，但我什麼也沒說，什麼也沒做。孩子的事是這樣的，如果他們想要抓住金戒指，你就必須讓他們這麼做，什麼也別說。如果他們摔下來，他們就是摔下來了，但如果你對他們說了什麼就不好。）

✚ 用語解析

本書中作者使用了不少青少年的俚俗語，此處列出一些，幫助瞭解其語言與深入的閱讀。

- kills me：「我受不了」。Holden 只要覺得某些事情讓他情緒受影響，尤其是痛苦的感覺，他就會說：That kills me.
- ace：高品質，很優秀的。
- flunk：當掉，成績不及格。
- cut class：蹺課，現在很多人使用 skip class。
- fell lousy about：覺得很不舒服、很差勁。
- dough：錢 money。
- get wise with：原意指「懂得某些事」，小說中指得是，知道如何向異性示好、占便宜。

· phony：虛偽、膚淺的，從 Holden 的觀點，他覺得很多大人都是非常 phony。

· neck：摟抱（對方的脖子）、接吻、溫存等親密動作，當動詞用。

📖 結局賞析

　　失落的男主角，最後還是回到了成長的道路。他回家接受治療輔導，準備繼續下一個階段的洗禮。即使在迷失的過程中，他仍然看到了其妹妹的純真與愛的呈現：

　　"I felt so damn happy all of a sudden, / the way old Phoebe kept going around and around. / I was damn near bawling, / I felt so damn happy, / if you wan to know the truth. / I don't know why. / It was just that she looked so damn nice, / the way she kept going around and around, / in her blue coat and all. / God, I wish you could've been there."

　　（「我突然感到非常快樂，/ Phoebe 在那邊繞來繞去（坐在旋轉木馬上）/，我幾乎是號啕大哭，/ 我感到非常快樂，/ 如果你想知道怎麼回事。/ 我不知道為什麼。/ 只是她看起來那麼美好，/ 她不斷地旋轉、旋轉，/ 穿著藍色的外套。/ 天啊，真希望你能在現場！」）

　　坐在旋轉木馬的妹妹 Phoebe，穿著藍色的外套，那種純潔與真誠的意象，將孤寂的 Holden 拉回了愛的擁抱，也提供了他治療的力量！

適合閱讀程度：

高二以上程度；高一生或國中生可以閱讀簡易版。

延伸閱讀／推薦書單、電影：

小說：

The Lovely Bones（《蘇西的世界》）

Life of Pi（《少年 Pi 的奇幻之旅》）

《華氏451度》

Fahrenheit 451

(1953)

Ray Bradbury

📖 作者簡介

　　美國作家雷‧布萊伯利（Ray Bradbury, 1920～）現年 91 歲，仍住在加州。11 歲開始寫作，高中畢業後，靠著圖書館自學，不斷地創作。於 1938 年第一次在雜誌出版小說，爾後創作不斷，主要以科幻小說為主，並嘗試為驚悚的電視影集寫作劇本。

　　1950 年的春天，布萊伯利在加州大學洛杉磯分校的圖書館地下室，開始撰寫這本《華氏 451 度》，歷時 9 天完成。這本小說一開始開始以《消防隊員》（*The Fireman*）為名，並於 1953 年出版，馬上成為他最受歡迎的小說，日後並被拍成電影。布萊伯利獲得很多的文學獎項，他的科幻預言小說見解獨到、寫作風格略帶感傷，1950 年出版的《火星人記事》（*The Martian Chronicles*）更是奠定他在美國科幻小說的不朽地位。

📖 小說介紹

　　Books were only one type of receptacle where we stored a lot of things we were afraid we might forget. There is nothing magical in them at all. The magic is only in what books say, how they stitched the patches of the universe together into one garment for us.

　　（書只不過是某種容器，儲存很多我們害怕會忘記得事物。沒有任何神奇的事物，唯一神奇的就是書裡面所說的，如何將宇宙的一些零碎，為我們整理、織成一件衣服。）

　　「書本將這世界上一切支離破碎的布片，有系統的編織成一完整的衣服，將雜亂的資訊系統整理成有用的知識。」布萊伯利在這本 1950 年出版的未來預言小說中，提到書本的重要性。他認為在未來圖像與聲音充斥、文字不受重視的時代裡，到底文字能帶給我們什麼意義呢？21 世紀的今天，網路影像越來越盛行，傳統的書本漸漸被電子媒體所替代，布萊伯利的焦慮與恐慌，無疑可以看出一種文明死亡的悲哀。

　　小說一開始，讀者面臨巨大的震撼：未來的世界裡，紙本的書籍是違禁品。所有的書籍均被燒燬，人類只能閱讀圖像或漫畫。華氏451度就是書籍燃燒的溫度。主人翁 Montag 是個 fireman（消防員或放火員？），他的工作不是救火，而是放火，燒毀任何書籍，逮捕擁有書籍的居民。這是個令人震驚的未來，這是個放棄文字的世界！

📖 主題分析

✚ 知識（痛苦？）vs. 無知（快樂？）

　　小說以預言的方式，提出未來社會由於對書本（或知識）的反感，燒毀了所有書籍，而僅保留了漫畫、電視與聲音。書中的 fireman 隊長 Beatty 批評書本為人類帶來痛苦與衝突，因此認為燒毀書籍反而帶來快樂：

No everyone born free and equal, / as the Constitution says, / but everyone **made** equal. / Each man the image of every other; / then all are happy, / for there are no mountains to make them cower, / to judge themselves against. / So! / A book is a loaded gun / in the house next door. / Burn it. / Take the shot from the weapon. / Breach man's mind.

　　（不是所有人都生而自由平等，/ 如憲法所說的；/ 但是每個人可以獲得平等。/ 每個人都跟其他人一樣；/ 這樣所有人都快樂，/ 沒有高山讓他們畏縮，/ 或與之相比。/ 好了！/ 書就像一把上膛的槍，/ 在鄰居家中。/ 燒掉它。/ 受到此武器的打擊，/ 傷害心靈。）

　　書本帶來批判與思考，有如一把上膛的槍，讓心靈受到傷害；知識帶來痛苦，讓我們無從快樂。在 Beatty 的眼中，生命是即時的，只有工作及娛樂，學習無知，忘掉一切知識：

"Life is immediate, the job counts, pleasure lies all about after work. Why learn anything save pressing buttons, pulling switches, fitting nuts and bolts?"

（何必學習任何事情，只要會按按鈕、拉拉開關、轉轉螺絲即可。）

生命真的只是 pressing buttons, pulling switches, fitting nuts and bolts 嗎？Montag 面對這種短暫的生命，開始偷偷地閱讀書籍去尋找答案，他讀得越多，問題越多。於是他去請教 Faber 教授，開始一連串對話與追尋。Faber 指出書本的重要性，不在於資訊本身，這些電視影像、漫畫或聲音都可以告訴你，而是書本帶來的質感，深入生命的本質，告訴我們一些生命的細節（detail），活生生的細節（fresh detail）：

"Do you know / why books such as this / are so important? / Because they have quality. / And what does the word quality mean? / To me / it means texture. / This book has pores. / It has features. / This book can go / under the microscope. / You'd find life under the glass, / streaming past in infinite profusion. / The more pores, / the more truthfully recorded details of life / per square inch you can get on a sheet of paper, / the more "literary" you are. / That's my definition, anyway. / Telling detail. / Fresh detail. / The good writers touch life often. / The mediocre ones run a quick hand over her. / The bad ones rape her / and leave her for the flies."

（你知道／為何像這樣的書本／這麼重要？／因為它們有質感。／所謂質感這個字什麼意思？／對我來說，／就是組織結構。／這本書有毛孔。／有特徵。／這本書可以放在／顯微鏡下。／你可以在玻璃下發現生命，／大量地流動。／有越多的毛孔，／就有越多真實記載的生命細節，／你在一片紙上的每 1 平方英吋可以找到，／你就越「有學問」。／總歸，這是我的定義。／告訴你細節，/ 活生生的細節。/ 好作家經常碰觸生命；/ 平庸的作家對生命輕描淡寫；/ 壞作家強暴生命，/ 留給蒼蠅叮食。）

與影像及聲音不同，書本是有毛孔的（pores），每個毛孔記載人類生命的記憶、生命的細節。這裡作者利用顯微鏡的意像，具體地指出紙本書籍與其他媒體資訊的不同，握著紙本所感受的生命質感（quality），說明了書本的重要性。書本對我們的幫助又是如何呢？ Montag 這麼問：

"Would books help us?"
（書本會幫助我們嗎？）
"Only if the third necessary thing could be given us. / Number one, as I said: / quality of information. / Number two: leisure to digest it. / And number three: the right to carry out actions / based on what we learn / from the interaction of the first two."
（只有我們被付予第三件必須辦到的事。/ 第一是，我說過的：/ 資訊的質感；第二：有時間去吸收消化這些資訊；/ 第三：有權去付諸行動，/ 依照我們所學到的，/ 從前面兩者交互運作中。）

這裡提出了書本閱讀的意義：一是閱讀有質感的內容；二是要有時間去消化咀嚼；三是付諸行動的權利。透過閱讀書本的意義，主人翁 Montag 放棄過去的無知（或無書），重新思考文明的復甦：書本成為文明的重要圖騰（totem）。

在網路氾濫、Youtube 掛帥的時代，思考布萊伯利的質感理論，您是否有拿起紙本書籍閱讀的衝動呢？

📖 精彩片段賞析

　　主人翁 Montag 有次在家裡，看到太太與友人看電視，輕浮且無知地討論戰爭，他拿起 19 世紀詩人 Matthew Arnold 的一首詩 "Dover Beach" 敘述戰爭的殘忍與人世的荒謬：

Ah, love, let us be true
（啊，愛人，讓我們忠誠）
To one another! For the world, which seems
（對待彼此！因為這世界似乎是）
To lie before us like a land of dreams,
（展現在我們面前，有如夢境般）
So various, so beautiful, so new,
（這樣多變、這樣美、這樣新）
Hath really neither joy, nor love, nor light,
（其實，並無喜悅、亦無愛、亦無光亮）
Nor certitude, nor peace, nor help for pain;
（亦無真實、亦無和平、亦無法解決痛苦）
And we here as on a darkling plain
（我們在此，有如置身暗無天日的平原上）
Swept with confused alarms of struggle and flight,
（吞噬於掙扎與逃亡的混亂驚慌中）
Where ignorant armies clash by night.
（陷身於無知的軍隊，在黑夜中廝殺）

　　聽到這首詩，其中的 Mrs. Phelps 感受這首詩的悲愴，突然痛哭，驚嚇了所有的人：

Mrs. Phelps was crying....

（Mrs. Phelps 在哭泣）

"Sh, sh," said Mildred. "You're all right, Clara, now, Clara, snap out of it! Clara, what's wrong?"

"I— I," sobbed Mrs. Phelps, "don't know, don't know, I just don't know, oh, oh...."

Mrs. Bowels stood up / and glared at Montag. "You see? / I knew it, / that's what I wanted to prove! / I knew it would happen! / I've always said poetry and tears, / poetry and suicide and crying and awful feelings, / poetry and sickness; / all that mush!"

（Mrs. Bowels 站起來，/ 瞪著 Montag：「你看，/ 我就知道，/ 這就是我想 證明的，/ 我知道這會發生，/ 我總是說詩引起眼淚，/ 詩引起自殺、哭泣還有可怕的感覺，/ 詩引起病態；/ 這一切的感傷！」）

沒錯，詩觸動了我們的感傷，也觸動了我們對外在世界的認知。然而是否因為知識帶來覺醒與痛苦，我們就應該放棄知識呢？ Montag 對生命認知的渴望，還是讓他繼續擁抱書本。最後妻子及友人密報，他匆忙地逃離家園，仍然拯救心愛的書本：

Montag took the four remaining books, / and hopped, / jolted, / hopped his way / down the alley / and suddenly fell / as if his head had been cut off / and only his body lay there. / Something inside had jerked him / to a halt / and flopped him down. / He lay where he had fallen / and sobbed, / his legs folded, / his face pressed blindly to the gravel.

（Montag 帶著 4 本留下來的書，/ 跳脫、/ 搖晃、/ 逃離 / 到巷子，/ 突然他跌倒在地，/ 似乎頭被砍掉，/ 只有身子躺在那。/ 腦子裡有件事扯著他 / 停下來，/ 把他拉倒。/ 他趴在跌倒的地方，/ 低泣，/ 腳縮著，/ 臉茫然地壓在地上的碎石。）

心中的覺醒讓他停住。作者使用生動的幾個節奏性非常快速的動詞如 hopped、jolted、fell、cut off、jerked、flopped、sobbed、folded、pressed 來強調這一瞬間的連續動作，簡潔明快，點出那時 Montag 的頓悟。

Montag 抱著書本，逃離機器的文明（書中以 helicopters 及擅長追蹤的機器狗 The Mechanical Hound 做為代表），進入了反省的階段。作者以燃燒的意象來說明 Montag 的文明的反思：

The sun burnt every day. / It burnt Time. / The world rushed in a circle / and turned on its axis / and time was busy / burning the years and the people anyway, / without any help from him. / So / if he burnt things with the firemen / and the sun burnt Time, / that meant that everything burnt!

（太陽每天燃燒，/ 燃燒時間，/ 這世界匆忙地繞圈，/ 順著自己的軸線，/ 時間忙著 / 燃燒歲月與人們，/ 無需他的協助。/ 所以 / 如果他也跟其他放火員一起燒東西，/ 太陽也在燃燒時間，/ 那就表示一切都會燃燒起來！）

所有文明的世界，都隨著時間的流逝（the sun and Time）而被消失（被燃燒），如果人類自己也在燃燒文明（書本），那所有的一切將消失無蹤！書本保留文明的記憶，知識見證人類文命存在的價值。Montag 揚棄過去燃燒記憶的過失，加入了保留文明記憶的行列。他在鄉間遇到了一群知識難民 （renegade intellectuals），也就是所謂的 Book People（書人），每個人在腦中記憶一本書：We are all bits and pieces / of history and / literature and / international law. / Byron, / Tom Paine, / Machiavelli, / or Christ,/ it's here.（我們都是一小塊、一小片，/ 歷史、/ 文學 / 或國際法。/ 拜倫、/ 潘恩、/ 馬基維立、/ 或耶穌基督，/ 都在此）。Montag 腦中背下聖經的傳道書（the Book of *Ecclesiastes*），誠如其中的成員 Granger 所說的，他們都在等待文明的復甦：

And when the war's over, / someday, some year, / the books can be written again, / the people will be called in, one by one, / to recite what they know / and we'll set it up in type / until another Dark Age....

（當戰爭結束，／哪一天，哪一年，／書可以重寫，我們這些人會一個一個被召喚，／去背誦所知道的，／我們會把它印下來，／直到另一個黑暗時期。）

人類的知識與記憶，充滿著韌性，在人類歷史中即時曾經被壓抑（如西方中古世紀的書禁及東方的焚書），但都能不斷地延續。這本雖是未來預言小說（預言文字與紙本的消失），但不也訴說過去書本知識的一段歷史？

📖 結局賞析

小說最後以古老的傳說意象 phoenix 來結束，從火的灰燼中，人類文明將再起。但是 Granger 則希望人類比鳳凰聰明些，不要老是犯下歷史的錯誤，不斷地毀滅自己的文明：

"There was a silly damn bird /called a phoenix / back before Christ, / every few hundred years / he built a pyre and / burnt himself up. / He must have been first cousin to Man. / But every time he burnt himself up / he sprang out of the ashes, / he got himself born all over again./ And it looks like / we're doing the same thing, / over and over, / but we've got one damn thing / the phoenix never had. / We know the damn silly thing we just did. / We know all the damn silly things / we've done for a thousand years / and as long as we know that / and always have it around where we can see it, / someday we'll stop making the goddamn funeral pyres / and jumping in the middle of them."

（有隻愚蠢的鳥／叫鳳凰，／生在基督之前，／每幾百年／就會建個火堆，／燃燒自己。／他一定是人類的近親。／不過每次他燒了自己，／就會從灰燼跳出來。／重新再生。／似乎我們／也在做同樣的事，／一而再、再而三，／但是我們有件事，／鳳凰不會有。／我們知道我們做的蠢事。／我們知道這些愚蠢事，/ 過去幾千年做的。/ 只要我們知道，/ 留在我們看得到的地方，/ 有天我們會停止做這些埋葬的火堆，/ 跳入其中。）

幾千年來，人類不斷毀滅自己、毀滅文明，我們真的知道自己所作的蠢事嗎？即使知道做了些蠢事，我們真的可以停止嗎？布萊伯利很樂觀地指出人類與鳳凰的不同，但是同時他也正暗諷人類的愚蠢：人類真的比愚蠢的鳳凰鳥聰明嗎？

適合閱讀程度：
　高二以上學生及社會人士
延伸閱讀／推薦書單、電影：
小說：
Brave New World（《美麗新世界》）
1984（《1984》）

《覺醒》

The Awakening
(1899)

Kate Chopin

courtesy of the Missouri History
Museum, St. Louis, Missouri, USA

📖 作者簡介

　　美國作家凱特・蕭邦（Kate Chopin, 1850 ～ 1904）生於聖路易，她的成長過程中，大都跟一些獨立、有智慧的女性相處，其父親及兄弟均早夭，因此缺乏男性長輩的照顧。對於女性順從的傳統甚少接觸，養成其獨立自主的人格。在學校表現優異，之後從學校畢業後，即踏入聖路易的社交圈。1870 年嫁給路易斯安那富裕家庭的兒子，婚姻生活美滿。即使生了 6 個小孩且對於家庭非常盡責，蕭邦仍然享受獨立自由的生活，活躍於紐奧良。丈夫在 1882 年因病過世後，她獨立地過著生活。

　　1889 年蕭邦開始寫作，表達其對女性議題及婚姻與性的一些看法。她的小說以法國移居美國的家庭為主，場景大都在紐奧良。小說出版後，受到很大迴響。主要是小說中表現出的女性獨立、自由及熱情。1899 年《覺醒》出版時，引起很大的爭議。讀者對於書中描寫女性的性意識與性覺醒甚為震驚。之後，受到負面的攻擊。蕭邦的出版著作甚少，1904 年死於腦出血。

　　蕭邦早期被認定為地方作家，因為她的作品著重於紐奧良的文化風格人物。直到《覺醒》被當代批評家重新定位，才奠立她在美國文壇的地位，尤其是對於女性主義運動的激發，有絕大的貢獻。

📖 小說介紹

　　With a writing motion she settled herself more securely in the hammock. She perceived that her will had blazed up, stubborn and resistant. She could not at that moment have done other than denied and resisted. She wondered if her husband had ever spoken to her like that before, and if she had submitted to his command. Of course she had; she remembered that she had. But she could not realize why or how she should have yielded....

　　（身體扭曲移動，她更安全地坐進帆布椅內。她感覺到她的意志已經燃燒起來，固執、反抗。她這時，無法做其他事，只能拒絕、抵抗。她懷疑她先生是否還曾跟她這麼說話，像之前那樣，是否她會屈服於他的指令。當然，她曾經有，她記得她曾有過。但是，她無法理解為何、怎麼她該屈服。）

意志已經燃燒起來（her will had blazed up），變得固執與反抗（stubborn and resistant）。女主角從之前屈服丈夫命令（submitted to his command）的角色，開始轉變，成為一個獨立自主的女性。

這是一本描寫女性獨立與孤獨的小說。小說中的女主角面對傳統社會對她的要求，如善盡妻子的角色、服從丈夫的需求等，逐漸引起了反抗的心。在緩慢的成長與覺醒的過程中，她漸漸地從認識自己的定位到情欲與感情的衝擊，這些都顯示出現代女性的成長。

📖 主題分析

✚ 獨立與孤獨（independence vs. loneliness）

追求獨立自主的人總是孤單的，因為要反抗傳統社會的壓力。女主角 Edna 從小就生活在孤獨的世界裡：

Mrs. Pontellier was not a woman / given to confidence, / a characteristic hitherto / contrary to her nature. / Even as a child / she had lived her own small life / all within herself. / At a very early period / she had apprehended instinctively / the dual life— / that outward existence / which conforms, / the inward life / which questions.

（Mrs. Pontellier 不是一個女性，/ 給人信任的感覺。/ 這種信任（或推心置腹）的特質 / 違反她的本性。/ 即使在小時候，/ 她過著自己狹小的生活，/ 在自己裡面。/ 在很早的時候，/ 她已經直覺地體會 / 這種雙重生活—— / 外在的存在，/ 順從；/ 內在的生活，/ 懷疑。）

　　從小，Mrs. Pontellier 就是生活在自我的小圈圈中，不是一個可以跟她吐露心情，分享心事的人（not a woman to confidence），此句後面的 a characteristic hitherto contrary to her nature（一種違反她本性的特質）是用來解釋說明前面這個 confidence 這種特性的。一般來說，女性被期望能一起分享、一起談些心事。但是 Edna Pontellier 從小表現的跟一般女性不同，表面上她是順從的，然而內心中，對這些女性被迫去接受的事物，抱著懷疑的態度。

　　對女性的壓迫，作者使用有如陰影（shadow）的比喻，籠罩在 Edna 的靈魂上，讓她喘不過氣來。然而她並不是怪罪丈夫，也不是怨恨命運，這種內斂及自我壓抑的個性，形成了她孤獨及自我疏離的心境：

An indescribable oppression, / which seemed to generate / in some unfamiliar part of her consciousness, / filled her whole being / with a vague anguish. / It was like a shadow, / like a mist / passing across her soul's summer day. / It was strange and unfamiliar; / it was mood. / She did not sit there / inwardly unbraiding her husband, / lamenting at Fate, / which had directed her footsteps / to the path which they had taken. / She was just having /a good cry all to herself. / The mosquitoes made merry over her, / biting her firm, round arms / and nipping at her bare insteps.

　　（一種無法形容的壓迫，/ 似乎形成，/ 在她內心一些陌生的角落，/ 擴展至她全身 / 一種模糊的痛苦。/ 有如陰影，/ 像霧般，/ 穿越她靈魂的夏日。/ 很奇怪也很陌生，/ 一種心情。/ 她並不會坐在那，/ 內心譴責先生，/ 哀悼命運，/ 指導她的腳步 / 來到現今的道路。/ 她僅僅 / 好好的自己痛哭一番。/ 蚊子在她身上取悅，/ 叮咬堅實、圓潤的手臂，/ 囓咬她裸露的腳背。）

　　此處，作者用了兩個譬喻，一個是修辭學上所說的明喻（simile），以陰影有如霧般（like a mist），穿透了她開朗、有如夏日的靈魂（her soul's summer day），形成一種奇怪陌生的情緒。 利用陰影與陽光形成一種強烈的對比，本來她個性像陽光的，但由於那種性別的壓迫感，讓她無法開朗，陽光被壓住了。最後，利用蚊子的暗喻（metaphor），來描寫那種壓迫所產生的痛苦或命運，蚊子叮咬她的全身，摧殘她裸露在外的身體（biting her firm, round arms and nipping at her bare insteps）。不僅是內心的痛苦，還將內心的痛苦轉化成外在的傷害。

然而她也不是整日的哀傷。一個獨立有想法的女性，會去發覺一些內心的喜悅，去尋找自己的空間。她投身在繪畫，希望透過畫畫能舒解內心的壓力，找到自己自由呼吸的空間：

There were days / when she was very happy / without knowing why. / She was happy / to be alive and breathing, / when her whole being seemed to be one / with the sunlight, the color, the odors, the luxuriant warmth / of some perfect Southern day. / She liked then / to wander alone / into strange and unfamiliar places. / She discovered many a sunny, sleepy corner, / fashioned to dream in. / And she found it good / to dream / and to be alone / and unmolested.

（有些時候，/ 她很快樂，/ 不知道原因。/ 她很高興自己活著、呼吸，/ 全身似乎合而為一，/ 與陽光、顏色、氣味、舒適溫馨，/ 某個完美的南方日子。/ 那時，她喜歡 / 孤獨地漫步，/ 進入奇怪、陌生的地方。/ 她發現一些快活、令人沉睡的角落，/ 適合做夢。/ 她覺得很好，/ 做夢、/ 孤獨、/ 不受打擾。）

最快樂的時光莫如一個人在家，將家裡全部占為己有，家有如自己個人的聖殿，闖進去，卻有千萬的聲音要她出去！

Within the precincts of her home / she felt like one / who has entered / and lingered within the portals / of some forbidden temple / in which a thousand muffled voices / bade her begone.

（在她家的範圍內，／她感覺自己就像／進入／閒蕩在門廊裡，／某個禁止進入的廟堂，／在裡面，／數千的低沉聲音，／命令她出去。）

這是否意味著她不喜歡自己的先生小孩呢？不，獨立自主的女性仍有其溫柔感性與付出的一面，但是愛先生與小孩，並不代表他們能夠完全占有她。當一個生活的藝術師，她必須擁有勇氣，去挑戰一切，承擔一切：

She thought of Leonce and the children. / They were a part of her life. / But they need not have thought / that they could possess her, / body and soul.... / The artist must possess the courageous soul / that dares and defies.... /

（她想到 Leonce 及小孩。／他們是她生命的一部分。／但是他們無須認為他們可以擁有她，／身體與靈魂……／藝術家必須擁有勇敢的靈魂，／敢挑戰、／敢反抗。）

當一個鬥士、當一個生活的藝術家，她就必須面對自己的孤獨與外在不同聲音的刺激，她是否能夠承擔呢？她是否能在世俗的壓力下，走出自己的一條路呢？

📖 精彩片段賞析

✚ 女性性意識的覺醒

選擇走自己的路，不但是辛苦的，也是寂寞的。對於女性更是如此，女主角需要不斷地發覺自己要什麼，自己內心的需求。此處，作者以自身的生活經驗與社會投入，提出了一個很大膽的訴求：女性身體的覺醒與性意識的抬頭。這個訴求對於 19 世紀的美國傳統社會無疑是個很大的衝擊。Edna 從年輕就很清楚的感受自己豐富的情感與情欲：

Edna often wondered at one propensity / which sometimes had inwardly disturbed her / without causing any outward show or manifestation / on her part. / At a very early age—/ perhaps it was when she traversed the ocean of waving grass—/ she remembered / that she had been passionately enamored of / a dignified and sad-eyed cavalry officer / who visited her father / in Kentucky.

（Edna 經常驚訝一種傾向，有時在內心困擾著她，/ 但並不會從在外在表現出來，/ 在她這方面。/ 在年紀小的時候，/ 或許，那是當她橫越一大片的草地時──/ 她記得 / 她狂熱地迷戀 / 一個有威嚴、眼帶哀傷的騎士軍官，/ 來拜訪她爸爸，/ 在肯塔基。）

那時他像個野孩子，喜歡在草地狂奔，享受那種自由狂野的感覺。從那時，她已經感受到那種強烈情欲的傾向（one propensity），困擾她的內心。這種強烈情欲的傾向，不斷增強，從內心到肉體。對於 19 世紀的讀者來說，作者大膽地描寫女主角 Edna 對身體的自覺，無疑是非常震驚，挑戰了傳統對女性壓抑性慾的觀念。我們似乎目睹一場女性的情欲秀：

Edna, / left alone in the little side room, / loosened her clothes, / removing the greater part of them. / She bathed her face, her neck and arms / in the basin / that stood between the windows. / She took off her shoes and stockings / and stretched herself / in the very center of the high, white bed. / How luxurious it felt / to rest thus in a strange, quaint bed, / with its sweet country odor of laurel / lingering about the sheets and mattress! / She stretched her strong limbs / that ached a little. / She ran her fingers / through her loosened hair / for a while. / She looked at her round arms / as she held them straight up / and rubbed them one after the other, / observing closely....

（Edna，/ 孤單地留在邊間的小房間裡，/ 鬆開衣服，/ 脫下大部分的衣服。/ 她清洗臉頰、頸部及手部，/ 在面盆裡，/ 位於窗戶間。/ 她脫掉鞋子、襪子，/ 伸展自己，/ 在高架、白色的床中。/ 多麼奢侈的感覺，/ 在陌生、奇妙的床上休息，/甜美月桂的鄉村味道，/停留在床單與床墊上。/她伸展強壯的四肢，/稍微酸痛。/手指穿越鬆下來的頭髮/一會兒。/看著自己圓潤的手臂，/高舉著，一隻一隻地撫摸著，/仔細觀察……）

幾近全裸地撫摸自己的身體，感受身體的每一部分，這是女性自我意識覺醒的重要一步。從內在與外在軀體的需求，她展現自己情欲的部分，與年輕 Robert 的曖昧關係，只是她情欲世界的一部分。與其說她迷戀 Robert，不是說 Robert 只是她情欲的轉移對象，猶如之前父親時代的騎士軍官，她愛上的是自己情欲解放的感覺：

"Don't part from me / in any ill humor. / I never knew you to be out of patience with me / before."

（「不要離開我，/以情緒不佳的方式；/我從來不知你會對我沒有耐心，/之前。」）

"I don't want to part in any ill humor," she said. / "But can't you understand? I've grown used to seeing you, / to having you with me all the time, ..."

（「我不想這樣情緒不好的跟你分手。」/她說。「不過你不瞭解嗎？/我已經習慣看到你，/習慣你總是在我身邊。」）

"Good-by, my dear Mrs. Pontellier; / good-by. / You won't—I hope you won't completely forget me." / She clung to his hand, / striving to detain him.

（「再見，親愛的 Mrs. Pontellier /再見；/你不會，/我希望你不會完全忘記我。」/她抓住他的手，/試圖要留下他。）

兩人的曖昧建立在迷戀的基礎上，並不是 Edna 喜歡這個人的特質，而是這種異性存在的吸引力，那種迷戀的感覺，激起了 Edna 女性的情欲特質：

As Edna walked along the street / she was thinking of Robert. / She was still under the spell of her infatuation. / She had tried to forget him, / realizing the inutility of remembering. / But the thought of him was like an obsession, / ever pressing itself upon her. / It was not that she dwelt upon details of their acquaintance, / or recalled / in any special or peculiar way / his personality; / it was his being, his existence, / which dominated her thought, / fading sometimes / as if it would melt into / the mist of the forgotten, / reviving again with an intensity / which filled her with an incomprehensible longing.

（當 Edna 沿著街道行走，/ 她想到 Robert。/ 她仍然在迷戀的魔力下。/ 她試圖忘記他，/ 知道記得他也是無濟於事。/ 但是，想起他成為一種迷亂（執著），/ 不斷地壓迫她。/ 並不是她一直想著兩人相識的細節 / 或是回憶，/ 以特別或特殊的方式，/ 他的個性；/ 而是他整個人，整個存在，/ 佔據了她的心思，/ 有時消退，/ 好像溶入了失憶的迷霧中，/ 又再度復活，非常強烈，/ 讓她充滿一種無法理解的渴望。）

　　從 infatuation（迷戀）到 obsession（迷亂或執著），強調 Edna 對 Robert 的迷戀其實是自我對情欲的一種執著（也可以用 obsession），最後變成強烈的渴望（longing）。這段的描寫是 Edna 獨自散步，邊走邊想的心路歷程與內心獨白。作者使用 4 個 S+V, Ving 的句型（如 She had tried to..., realizing...; the thought of him..., pressing itself upon; it was his being..., fading sometimes; it would melt into, reviving again...）來呈現女主角邊走邊分析的情境，從主要的句子開始思考，而後用 Ving 的形式來表達思考後的結果，4 個類似的句法放在此段，引導我們一起跟 Edna 來散步，一起來思考。

　　Edna 的情欲覺醒與身體的自覺，讓她彷彿得到新的生命。她不僅是人妻，更是個新女性，開啟了新的視野，有如新生命般，裸身的進入這個世界：

How strange and awful / it seemed to stand naked / under the sky! / How delicious! / She felt like some new-born creature, / opening its eyes / in a familiar world / that it had never known.

（多麼奇特、多麼令人驚訝，/ 裸體地站 / 在天空下。/ 多麼的愉悅！/ 她感覺自己像個新生命，/ 打開眼睛，/ 在一個熟悉的世界，/ 之前從來不知認識。）

📖 結局賞析

　　本書打破禁忌，超越女性原來的格局，Edna 大膽的嘗試發覺自己的情欲與內心的世界。並非她不滿足先生及小孩的生活與世界，而是她要去開創自己的視野。她搬出先生的家，自己創造自己的空間，可以盡情繪畫，可以解放自己，回應了 20 世紀初女性作家維吉尼亞 ‧ 吳爾芙（Virginia Woolf）所主張的：女性應該有自己的房間（a room of one's own）。然而，到了後面，社會的輿論壓力，周遭朋友的不諒解，她是否有能力去對抗、去挑戰了。小說結局，作者呈現了一個非常模糊的空間，Edna 赤身走入海中，到底是自殺呢？還是象徵一種海的洗禮與女性的再生呢？歷年來的批評家，都有不同的詮釋。讀者，請妳閱讀這一段，說出你自己的感覺吧！

　　赤身走入海中，　那間，Edna 回到童年的時光，聽到了童年的呼叫：

She looked into the distance, / and the old terror flamed up / for an instance, / then sank again. Edna heard her father's voice / and her sister Margaret's. / She heard the barking of an old dog / that was chained to the sycamore tree. / The spurs of the cavalry officer clanged / as he walked across the porch. / There was the hum of bees, / and the musky odor of pinks / filled the air.

　　（她望著遠方，/ 古老的恐懼燃起，/ 一下子，/ 然後又下沉。/ Edna 聽到父親 / 及妹妹 Margaret 的聲音。/ 她聽到老狗的叫聲，/ 拴在無花果樹下。/ 騎士軍官的馬刺叮噹作響，/ 當他走過走過玄關。/ 蜜蜂的嗡嗡聲，/ 石竹的麝香味 / 瀰漫在空氣中。）

適合閱讀程度：

大一以上程度及社會人士

延伸閱讀／推薦書單、電影：

小說：

To Room Nineteen（《到 19 號房》）

The Color Purple（《紫色姊妹花》）

《黛斯姑娘》

Tess of the D'Urbervilles
(1891)

Thomas Hardy

📖 作者簡介

英國作家湯瑪士・哈代（Thomas Hardy, 1840 ～ 1928）出生在英國西南方鄉村 Dorset，此地方後來成為他大部分小說場景的背景。哈代的父親從事蓋房子的工作，所以他從年輕時，也成為建築師的學徒。日後他曾經進入大學念書想成為教會人士，但由於後來喪失宗教熱誠，也缺乏經濟基礎，於是開始寫作，希望能以寫作為生。直到 1984 年出版的《遠離塵囂》（*Far From the Madding Crowd*）成功後，才真正能以寫作為生。

哈代內心想成為詩人，小說寫作只是作為謀生的方式。他的寫作風格介於 19 世紀與 20 世紀的作家間，遊走於傳統維多利亞的小說形式與 20 世紀的創新手法。1891 年出版的《黛絲姑娘》確立他在文壇的地位。

《黛絲姑娘》呈現作者對英國下階層社會的同情與關懷，並對當時社會的虛偽及性觀念諸多批判。英國當時面對傳統與現代經濟與社會的劇烈轉變，從一個以農業主導的社會轉變成工業與商業運作的現代情境，此本小說展現的就是這方面的巨大改變。小說中的觀點引起當時社會的極大震撼，也引起相當多保守勢力的攻擊。在下一本小說《石匠玖德》（*Jude the Obscure*）出版後，哈代就完全放棄小說寫作，專職寫詩。

哈代的作品充滿悲觀的論點，極力描寫人類與環境交雜出現的悲劇場景，誠如他在作品中，一再強調他無法相信這個世界是由仁慈的上帝所主導。這種悲觀的論點，著重在上帝的消失（disappearance of God），這樣的論點在 19 世紀末期甚為流行。而支持人類繼續在這不仁慈的自然中生存的，卻是人與人間互相的關懷與同情，及人類在這個困難中所堅持的尊嚴。

📖 小說介紹

... in the present case, / as in millions, / it was not the two halves of a perfect whole / that confronted each other / at the perfect moment; / a missing counterpart wandered independently / about the earth / waiting in crass obtuseness / till the late time came.

（在現在這個案例上，／有如其他數以萬計的例子一樣，／不是完美的整體的兩半，／面對彼此，／在完美的時刻。／短缺的另一半單獨地流浪，／在世上，／愚蠢地等待，／直到時間太晚了！）

完美的愛情通常指發生在兩個完美的男女，在完美的時刻相遇，墜入情網，產生愛情的火花。然而，世事並非如此，作者在此段中，明顯指出，本故事的案例跟世上其他事情一樣的，完美的兩半（two halves of a perfect whole），並沒有在適當的時刻相遇。反而，另一半在愚蠢地流浪，直到時不我與。《黛絲姑娘》的男女主角就是在這樣的命運作弄下，造成了無法挽回的悲劇。讀者不禁要問，為何兩人不早點相遇，不在完美的時刻面對彼此呢（confronted each other at the perfect moment）？

《黛絲姑娘》這本小說完整呈現當時英國農村下層勞工的生活困境，以女主角 Tess 為主線，深刻進入這些弱勢族群的生活中，點出其人類生存的不義與男女價值觀念的扭曲。Tess 一生的悲慘命運，為環境與男人所作弄，最後遭受死亡，令人黯然。

📖 主題分析

✚ 真愛 vs. 理想的愛

整本故事圍繞著女主角 Tess 的一生。一個農場的貧窮女孩面對家庭的經濟壓力，不得不前往有錢人家求助。然而遇上了不懷好意的 Mr. Alec，注定了悲慘命運的開始：

He watched her pretty and unconscious munching / through the skeins of smoke / that pervaded the tent, / and Tess Durbeyfield did not divine, / as she innocently looked down at the roses in her bosom, / that there behind the blue narcotic haze / was potentially the tragic mischief / of her drama.

（他看著她美麗、無意識的咀嚼，/ 透過煙霧中，/ 瀰漫在帳篷內。/ Tess 無法預測，/ 當她天真地看著胸前的玫瑰，/ 在藍色、令人麻醉的煙霧後，/ 隱藏了悲劇的作弄，/ 她人生這場戲。）

Alec 看著天真可愛的 Tess，心懷鬼胎，然而在迷霧中的 Tess 渾然不知自己未來悲慘的命運。在不對的時間碰到不對的人，這是悲劇的開始。在一次的刻意安排下，純真的 Tess 喪失了童貞，成為 Alec 的女人。

然而，迷失的另一半卻在癡癡地等待。離開了 Alec，Tess 來到一農莊工作，碰到了充滿理想的 Clare Angel。看到了純潔天真的 Tess，Angel 不顧父母的反對，投入了這場充滿理想的愛情裡。

He observed his own inconsistencies in dwelling / upon accidents in Tess's life / as if they were vital features. / It was for herself that he loved Tess; / her soul, her heart, her substance— / not for her skill in the dairy, / her aptness as his scholar, / and certainly not for her simply formal faith-professions. / Her unsophisticated open-air existence / required no varnish of conventionality / to make it palatable to him.

（他觀察自己前後的矛盾，/ 強調 Tess 生活中的意外，/ 好像這是關鍵的特色。/ 就是她本身，他愛上 Tess；/ 她的靈魂、心靈、本體—— / 並不是她在酪農場的技巧，/ 或她成為他的老師，/ 更不是她簡單、正式的信仰表白。/ 她未經事故、生活在戶外，/ 無須傳統繁文縟節的修飾，/ 讓他覺得愉悅入口。）

這段的內心描述，生動地點出了 Angel 對 Tess 愛情的本質。一方面他很重視他生活中的一些事情（accidents in Tess's life），一方面他又強調是她本人，而非外在的一些事物或條件，讓他愛上她。所以，他自己也看到了自我的矛盾（inconsistencies）。這裡，作者用了對稱的句法來表達 Angel 內心衡量對 Tess 的感情：It was for ..., not for ...。最後以 palatable 這個口感十足的字眼來強調 Tess 在她心目中的角色：仍是由男性品嘗的事物。

也就是了解 Angel 這種自我中心的愛戀，Tess 在最後不敢面對未婚夫，告訴他之前與 Alec 的一段生活：

She had not told. At the last moment her courage had failed her, she feared his blame for not telling him sooner; and **her instinct of self-preservation was stronger than her candor.**

（她自我保護的本能強過了坦白。）

Tess 知道，Angel 愛上的是理想的天使情人，是他心中幻想的靈魂與心靈，而非真正的她；這是真愛？還是理想虛幻的愛？此段點出了整本小說的重要訊息，也是作者一再強調的主題：

"O my love, my love, / why do I love you so!" / she whispered there alone; / "for she you love is not my real self, / but one in my image; / the one I might have been!/"

（「我的愛人，/ 我的愛人，/ 你為何這樣愛我。」/ 她孤獨地喃喃自語，/「你愛上的並非真正的我，/ 而是我的意象，可能的我！」）

從一開始，Angel 為了追求自己理想的愛情，在 Tess 身上建構了理想天使的形象，愛上了這個形象，而非真正的 Tess。所以當他知道 Tess 不是處女，也非純潔的天使，他的整個愛情信念崩潰。他無法原諒 Tess：

"Forgive me as you are forgiven! I forgive you, Angel."
（「原諒我，誠如我原諒你，我原諒你。」）

"You—yes, you do."

（「你，是的，你原諒我。」）

"But you do not forgive me?"

（「但是你不原諒我？」）

"O Tess, forgiveness does not apply to the case! You were one person; now you are another. My God—how can forgiveness meet such a grotesque—prestidigitation as that!"

（「喔，Tess，原諒無法用在這上面。你以前是那樣的，現在你變成另一個人。天啊，原諒怎麼可能碰上這麼怪異的——戲法！」）

"What have I done—/ what have I done! .... / It is in your own mind / what you are angry at, Angel; / it is not in me. / O, It is not in me, / and I am not that deceitful woman you think me!"

（「我做了什麼——/ 我做了什麼！/ 在你的內心，/ 你為了什麼生氣，Angel，/ 並不是在我身上，/ 喔，不是在我身上，/ 我不是你想的那樣，欺騙你的女人。」）

Tess 展現了智慧，告訴 Angel，他所生氣的並非 Tess 本人，而是對自己信念的氣憤。儘管 Angel 自認是個突破傳統、追求獨立思考的年輕人，但是碰到關鍵的時刻，他仍然回到過去陳腐的觀念：要求自己的妻子是個純潔的天使與處女：

With all his attempted independence of judgment / this advanced and well-meaning young man, / a sample product of the last five-and twenty years, / was yet the slave to custom and conventionality / when surprised back into his early teachings.

（儘管其企圖建立獨立判斷，/ 這個觀念先進、心地善良的年情人，/ 過去 25 年來的好樣本，/ 仍然是習慣與傳統的奴隸，/ 驚嚇地回到早期的教養上。）

小說的敘述者，跳入故事中，對 Angel 的個性做了嚴格的批判。Angel 的迂腐讓他盲目，讓他無法面對自我。等到他流浪海外，瞭解自己的錯誤，再回到家鄉尋找 Tess，面對真愛的時候，一切都已經太晚了。

📖 精彩片段賞析

✚ nature vs. human society

真摯的愛情碰上了世俗的想法，產生了無可彌補的悲劇。難道是命運作弄人嗎？小說家不斷在敘述中，強調大自然的美，尤其是在酪農場中，Tess 與 Angel 的愛情就是在這種天然的環境中滋長的：

On one of these afternoons / four or five unmilked cows chanced to stand apart / from the general herd, / behind the corner of a hedge, / among them being Dumpling and Old Pretty, / who loved Tess's hands / above those of any other maid. / When she rose from her stool / under a finished cow, / Angel Clare, who had been observing her for some time, / asked her if she would take the aforesaid creatures next./ She silently assented, / and with her stool at arm's length, / and the pail against her knee,/ went round to / where they stood. / Soon the sound of Old Pretty's milk / fizzing into the pail / came through the hedge, / and then Angel felt inclined to go round the corner also, / to finish off a hard-yielding milcher / who had strayed there, / he being now as capable of this as the dairyman himself.

（有一次下午，/ 4、5 隻未被擠奶的母牛恰好站得 / 遠離一般牛隻。/ 在籬笆角落後，/ 其中有 Dumping 跟 Old Pretty 兩隻母牛，/ 他們喜歡 Tess 的手，/ 超過其他女工。/ 當她從凳子上站起來，/ 完成了一隻牛，/ Angel，/ 已經觀察她一段時間，/ 問她是否願意接下去接受前面那些牛隻。/ 她靜靜地同意。/ 帶著凳子，/ 水桶靠著膝蓋，/ 她來到了那些牛隻 / 所站的地方。/ 很快地，Old Pretty 的奶水聲滴到水桶，/ 穿過籬笆。/ 然後 Angel 也想繞過角落，/ 去完成一隻很難屈服的母牛，/ 迷路到這個地方，/ 他現在也是有如酪農般有能力辦到。/ ）

但是這種大自然的美卻無法挽救 Tess 的命運。大自然是無法對抗人類社會加諸的價值觀，也就是像 Tess 這種大自然小孩（child of nature）是無法生活在混亂的人類社會中。小說中，不斷強調 Tess 的大自然傾向，尤其是 Tess 在酪農場擠奶的一段，更是看出 Tess 與自然和諧一致，純樸天真的一面：

All the men, / and some of the women, / when milking, / dug their foreheads into the cows / and gazed into the pail. / But a few— / mainly the younger ones — / rested their heads sideways. / This was Tess Durbeyfield's habit, / her temple pressing the milcher's flank, / her eyes fixed on the far end of the meadow / with the quiet of one / lost in meditation. / She was milking Old Pretty thus, / and the sun chancing to be on the milking-side, / it shone flat upon her pink-gowned form / and her white curtain-bonnet, / and upon her profile, / rendering it keen as a cameo / cut from the dun background of the cow.

（所有的男人，/ 還有一些女人，/ 在擠牛奶時，/ 將前額埋到母牛下，/ 瞪著水桶。/ 但是少數── / 主要是年輕的，/ 頭靠邊。/ 這是 Tess 的習慣，/ 她的太陽穴壓著母牛的側腹，/ 眼睛望著遠方的草地，/ 帶著寧靜，/ 一個人陷在沉思中。/ 她是這麼擠 Old Pretty，/ 太陽剛好落在擠奶這邊，/ 平平地照在她粉色外衣的形體、/ 白色垂幕的邊帽，/ 照在她的身影，/ 有如鮮明的浮雕，/ 從暗褐色的牛隻背景切出。）

這段文字中，光線的變化，造成一幅浮雕的景色（a cameo），將 Tess 與母牛合而為一，象徵 Tess 就是大地的女兒，跟自然跟母牛共存的美，表現無遺。顏色非常重要：pink、white、dun 等，都是透過光線產生一種朦朧的美。

除了顏色與光線所構成的視覺之外，Tess 與大自然的結合，還呈現一種大自然的脈動：

The stillness of her head and features / was remarkable: / she might have been in a trance, / her eyes open, / yet unseeing. / Nothing in the picture moved / but Old Pretty's tail and Tess's pink hands, / the latter so gently / as to be a rhythmic pulsation only, / as if they were obeying a reflex stimulus, / like a beating heart.

（她的頭與外觀展現出的寧靜 / 非常引人注目。/ 可能陷入一種恍惚的狀態，/ / 眼睛開著，/ 卻看不到。/ 畫面上沒有東西移動，/ / 只有 Old Pretty 的尾巴及 Tess 粉紅的雙手。/ / 雙手輕柔的，/ / 展現韻律的脈動，/ 似乎順著一種自然反應的刺激，/ / 好像跳動的心臟。）

以上這幾段描寫 Tess 與母牛的律動、與大自然顏色的協調，可說是整本小說最精彩的文字，有如詩的描寫。在小說中穿插田園風光的詩意描寫，凸顯小說家的詩人風格，也造就這本小說文字的美。一些片語的分割，如（her eyes open, yet unseeing, as if they were obeying, like a beating heart），讓閱讀間斷，但也讓節奏慢了下來，讀者慢慢讀來，有如漫步於自然中，與小說人物一起倘佯於大自然裡。對於這種意境的想像也是閱讀小說最大的樂趣。

在使用這麼多詩意的語言後，作者很直接的就點出 Tess 就是大地的女兒，並不是人工刻畫出來的藝術品：

It seemed natural enough to him / now / that Tess was again in sight / to choose a mate from unconstrained Nature, / and not from the abodes of Art.

（很自然地對他來說，/ / 現在，/ / Tess 再度出現眼前，/ / 挑選伴侶，/ 從奔放的自然中，/ 而非從藝術的處所。）

📖 結局賞析

　　小說的最後，重新擁抱 Tess，也重新認識真愛的 Angel，帶著殺死同居人的 Tess，來到了荒野。Tess 到了大自然的懷抱外，回復到之前的寧靜，面對當地司法的追捕：

　　"What is it, Angel?" she said, starting up. "Have they come for me?"

　　（「那是什麼，Angel？」她說著起身。「他們是來找我們的嗎？」）

　　"Yes, dearest, " he said. "They have come."

　　（「是的，親愛的。」他說。「他們來了。」）

　　"It is as it should be," she murmured. "Angel, I am almost glad—yes, glad! This happiness could not have lasted. It was too much. I have had enough; and now I shall not live for you to despise me!"

　　（「該來的就來吧。」她低聲說，「Angel，我相當快樂，是的，快樂！這種快樂幾乎無法持久，太多了，我已經擁有夠了。現在，我不要活著，讓你鄙視我。」）

　　She stood up, shook herself, and went forward, neither of the men having moved.

　　（她站起來，抖一抖，往前傾，兩人都沒有移動。）

　　"I am ready," she said quietly.

　　（我準備好了，她平靜地說。）

　　面對自己的命運，有如殉道者般來到了生命的終點，純真的大地女兒 Tess，面對人類社會僵化的價值，不管是 Alec 的摧殘與利用，或是 Angel 的懦弱與幼稚，她都要勇敢地準備好，去承擔這些人類的罪惡！

適合閱讀程度：

適合閱讀程度：大二以上程度；大一或高中可以閱讀簡易版。

延伸閱讀／推薦書單、電影：

小說：

Jude the Obscure（《石匠玖德》）

Daisy Miller（《黛絲米勒》）

附錄

以小說為題材拍攝之電影（按字母順序排列）

小說：*The Adventures of Sherlock Holmes*《福爾摩斯冒險》

電影：*The Adventures of Sherlock Holmes*《福爾摩斯歷險記》

（1939, starring Basil Rathbone, Nigel Bruce and Ida Lupino）

小說：*The Awakening*《覺醒》

電影：*The Awakening*《覺醒》

（1980, starring Charlton Heston, Susannah York and Jill Townsend）

小說：*The Da Vinci Code*《達文西密碼》

電影：*The Da Vinci Code*《達文西密碼》

（2006, starring Tom Hanks, Audrey Tautou and Jean Reno）

小說：*Charlie and the Chocolate Factory*《查理的巧克力工廠》

電影：*Charlie and the Chocolate Factory*《巧克力冒險工廠》

（2005 starring Johnny Depp, Freddie Highmore and David Kelly）

小說：*Fahrenheit 451*《華氏 451 度》

電影：*Fahrenheit 451*《華氏 451 度》

（1966, starring Oskar Werner, Julie Christie and Cyril Cusack）

小說：*Frankenstein*《科學怪人》

電影：*Frankenstein*《科學怪人》

（1994, starring Robert De Niro, Kenneth Branagh and Helena Bonham Carter）

小說：*Great Expectations*《遠大前程》

電影：*Great Expectations*《烈愛風雲》

（1998, starring Ethan Hawke, Gwyneth Paltrow and Hank Azaria）

小說：*The Great Gatsby*《大亨小傳》

電影：*The Great Gatsby*《大亨小傳》

（1974, starring Robert Redford, Mia Farrow and Bruce Dern）

小說：*Gulliver's Travels*《格列佛遊記》

電影：*Gulliver's Travels*《格列佛遊記》

（2011, starring Jack Black, Emily Blunt and Jason Segel）

小說：*Interview with the Vampire*《夜訪吸血鬼》

電影：*Interview with the Vampire*《夜訪吸血鬼》

（1994, starring Brad Pitt, Tom Cruise and Antonio Banderas）

小說：*I, Robot*《機械公敵》

電影：*I, Robot*《機械公敵》

（2004, starring Will Smith, Bridget Moynahan and Bruce Greenwood）

小說：*Message in the Bottle*《瓶中信》

電影：*Message in the Bottle*《瓶中信》

（1999, starring Kevin Costner, Robin Wright and Paul Newman）

小說：*Needful Things*《必需品專賣店》

電影：*Needful Things*《勾魂遊戲》

（1993, starring Max von Sydow, Ed Harris and Bonnie Bedelia）

小說：*Of Mice and Men*《人鼠之間》

電影：*Of Mice and Men*《人鼠之間》

（1992, starring John Malkovich, Gary Sinise and Ray Walston）

小說：*Pride and Prejudice*《傲慢與偏見》

電影：*Pride and Prejudice*《傲慢與偏見》

（1940, starring Greer Garson and Laurence Olivier）

  Pride and Prejudice《傲慢與偏見》

（2005, starring Keira Knightley and Matthew Macfadyen）

小說：*Silas Marner*《織工馬南傳》

電影：*Silas Marner*

（1922, starring Crauford Kent, Marguerite Courtot and Robert Kenyon）

Silas Marner: The Weaver of Raveloe《塞拉斯馬尼爾》1985 starring Ben Kingsley,

Jenny Agutter and Patrick Ryecart

小說：*Tess of the d'Urbervilles*《黛絲姑娘》

電影：*Tess of the d'Urbervilles*《黛絲姑娘》

（1913, starring Minnie Maddern Fiske, Raymond Bond and David Torrence）

Tess of the d'Urbervilles《黛絲姑娘》

（1924 starring Blanche Sweet, Conrad Nagel and Stuart Holmes）

Tess of the d'Urbervilles《黛絲姑娘》

（TV 1913, starring Justine Waddell, Jason Flemyng and Oliver Milburn）

小說：*Twilight*《暮光之城》

電影：*Twilight*《暮光之城》

（2008, starring Kristen Stewart, Robert Pattinson and Billy Burke）

Linking English
一生必讀的英文小說：經典&大眾小說導讀賞析

2011年4月初版   定價：新臺幣350元
2017年8月初版第八刷
有著作權・翻印必究   著　　者　陳　超　明
Printed in Taiwan.   叢書主編　李　　　芃
                                      校　　對　張　靜　芬
                                      封面設計　江　宜　蔚
                                      內文排版　江　宜　蔚

出　版　者　聯經出版事業股份有限公司   總編輯　胡　金　倫
地　　　址　台北市基隆路一段180號4樓   總經理　陳　芝　宇
編輯部地址　台北市基隆路一段180號4樓   社　長　羅　國　俊
叢書主編電話　(02)87876242轉226   發行人　林　載　爵
台北聯經書房　台北市新生南路三段94號
電　　　話　(02)23620308
台中分公司　台中市北區崇德路一段198號
暨門市電話　(04)22312023
郵政劃撥帳戶第0100559-3號
郵撥電話　(02)23620308
印　刷　者　文聯彩色製版印刷有限公司
總　經　銷　聯合發行股份有限公司
發　行　所　新北市新店區寶橋路235巷6弄6號2F
電　　　話　(02)29178022

行政院新聞局出版事業登記證局版臺業字第0130號

本書如有缺頁，破損，倒裝請寄回台北聯經書房更換。　ISBN　978-957-08-3770-4 (平裝)
聯經網址 http://www.linkingbooks.com.tw
電子信箱 e-mail:linking@udngroup.com

國家圖書館出版品預行編目資料

一生必讀的英文小說：經典＆大眾
小說導讀賞析/陳超明著．初版．臺北市．
聯經．2011年4月（民100年）．232面．
17×23公分（Linking English）
ISBN 978-957-08-3770-4（平裝）
[2017年8月初版第八刷]

1.英語 2.讀本

805.18　　　　　　　　　　100002584

《一生必學的英文閱讀》系列
Readings for Life

經典重現、搭配聲效俱佳朗讀CD & 精美插畫、連結經典與當代

厚重的英語經典文學作品是不是常讓人望之卻步？以為只有英文系的學生才看得懂原文的經典文學？其實，英國經典文學作品讀起來也可以easy & fun！尤其在學習語言的階段中，閱讀經典更是培養語感重要的一步。

聯經自 2009 年起隆重推出《一生必學的英文閱讀》，全系列分為「珍‧奧斯汀系列」、「狄更斯系列」與「科幻冒險系列」，以及未來的「莎士比亞系列」等等，本本皆是英國文壇史上的必讀經典，題材涵蓋從浪漫愛情、寫實批判、奇幻冒險乃至驚險懸疑等。

經典重現
《一生必學的英文閱讀》以中英對照的方式呈現，原文部分由熱愛英國文學且經驗豐富的英國籍老師在保留原著精神的前提之下，以淺顯易懂的文字改寫而成。原版由英國 Real Reads 出版社發行。本版並邀請陳超明教授為每一本做導讀、解析。

搭配聲效俱佳朗讀 CD & 精美插畫
文字搭配生動活潑的插圖以及依據情節不同而變化的豐富音效，把閱讀變成一場視覺與聽覺的文學盛宴，讓讀者不再視文學作品為畏途，而能在輕鬆、活潑又有趣的氛圍下逐步提升「英語閱讀力」！

連結經典與當代
大師的經典之作蘊含文化價值觀，跨文化的閱讀可以讓讀者了解重要的文化、歷史背景。《一生必學的英文閱讀》每本書都有 Taking things further 單元，提供與該書相關的人文、歷史導引、內容豐富的資訊連結，讓讀者除了閱讀文字，讀後還能夠延伸思考。

A fantastic way to introduce you to classic literature~

珍・奧斯汀系列  *Jane Austen*

珍・奧斯汀被譽為英國最偉大的女性作家。自小便熱愛閱讀且沉浸在文學世界中，十二歲開始嘗試寫作，自此展露卓越的文筆和才華。珍・奧斯汀一生幾乎從未離開家鄉，卻能在自己的一方小天地裡，運用天生的觀察力與洗練文筆激盪出許多題材，在平凡的人、事、物中粹取出引人入勝的故事情節。珍・奧斯汀擅於描寫犀利的對話與細膩的人性刻畫，小說情節的起伏有如戲劇一般，而對白及文字的使用生動，令人激賞。

《傲慢與偏見》 *Pride and Prejudice*
生動的個性描寫、機智對話已是英國古典文學史上最具代表性的愛情經典，也是英國人心目中的頭號愛情聖經。

《理性與感性》 *Sense and Sensibility*
書中細膩的感情、人物的刻畫在在讓人印象深刻，是家喻戶曉的經典小說，故事內容也一再被翻拍成電影等作品。

《艾瑪》 *Emma*
活潑的筆觸，呼應了主角捉摸不定的個性，捕捉了最真實的「人性」，讓讀者得到共鳴。

狄更斯是英國小說的泰斗人物，我們常說，要了解英國文化、要體會英文之美，一定要讀狄更斯。

刻畫幻想與現實

狄更斯的小說，大都描寫十九世紀英國中下階層的生活，從家庭的關係到社會的溫情，透過孤兒主角的成長，小說中的人物，面對艱難的生活挑戰，建立人與人之間的信任與愛，令人回味無窮。儘管故事主題溫馨感人，但是故事情節曲折動人，有驚奇的冒險、懸疑的探索，也有意想不到的奇幻之旅。人物生動活潑、對話充滿機智、情節出人意表。

《小氣財神》 *A Christmas Carol*
饒富聖誕佳節的深刻教化意義，有如奇幻故事，帶領讀者穿越時空

《孤雛淚》 *Oliver Twist*
讓讀者進入倫敦的地下社會，感受罪犯的邪惡與救贖

《塊肉餘生記》 *David Copperfield*
探索青少年的感情世界，勇敢面對世俗的誘惑

《遠大前程》 *Great Expectations*
充滿驚奇，從貧窮到浮華，青澀的成長，如何迷失在都市的頹廢與愛情的迷惘，最後找回了失去的良知。

科幻冒險系列 *Science Fiction*

閱讀科幻小說絕對是雙重的閱讀享受，不但可以進入小說天馬行空的幻想世界之中，又可以期望這些科幻的敍述早晚會成真。不管是機器人、地心旅行或外星探險，也似乎正在我們周遭發生！科技的發展帶來很多的想像空間，也提供了小說家很多創作的題材。結合科學的論述與極高的想像力，開展了科幻小說的浪漫之旅。

科幻小說充滿了科學的論辯或科學中的理論敍述，在閱讀之前，我們可能對於這些科學概念充滿幻想，可是在閱讀的過程中，我們卻不斷地去挑戰與修正這些看法與觀點，例如在《科學怪人》的小說中，我們一開始讚歎科學的成就，可以創造出一個新的人類，但是這個新人類卻成為暴力怪物，爾後這個暴力怪物又不斷地為自己辯解，我們到底要同情他還是要譴責他呢？我們也開始懷疑這種科學創造人的神話，到底可行嗎？人類要繼續研究機器人嗎？讀者一方面以理性科學的閱讀角度，一方面卻又會投入感性的思維，勾畫出閱讀科幻小說的趣味。

《化身博士》 *Dr Jekyll and Mr Hyde*（by Robert Louis Stevenson）

討論善惡二元對立的精采小說，這種概念，在不同的科幻或奇幻小說中，常被套用與挪移，可說是善惡原形的經典之作。

《世界大戰》 *The War of the Worlds*（by H. G. Wells）

人類面臨火星人的入侵該如何面對？在強大的武力入侵下，人們無助又懦弱，但在面對世界毀滅的過程中，也更能互相扶持。

《失落的世界》 *The Lost World*（by Arthur Conan Doyle）

恐龍真的絕種了嗎？人類對於過去文明的消失，一直想找到答案，也一直懷念過去文明或蠻荒世界的種種驚奇。

《時光機器》 *The Time Machine*（by H. G. Wells）

時間旅行一直是科學界的熱門話題，時光旅人經歷了多重時空的旅程，來到了一個他無法處理的世界，到底這個世界對他的衝擊為何？回到旅行的原點，又該如何面對不一樣的自我？

《吸血鬼德古拉》 *Dracula*（by Bram Stoker）

開啟了我們對於「異形世界」的好奇，其中暴力美學與細膩的情景描寫也非常引人入勝，刻畫了經典的吸血鬼形象。

《科學怪人》 *Frankenstein*（by Mary Shelley）

追求超越人類知識極限的科學家，扮演起上帝的角色，創造了活生生的生命。但卻成為其生命的夢魘。一連串的暴力與親人的喪生，讓科學家懷疑自己科學實驗的正確性。然而充滿暴力的惡魔，如何為自己辯解？讀者到底要同情科學家？還是憐憫被社會遺棄的孤兒？